Honey, Hairballs, and Murder

A Cozy Magic Midlife Mystery

Silver Circle Cat Rescue Mysteries
Book 2

Leanne Leeds

Honey, Hairballs, and Murder
Silver Circle Cat Rescue Mysteries #2
ISBN: 978-1-950505-84-5

Published by Badchen Publishing
2709 N Hayden Island Dr.
STE 103131
Portland, Oregon, 97217

I have studied many philosophers and many cats. The wisdom of cats is infinitely superior.
  Hippolyte Taine

Contents

Chapter One

THE SUN WAS JUST SETTING AS I STOOD WITH MY daughter Evie in the gallery on the second floor overlooking the main room of the Silver Circle Cat Rescue, a large, airy space filled with tables, couches, and chairs.

"I still can't believe it, Mom," Evie said, her eyes wide with amazement. "I mean, look at this place!"

I gazed out at the bustling cat café, a sense of pride swelling in my chest. Warm hues of orange and pink seeped through the large windows, painting the room in a soft glow. People sipped on steaming cups of coffee, nibbled at fresh pastries, and snuggled with the adorable feline residents who eagerly walked through the room seeking attention and cat treats.

"I know, sweetheart," I agreed, unable to suppress a grin. "I wasn't sure about the whole cat café concept, but you outdid yourself with this idea."

Before we could say more, staff and board member

Matt Garcia walked over, his auburn hair a wild mess. "Evie, I've got to hand it to you. The cat café was a stroke of genius."

"Oh, it was nothing." She blushed, tucking a stray strand of light brown hair behind her ear. "Thanks, Matt. I thought it would be a nice way to bring people in and help the cats find homes. You guys voted for it, though."

"We did." Matt smiled at Evie's response, a spark of admiration in his eyes. "But it's not nothing. This is definitely not nothing."

Evie's cheeks grew pinker as she glanced down shyly at her feet, but I could tell she was enjoying the praise. I proudly put my arm around her shoulder as Matt continued to gush about the success of the cat café and how happy his grandmother was to help out with the delicious baked goods and snacks.

As I glanced around the room, I couldn't help but marvel at what Fiona's mansion had transformed into.

Plush cushions and cozy nooks beckoned visitors to curl up with a cat and a book. At the same time, floor-to-ceiling shelves showcased an array of cat-related trinkets and treasures, and books encased in see-through cabinets interspersed between cat cubbies. The walls were adorned with whimsical cat paintings and photographs done by the kids at the local high school, lending a quirky charm to the room.

Estella Garcia provided cases of conchas, churros,

and polvorones to go with the fresh coffee sold behind the counter at one end of the café.

And, of course, there were the cats themselves, some snoozing in comfortable hammocks, others batting at toys or exploring the various perches and climbing structures that local contractor Landon Rogers built. After all, the felines were the real stars of the show, each one hoping to find their forever home.

My gaze wandered to the corner of the room, where Belladonna perched regally atop a ledge, surveying her domain like a queen on her throne. Her sleek black fur glistened in the dim light, and her piercing yellow eyes locked onto mine with an air of superiority. It was as if she were silently contemplating her next command, assessing my worthiness thus far and how long she would allow it to continue.

Well.

Not every cat was hoping to find their forever home.

Some, like the enigmatic Belladonna, seemed perfectly content to rule their little corners of the world, commanding the attention and admiration of all who crossed their path.

"Landon did a fantastic job with the renovations, didn't he?"

Evie nodded enthusiastically. "He really did, Mom. Everything looks better than I ever imagined it could."

Matt leaned against the wall. "And the best part is, we're helping these cats find loving families. That's what it's all about, right?"

"You're absolutely right, Matt," I said. Watching the cats interact with their human visitors, I knew we were making a real difference in their lives.

At that moment, the door to the café creaked open, and Deputy Don Markham strode in with purpose. He was a tall, broad-shouldered man, his clean-shaven face exuding a rugged confidence that was difficult to ignore. Clad in his crisply pressed uniform, he appeared some-what out of place amid the whimsical atmosphere of frol-icking cats and vibrant decor that enveloped the café.

"Deputy!" I called, waving him up to the balcony. "What brings you here today?"

He smiled as he approached us, his eyes taking in the lively scene as he ascended the curved stairs. "I must admit, I was curious about this cat café everyone's been talking about." He winked. "I thought I'd drop by and see it for myself."

"Well, you're more than welcome here," Evie said, offering him a warm smile.

"Thank you," he replied, nodding his appreciation. "I must say, you've done a remarkable job with this place."

As we engaged in conversation, Marmalade, a cunning calico with a mischievous glint in her eyes, crept toward the deputy like a miniature orange and black ninja. Her movements were stealthy, her intent clear—she had set her sights on her next unsuspecting victim. She leaped onto Don's shoulder in a swift, fluid motion, catching him completely off guard.

He muttered through clenched teeth, taken aback but trying to maintain his composure, "I suppose for some folks, the café holds its own... peculiar allure." He managed a tight smile, though his eyes betrayed a hint of surprise at Marmalade's unexpected ambush.

Seeing the rugged deputy and the bold calico locked in their unlikely encounter was a comical sight. "I think she likes you, Deputy," I told him as Marmalade nuzzled her head against his neck.

He cast a sidelong glance at Marmalade, who had settled comfortably on his shoulder, her fur blending seamlessly into the fabric of his dark jacket. "If that's true," he grumbled, doing his best to maintain a stoic expression, "then it's a real shame because I don't like cats."

Seemingly unfazed by Don's admission, Marmalade let out a triumphant meow as if to assert her dominance over the situation.

The four of us laughed.

It was pretty odd, the life I found myself in, I thought as I stood there overlooking the rescue's first open day in its new home. A grand mansion bequeathed to Silver Circle by a murder victim I barely knew, a room ingeniously designed to indulge feline whims... it was terrific.

Especially since the cat preferences came through another aspect of Fiona Blackwell's peculiar inheritance to us—what Evie playfully dubbed "the talking plate." It was a platter adorned with a luminescent crystal that, when a cat stood upon it, amplified their voice, making it intelligible to human ears.

If I was to recount this experience to someone, they'd surely brush it off as a wild yarn. A tall Texas tale that was far too outlandish to be real.

Yet, as I stood there among the laughter, the purring cats, and the local folks sipping coffee and eating Mexican sweet breads, I knew that this unbelievable tale was not just a story but our reality.

And at that moment, I couldn't imagine a more perfect, extraordinary life.

That moment of peace lasted precisely three days.

Three days later, Evie and I walked into Ben's Honey Pot, a cozy little shop tucked away on the outskirts of our small town of Tablerock, Texas. Ben's honey had been far more popular in the café than we'd expected, and we'd come to pick up some more of the local nectar for the cat café.

I loved this little place.

The warm, golden light from the vintage lamps cast a soft glow on the wooden shelves lined with jars of amber honey. The array of colors glistened under the light like jewels, their sweet aroma permeating the air.

"Mom, look!"

Evie and I stared, our eyes fixed on Ben Tyson—who lay sprawled face down on the floor.

"Is he... dead?" Evie whispered, her eyes widening with a potent mixture of fear and disbelief.

Ben Tyson, the beekeeper and owner of the store, lay on the cold, hard floor, his body rigid and unmoving. His arms were spread out awkwardly at his sides. A disheveled mess of honey-coated hair partially obscured his face, which was pressed into a large, shallow pan filled with thick, gooey honey.

An orange and white cat was perched atop the motionless man's back, its eyes wide and alert, seemingly aware of the gravity of the situation. The feline's fur appeared soft and vibrant under the light, giving it an almost ethereal quality amid the somber scene. Its tail twitched inquisitively, betraying a sense of curiosity or unease, as its paws rested gently on the man's shoulder blades.

I slowly, carefully felt for a pulse under its watchful stare, but there was none.

Poor Ben.

"I need to call the Tablerock Police," I said, my hand trembling slightly as I pulled out my cell phone from the pocket of my jeans. "The poor man must have tripped."

Evie nodded in agreement, her gaze shifting to the orange and white cat watching us with tense suspicion. The cat's yellow eyes stared back at her, unblinking and full of wariness. She spoke softly to the feline, trying to comfort it without daring to approach it.

"What's your emergency?" a woman on the other

end of the line inquired, her voice professional and steady. The calmness in her tone felt almost jarring.

I took a deep breath, steadying my nerves before I replied. "My daughter and I are at Ben Tyson's honey store on the edge of Tablerock. We found Ben lying face down in a honey pan, and we think he might be dead." I paused and then sighed. "No, I'm sure he's dead. He's not breathing. I checked for a pulse, and there was no pulse. He didn't feel warm. We don't know what happened, but we need help immediately."

As I relayed the information, the details of our grim discovery felt all the more real. After what happened with the mayor's son just a few months ago, I couldn't help but feel a sense of foreboding settling in my chest.

The woman on the phone assured me that help was coming, and I thanked her before hanging up.

With the call complete, I turned to Evie, who continued to murmur comforting words to the orange cat even though they had zero effect. The creature's eyes followed our every move with uncertainty as if it, too, was trying to make sense of the tragic and mysterious events that had unfolded in its domain.

Despite Evie's gentle coaxing, the cat remained stubbornly perched on Ben's back, its plump body pressing down on him like a protective shield.

"I didn't know Ben had a cat. That is Ben's cat, isn't it?" I asked.

Evie shrugged, her eyes never leaving the feline. "I don't know. I don't want to get close enough to it to read the collar tag in case she takes a swipe at me. I mean, obviously, something terrible happened here. The poor cat's probably traumatized from seeing its owner murdered—"

"Evie, we have no idea what happened. Poor Ben probably tripped.

"But what if he didn't?" she countered, her gaze flicking between the cat and me. She gestured to the orange feline with a worried expression. "We might be the only people who can tell the police what happened here. We can talk to her."

"Actually, it's likely a 'him,'" I pointed out. "There's about a 70 percent chance that cat's male, remember?" Orange fur is tied to the X chromosome; thus, female cats need two gene copies to be orange, while male cats only need one. Consequently, orange females are rare, while orange males are more prevalent. "And we're not just walking off with a cat. We'll talk to the police when they get here."

As I surveyed the honey shop, I couldn't help but notice that everything appeared to be in perfect order. No honey jars were broken or out of place, and there were no signs of any scuffle or commotion. The polished wooden shelves stood tall and immaculate, displaying their golden treasures in neat rows. I glanced at the cash register, and it appeared untouched.

"Besides, it doesn't look like anything happened here," I said, glancing at Evie. "There's no indication of a struggle or anything being knocked over. It's like Ben just...collapsed. Face down into a pan of honey."

"Which isn't exactly normal, Mom. He's in his early forties. People that age don't just collapse face down in the middle of a work day." Evie furrowed her brow, her gaze sweeping across the store as she took in the peculiar serenity of the scene. "But you're right," she agreed. "It's almost too calm. Like someone went out of their way to make sure everything was in order."

Oh, for goodness' sake. "Evie, that's not what I said—"

Our conversation was cut short by the wail of sirens, the sound growing louder as the police swiftly approached the honey store. The flashing lights of the police cars soon flooded the quaint shop through its large windows, casting eerie patterns on the walls and shelves.

From the vantage point of the parking lot, we observed the police officers moving methodically, processing the scene, and gathering evidence. Their stern faces and professional demeanor starkly contrasted with the honey store's warm, inviting atmosphere. The shop, with its cozy ambiance and the sweet scent of honey that usually wafted through the air, now seemed a world away from the tranquility it typically exuded.

"What do you think really happened in there?" Evie asked quietly, her voice barely audible above the hum of more approaching sirens and the murmur of officers speaking into their radios.

I sighed, my gaze fixed on the flurry of activity in the shop. "I don't know, Evie," I admitted. "I understand what you were saying before, though. Ben Tyson is young to have passed away so suddenly. And in such a strange way, too. I wonder if he drowned in that honey."

"He did not," a male voice offered.

I turned my head and saw Officer Mario Lopez approaching Evie and me. "Mario," I said with a warm smile. "Nice to see you again."

"Ellie, Evie."

Mario was a good friend of Landon Rogers, the contractor who had renovated the mansion for us. On his days off from the police force, Mario would often lend a hand to Landon, working alongside him to earn some extra money. His friendly demeanor and strong work ethic had endeared him to us during the renovation process.

"Good to see you two as well," Mario said, returning the smile with a hint of sadness in his eyes. "Wish it was under better circumstances, though."

"I know, right?" Evie nodded, her gaze drifting back to the shop. "Any idea what happened to Ben?"

Mario hesitated momentarily before responding as if weighing how much information to share. "Well, it's too early to say, but the preliminary assessment suggests he didn't drown in the honey. The coroner will examine some unusual marks on his body more closely as soon as we can get that cat off him."

"Unusual marks?" Evie asked.

"Yep," Mario said. "The marks on his lower back are quite distinctive." He paused, contemplating the most fitting description for the strange marks. "They create a circular pattern, almost, with a jagged, irregular outline. There are evenly spaced indentations inside the circle, almost like the impressions left by wheel spokes."

"How odd. Is the marking only on his lower back?" I asked.

"Well, we can't be sure about the rest of his back. You see, there's this stubborn orange cat that refuses to budge. Every time we try to grab it, the cat hisses and lunges at us. With its claws out."

As if to illustrate the truth of Mario's statement, a cacophony of feline noises erupted from the direction of the honey store's open front door. The fierce growls and frantic yowls interspersed with deep male voices shouting various four-letter words.

"As you can hear, we're having some trouble."

I looked at Mario.

He looked at me.

I raised an eyebrow.

He smiled.

"You're hoping we can remove the cat for you, aren't you?" I asked, raising an eyebrow in suspicion. "That's the real reason you came to talk to us."

Mario hesitated as if weighing his options. "Well, of

course, I wanted to say hello," he admitted, attempting to maintain an air of casual friendliness. But then his face broke into a sheepish grin, and he couldn't help but concede the truth. "But yes, we would be very grateful if you could coax that stubborn feline away from poor Ben's body." The grin dropped. "The guys are getting a bit more annoyed the longer this goes on, and I'd hate for Ben's cat to get hurt."

The earnest expression on Mario's face made it clear that he was genuinely concerned for the cat's well-being. It also revealed his faith in our ability to handle the situation.

It seemed that, once again, we were called upon to bring order to the feline chaos that plagued law enforcement in our peaceful little town, I thought sarcastically.

"What's the plan for the cat after we catch it?" Evie asked as I retrieved a sturdy cat carrier from the back of our rescue van.

Mario glanced around the honey store parking lot. He noted, no doubt, that we were the only vehicle in the lot beside the police cruisers. "Well, Ben lived alone, and none of his employees seem to be here," he said, rubbing his chin contemplatively. "Take it to your rescue center for now, and I'll let you know when I find out more."

Evie's eyes widened, and a sly grin hinted at the corners of her mouth. The anticipation radiated from her in electric waves. I could practically see my daughter salivating at the idea that she'd get to question the cat on the talking plate and find out more about Ben's death.

"Sounds good." I closed the van door with a reassuring thud and followed him into the store.

As we stepped through the doorway, a furry ball of rage met us with a menacing hiss. All eyes were on the aggressively agitated cat guarding Ben's body. His anger —and now that he stood I was sure it was a him—was unmistakable.

Evie stepped slowly toward the cat, her hands held carefully away from her body. The feline's fur bristled, its eyes wide with fear, but she continued softly speaking comforting words.

She knelt beside him, never taking her gaze off the cat, and stretched her hand toward him. It hissed louder, swatting furiously at the air before him warning her to keep back.

Evie kept talking, slowly inching closer until finally, the cat relaxed enough for her to slowly gather it into her arms and gently place it in the carrier.

With the cat safely contained, the coroner moved forward to perform his somber duty and gently, respectfully draped a sheet over Ben Tyson's body.

Chapter Two

EVIE AND I RETURNED TO THE RESCUE, THE CAT
safely contained within the carrier. We wasted no time
bypassing the bustling cat café on the first floor and went
directly to the second floor. After we ascended the stairs,
we headed toward a room off to the right, marked by a
sign warning people that there was no public access
beyond that point.

Upon reaching the restricted area, I couldn't help
but ask, "How's he doing?"

"He's quiet," Evie murmured, a hint of worry lacing
her voice. She gently shut the door to the room we
fondly called the 'talking plate room,' its walls adorned
with an eclectic mix of decorative plates so no one would
look too closely at the magic one. "He seems a little shell-
shocked, to tell you the truth."

The cat's wide, fear-filled eyes and tentative movements spoke volumes about its unease. Our eyes met,

conveying a mutual empathy as we considered the cat's ordeal. We knew all too well the importance of territory for felines and how the abrupt shift in surroundings would rattle even the most resilient creatures.

We meticulously arranged the cat's temporary refuge. We provided a soft, warm bed, a litter box, fresh water, and food, hoping to ease his transition and help him regain a sense of stability. Our gentle voices and soothing touches reassured the cat that he was safe and cared for in its new surroundings.

"Okay, that's everything," Evie declared with a nod, satisfied that we had provided all the comforts for our newest guest.

This isolation room was the first stop for all cats arriving at our rescue. We told curious visitors that the room was soundproofed and quiet, providing a safe haven where cats could decompress and adjust to their new surroundings — and while that was technically true, there was another reason for this room's existence.

It was the place where the cats could communicate with us after stepping onto a unique silver plate.

I still didn't fully comprehend how the talking plate had come to us. Well, I mean, I knew that Fiona Blackwell had bequeathed it to us — along with her mansion, substantial fortune, and enigmatic cat, Belladonna. The reasons behind her decision and the origins of the extraordinary device remained shrouded in mystery.

But one thing was clear – you don't need to know a thing's origins to use its capabilities.

And we certainly made use of the talking plate.

Once a cat came into contact with the large, silvery crystal platter, we could hear their words as if they were human and speaking to us in our own language. This remarkable phenomenon allowed us to understand the cats of the rescue — and their needs and emotions — on a level that would have been impossible otherwise.

So all cats stopped in this room first, allowing us to get acquainted with them and establish a relationship. It was also the last place they visited before leaving, a last check-in to ensure the cats were genuinely happy and comfortable with the people who sought to adopt them.

This room also served as a sanctuary they could return to whenever they needed to communicate with us. Despite this open invitation, most cats chose not to return to the talking plate room after settling into their new environment. They seemed content to express themselves through their body language and interactions with the other cats and us, as most felines naturally do.

"What is this?" a deep male voice asked as the cat stepped on the plate.

"Hello there," I said gently, trying to make the cat feel at ease. "My name is Ellie, and this is Evie. We run the cat rescue here and brought you to this room so you can have a quiet, comfortable place to settle in. The silver plate you're standing on allows us to communicate with you. It's a special tool we use to understand how our feline friends are feeling and what they need."

The cat stared back at me, his eyes filled with suspicion.

Evie said, her voice equally as soothing, "We're here to help you, and we want to make sure you feel safe and cared for. If you have any questions or concerns, please don't hesitate to share them with us."

The cat's eyes narrowed as he assessed our intentions, and then he said, "I watched a movie with Ben once. They threw humans into a hospital for crazy people. The nurses in that place talked to the crazy people like you're talking to me. All soft and calm. Like they were afraid the humans would rip their throats out." The cat tilted his head. "Is this a hospital for crazy cats?"

"No. This is a place for cats that don't have humans to care for them. I know you might be a little frightened and unsure of us right now," I said softly, "but please believe that we genuinely want to make sure you're safe and cared for. We're here to listen to you and to do everything we can to help you through this." I met his gaze steadily, trying to convey my sincerity and desire to help. "What's your name?"

The cat continued to eye us with a hint of suspicion, but it seemed our words had made some impact. "Honey. Ben named me Honey." The cat sneezed. "Not the most creative name in the world, but Ben wasn't the most creative human. Also, not the most masculine

name, but since he got my testicles chopped off, I
suppose it didn't have to be." Gradually, his tense
posture relaxed, and his eyes became more curious and
inquisitive. "Thank you for the food. Now leave me
alone. I need to think."

We did.

"Are you guys okay?" Darla's eyes widened with
concern as she joined our huddled group away from the
bustling cat café. "I can't believe Ben Tyson's dead. I was
just over at his shop the other day to get the wildflower
honey for my mom."

Evie sighed, her gaze downcast. "It was definitely
jarring," she admitted. She bit her lip, her brow furrowing. "And really strange. First, why would there be a pan
of honey? Second, why would it be on the floor? And
third, how did Ben Tyson's face end up on the floor in
the pan of honey?"

Matt's eyebrows shot up in surprise. "A pan? Like a
pot?"

"No, like a rectangular baking pan," Evie clarified,
using her hands to demonstrate the shape she described.
"And his face?" She clapped her hands sideways. "Right
down in it."

"How's the cat doing?" Matt asked, gesturing toward
the second floor.

"Stoic, like all cats, no doubt," Darla said.

"He's doing okay. He asked us to give him space, so we stepped away." Evie paused, a thoughtful expression crossing her features. "His name is Honey. He hinted at being Ben's cat, but we didn't delve too deep into the conversation. I didn't want to push him too hard."

I raised an eyebrow.

With a playful eye roll, Evie admitted, "Okay, fine, I was tempted to press him for more, but I restrained myself. I didn't want to be insensitive."

The four of us stood together, observing the bustling activity of the cat café. Laughter and lighthearted conversation filled the air, blending with the enticing aroma of freshly brewed coffee. I was glad I'd followed Josephine's advice and expanded our staff. It was definitely far more crowded than I expected. "I wonder if we should start serving sandwiches," I said.

"I could talk to my grandmother," Matt offered.

"That would be great, Matt. Thank you. It's so much busier than we thought, right?"

"Maybe busier than you thought. I knew this would work," Evie said.

Our latest hires, a diverse and dedicated group, were hard at work attending to their various duties. Behind the counter, the barista's nimble fingers danced across the espresso machine, pouring velvety streams of coffee into waiting cups. At the same time, another staff member efficiently cleared tables, wiped them down with a damp cloth, and ensured the entire dining area remained spotless.

A trio of caretakers circulated among the cats, each offering their unique brand of attention to the feline inhabitants. One dangled a feathered toy, engaging a cluster of playful kittens in a spirited game of chase. Another crouched beside a bashful cat, whispering soothing words and offering gentle strokes to coax the creature from its hiding place. The third caretaker circulated among the more outgoing cats, distributing treats that earned them an eager chorus of vocalizations.

Matt leaned in, his eyes sparkling with excitement. "So, when do we start working on the case?"

I froze in the middle of taking a sip, slowly lowering my coffee cup to the table. "What case are you talking about?"

"The one Evie texted me about."

"Ben's murder, of course," Darla added, a mischievous glint lighting up her eyes. "We've got the cat witness, the antique platter, and well-trained staff to keep the café running smoothly while we're occupied. What else could we possibly need?"

"I really want to get started, too." Evie thoughtfully tapped her index finger on the wooden table, her brows furrowed in contemplation. "But we should give Honey a few hours to settle into his new surroundings. Then, we can see if he will share any clues with us."

Clues.

Oh, dear.

The soft hum of conversation from other patrons in the background filled the room, but my attention was fixed solely on the impromptu detective team assembled around our small table. I was determined to rein in their runaway enthusiasm before they got carried away with wild theories and hasty decisions.

"Wait just a minute," I said, raising my hands to slow down the eager Catnip Conspirators assembled around me. "We don't even know if Ben Tyson was murdered. Heart attacks can happen to anyone, even someone as young as Ben. Sure, it's not the norm, but it's not impossible."

This was all because of that darn magic plate. Its secret had somehow slipped into the open, despite our best efforts to keep it under wraps.

Well, some effort. When Evie and I first discovered its unique ability, we solemnly promised each other to keep it a secret. And I really thought we would.

But, as it turned out, I couldn't resist confiding in Landon.

And then, of course, I had to tell my best friend, Laurie.

Evie, on the other hand, had shared the secret with Darla.

And eventually, she told Matt.

Telling Josephine was a necessity. Yes, she was a friend, but she was also the lawyer for our rescue operation. Anything we said to her was safeguarded by the attorney-client privilege.

Huh.

Okay, so maybe I did know how everyone knew.

Our little secret had spread among my and Evie's close-knit circles of friends like ripples on a pond's surface, weaving a web of intimate trust and intrigue. The rescue had become a hub of whispered conversations and shared secrets, a cozy sanctuary where we could discuss the mysteries that lived within a silver and crystalline serving tray.

Platter.

Whatever.

My eyes moved from one expectant face to another, each looking back at me with anticipation and curiosity. Obviously, the notion of solving a mystery had captivated them, but I knew I had to be the grown up voice of sanity.

"Listen, everyone," I said, "I know that the idea of solving a potential murder mystery is exciting, but we need to make sure we're not jumping to conclusions. Our first concern is Honey and his emotional well-being. Let's step back and approach this rationally without getting carried away." I glanced at their faces, hoping to see understanding and restraint begin to take hold.

But instead, I saw the opposite.

Their eyes widened with excitement, and their bodies shifted with expectation. The Scratching Post Sleuths weren't going to let this go so easily.

"Coming through!" Laurie called out as she entered the café after hours with a cat carrier securely held in her grasp. A fluffy black cat peered out through the front wire mesh, curiosity shining in its eyes. "The cat's owner insists up and down that this cat hasn't had chocolate, but she won't give me permission to run tests. I bet my new ultrasound machine that this little one ate a Hershey bar."

Dr. Laurie Gray, Tablerock's preeminent veterinarian, and my best friend, briskly walked through the now-closed cat café, her steps purposeful as she headed straight for the stairs leading to the second floor.

"Ben Tyson's cat is in the isolation room!" I called out while hurrying to catch up with her.

Laurie paused for a moment, her expression softening. "Oh, that poor thing. This won't take long, and I know Honey—I'm sure he'll be happy to see me. Maybe I can help while I'm here."

As she ascended the stairs, I couldn't help but admire Laurie's dedication to the well-being of the animals in her care. Her confident stride and genuine concern for the furry patients she treated were testaments to her passion for her work. At that moment, I felt grateful to have her as a friend and a professional resource.

While I was grateful for her expertise and friendship, Honey's gratitude for his doctor was an entirely different story.

You!" Honey cried out as Laurie opened the door to

the isolation room, his voice seething with anger. "What are you doing here? Haven't I been through enough today? Do I need Dr. Stick-Em-In-The-Butt-With-The-Pointy-End to finish me off?" The cat hissed and yowled, his frustration evident. "You already took my manhood, you witch! Are you coming for the rest of it? You'll need a magnifying glass!"

I could see the shock in Laurie's eyes as she tried to process the cat's outburst. It wasn't every day that a cat could so eloquently express its disdain for the veterinarian who had performed its neutering surgery.

I bit my lip, trying my best not to laugh at the unexpected insight.

"Honey, don't scare Creepers," Laurie told the cat. "Surely, you don't—"

"Get out! Leave me alone! Take your manhood-stripping scalpel and go!"

Laurie, being the professional she was, quickly composed herself and addressed Honey in a soothing tone. "Honey, I'm here to help another cat who might be in trouble. Creepers is sick, and I need to use the plate to find out what's wrong with him. I promise I'm not here to cause you any more distress."

"Are you wearing balls on your ears? Really, woman?" Honey remarked with a tone of indignation. "Balls? As decoration on your person? What kind of savage are you?"

I glanced at Laurie's earrings and realized they were small orange balls. They were undoubtedly designed to resemble fuzzy cat toys – a quirky and fun accessory for a cat-loving veterinarian.

However, the earrings took on a different, more unsettling meaning from Honey's perspective, given his past trauma.

Laurie's cheeks flushed with embarrassment as she self-consciously reached up to touch her earrings. "Oh, these? They're just for fun, Honey. I didn't mean any offense," she explained, attempting to smooth over the awkward moment.

Honey's eyes narrowed, and his hair stood on end.

Laurie gave up. She removed them and placed them in her pocket. "We good?"

"Not even close." Despite his words, his agitation appeared to subside slightly as he begrudgingly accepted her symbolic removal of the jewelry for his comfort. "Thank you. Though you should thank me. Those couldn't have been in worse taste for someone like you," the cat added, his voice dripping with disdain.

"Can I please use the tray you're sitting on?" Laurie asked politely.

Honey glanced at Creepers in the carrier, whose eyes pleaded for help as she emitted a pitiful whine.

"I'm doing this for her, not you," he grumbled. Honey sighed and stepped off the platter, his body language conveying reluctant cooperation. As he moved, the glowing light from the platter dimmed.

Laurie nodded appreciatively and carefully placed Creepers on the plate. "So, did you really only eat the highest quality kibble and soft food, or did you get into something you shouldn't have?" she asked Creepers, her tone empathetic.

"My mother," Creepers said with eyes narrowed and ears flattened against her head, "is nothing but a liar. She fed me chocolate ice cream despite my protests. Said it was for my birthday. Who gives a cat chocolate ice cream for their birthday? A fish, maybe. Octopus? Surely. But chocolate ice cream? What does that woman take me for, human? Then, on top of everything, she lied to your face when you asked about it!"

As Creepers recounted her mother's deception, I felt a pang of sympathy for the little cat. I knew all too well the pain of being lied to or lied about by someone you thought you could trust.

"That's terrible," Laurie said, her voice filled with compassion as she stroked Creepers' fur. "I'm sorry that happened to you. But now we know, and we'll get you fixed right up. I promise."

Honey, reacting to the distress of his fellow feline, hopped onto the glowing tray and rubbed his head against the black cat. "Yes," his voice came through, tinged with bitterness, "humans lie with an impunity that belies explanation — when you least expect it and to those you would least suspect."

"Quite," Creepers agreed.

Chapter Three

I OPENED THE DOOR TO THE SOUNDPROOFED ROOM, my furry charges' snores a reminder of the long day I'd had already. I was ready to crawl into bed, but a quick look at my watch told me it was only seven.

"You gonna hang out for a bit?" I asked.

"Yeah, but I'm not going back in there. I'm not sure I want to face the wrath of the altered duo in there without a drink," Laurie told me. Her lips curved into a half-smirk. "You have any bourbon down there?"

"We do not," I shook my head and smiled at her suggestion, my expression wry. "It's a cat rescue with a coffee counter. You won't find anything stronger than espresso shots here."

Laurie let out a small, resigned sigh, but her good humor remained. "Well, I suppose I'll have to make do with whatever you've got. You ought to think about stocking some for after hours."

"Not sure about that."

"You're no fun, Eleanor."

As we descended the stairs, I noticed that Evie and Matt had taken charge of the counter like professional baristas. They were chatting and handing decaf coffees to Darla. Oh, and Josephine, who must have arrived while we were upstairs.

It was the end of the day, and the rescue was closed to the public. The warm light of the setting sun spilled in through the windows, casting a golden glow over everything. The atmosphere in the room was no longer frantic; it was relaxed and inviting as we gathered together to unwind.

"Hey, Josephine." I waved. "What's up?"

Josephine thrust a stack of documents at me. Her imperious eyes were shrouded behind wire-rim spectacles, and her red power suit seemed to dominate the room. "I need your signature on these right now," she said.

"Of course, Josephine," I replied, taking the papers from her and grabbing a pen. As I signed my name on the dotted line, I couldn't help but note how all our lives had become so intertwined. "What am I signing?"

Her lips curled into a faint, knowing smile. "Does it matter?"

"In truth, no. I have faith in you," I said.

She chuckled. "Of course you do, but that's a careless answer. Never trust a lawyer." I handed the documents back to Josephine, who rolled her eyes. "I'm glad I stepped in through all this. I can't imagine what would have happened if someone with an agenda barreled in and took over."

"Wait just a sec. You mean to tell me you don't have some hidden agenda?" Laurie asked, cocking an eyebrow.

Josephine flashed a cheeky grin and said, "Oh, I've got an agenda, all right. Of course, I do. But my agenda is to protect you all. That's my agenda, and that's my only agenda. I've got Ellie's best interests at heart. I doubt anyone else would."

Landon Rogers, a friend of the rescue and resident handyman, swung open the front door and stepped into the mantrap, his tall frame casting a shadow against the twilight sky. I couldn't help but take note of his distinguished appearance — even in his fifties, there was a boyish charm about him that was hard to resist.

I knew he had a bit of a crush on me, but it wasn't something I entertained. After all, I had a lot going on with taking care of Evie and running the rescue. But still, occasionally, I caught a glimpse of his lingering gaze and wondered what it might be like to let those boundaries blur...

Just a little.

With a casual wave, Landon greeted the group. "Evening, folks," he said, sauntering over to grab a chair and join us at the table. Once settled, he asked Evie for soda water.

"Sure thing, Landon."

"Thank you," he told her. Landon's voice had a deep, soothing quality to it. It always reminded me of a steaming mug of hot chocolate on a frosty winter evening. "Did I somehow miss a memo about a board meeting?"

"Nope, we're just hanging out," I said, shrugging my shoulders. "Seems like it's been a crazy day for all of us, so we figured we could use a little downtime to decompress."

Landon nodded, his gaze shifting from one face to another. He looked over at my daughter. "I heard about the Ben Tyson situation, and Mario mentioned that you and Evie stumbled upon him in his store. You guys okay?"

"Why does everyone keep asking that?" Evie retorted, coming around the counter and handing Landon his fizzy water. "We're not the ones who got killed. We just walked into a store and found a dead guy on the floor. I mean, it's not that big of a deal, right?"

"Because most people get a little rattled after seeing someone they know all cold and lifeless like that," Landon replied, taking the soda water from Evie with an appreciative nod. "Reminders of our own mortality can be pretty unsettling."

Evie burst out laughing, her mirth bubbling over like a sparkling fountain. She paused to catch her breath, then said through her giggles. "Landon, I've had three open-heart surgeries. I have a tiny gadget in my chest that keeps me alive by telling my heart when to beat. Do you think finding a dead body on the floor will shake my sense of mortality? Give me a break!"

"No, ma'am." Landon's eyes fixed on Evie as he finished his soda water with a single swig. After a beat, he added in a low, even tone, "But I was asking you about your mom. I figured you might tell me the truth faster than she would."

Evie shot Landon a warm smile. "Oh, right. Yeah, that's true. Mom practically freaked out on the Tower of Terror at Disney World because there wasn't anything to hold onto. You're right. She gets pretty twitchy."

"I do not." I shot Evie a look. "It wasn't that bad. But I'll admit, coming across Ben's lifeless body was pretty... unnerving."

"You screamed," my daughter ribbed, smirking at me. "I didn't scream."

Landon leaned back in his chair, his face softening with sympathy. "Well, it's only natural to be shaken up by something like that. I'm just glad you're both okay."

"Look, no one needs to worry about me. When we found Ben, I didn't scream. I checked for a pulse, called the cops, and we waited. It was fine." My friends glanced at me, their faces full of knowing, as if they were privy to something I wasn't. "Evie, back me up here."

"I meant you screamed on the ride, Mom. Not today."

I exhaled in relief, realizing my mistake. "Oh, right. Sorry, I'm a bit frazzled after everything that's happened." I surveyed the café, my unease still lingering.

"I just can't wrap my head around the fact that Ben's gone."

Just then, Officer Mario Lopez strode into the shelter through the specially designed mantrap—a small, enclosed space installed to keep curious cats from sneaking out as people came in.

He moved with a sense of gravity that shifted the atmosphere in the room.

Evie leaned in, her eyes wide with excitement as she declared, "See? I told you he was murdered." The confidence in her voice was unmistakable.

The smugness was a little harder to detect.

I sighed, trying to remain levelheaded. "I didn't say Ben wasn't murdered, Evie. I didn't want to jump to conclusions without knowing all the facts."

Officer Lopez, a solid figure with broad shoulders and a meticulously pressed uniform, spoke with a somber tone that filled the front room. "Well, we don't have all the facts yet, Ellie, but we have enough to know that he didn't drop dead because the Almighty needed more beekeepers up in Heaven." He paused, his deep brown eyes searching mine as if to gauge my reaction.

I said nothing.

In fact, I don't think I even moved.

I was not interested in being caught up in yet another murder case.

Evie, however, was vibrating with excitement at hearing about poor Ben's untimely end. Which was a little gruesome. Her eyes sparkled with anticipation, her hands gripping the edge of her chair as if she were about to leap into action.

The contrast between her enthusiasm and my dread?

It couldn't have been more pronounced.

"I wanted to let you know," Mario continued, "so we could ask you to hold on to that cat until I know who to release it to—if anyone. You know how these things go." He nodded in agreement with his statement, a habit I had noticed many cops seemed to share. "We'll let you know as soon as we know."

"Of course, Mario," I told him. "We'll be happy to take care of Honey."

Mario's eyebrows furrowed. The creases remained on his forehead as he asked, "How did you discover the cat's name was Honey?"

Oops.

Darn it.

Incorporating a magical tabletop into my routine was one of the most daunting changes I'd ever encountered, and I'd already been through menopause. You wouldn't expect it to be that complex, but it was.

The challenge wasn't just about coming to terms with such a unique item but also remembering that the chatty cat room and the intel we gathered were secrets we had to guard closely.

Maintaining the secrecy of this information from those unaware around us was a never-ending mental balancing act. Everyday conversations became a high-wire act of discretion, made even more challenging by the reality that many of our close friends were in on the secret.

"He's one of my patients, naturally," Laurie interjected, stepping in when I didn't respond. "I told Ellie the cat's name. Makes sense, right?"

"Are you interrogating Ellie, Officer Lopez?" Josephine's voice sliced through the air, sharp and assertive. "Because I don't recall hearing any Miranda rights being read."

If Laurie excelled at easing tension, Josephine was a pro at...

Well, whatever the opposite of that was.

Sensing the gathering storm, Landon murmured under his breath, "Oh boy, here we go." He shot a sympathetic look at Mario, who returned a knowing nod. "Good luck, buddy."

Josephine's sharp ears caught the hushed words. "Did you say something, Landon?"

Landon shook his head, replying, "No, ma'am. That'd be pretty foolish of me."

Officer Lopez raised his hands placatingly, sensing the need to defuse the situation. His voice took on a soothing tone as if he were trying to calm a spooked animal. "No, Josephine. I'm not interrogating Ellie. When I saw her earlier today, she didn't know the cat's name. It didn't occur to me that Laurie would have told her."

"Well, the look on your face was a bit suspicious, Mario. But maybe we're all mistaken. Maybe you ate too many tacos from Pepper Jalisco's again," I said, attempting to inject some lightheartedness into the conversation.

Everyone at the table shifted their focus to the officer, their eyes curious and expectant.

Well, almost everyone.

Josephine Reynolds remained skeptical, her gaze narrowed as she scrutinized Mario.

Good grief.

Realizing he was the center of attention, Officer Lopez cracked a smile. He scratched his head, revealing a touch of vulnerability beneath his confident exterior.

"Apologies if my face was misleading," he said. "I didn't mean to cause any alarm, and no, of course, Ellie isn't a suspect in anything. Ben had a surveillance camera in the parking lot, and we're well aware y'all showed up when you claimed you did."

"One second." Josephine rummaged through her purse, rustling and clinking accompanying her search. After a moment, she pulled out a small digital tape recorder and clicked the button. Once activated, she shoved it toward Mario. "Can you say that whole thing again and be sure to enunciate? Thank you."

Caught off guard by the unexpected request, Mario

stared at the tape recorder for a moment before letting out a small chuckle.

Josephine's eyes were glued to him, recorder outstretched.

"Very funny." Mario shook his head.

Josephine continued to fix her gaze on Mario, her eyes expectant.

Mario's good-natured grin faded. "You're serious?" he asked, his eyebrows arching in surprise.

In response to Mario's surprise, Josephine shook the digital recorder, emphasizing her intent. She leaned closer, determination etched on her face, making it clear the attorney wasn't messing around. "As a heart attack, young man," she declared firmly. Suddenly, her face fell, and she turned to look at Evie. "Sorry about that. I wasn't thinking," she apologized.

Evie rolled her eyes. "That's my line!"

As was customary during our gatherings, our one big group split into smaller clusters separated by age. Evie, Darla, and Matt wandered over to the other side of the room to settle into a comfortable corner seating area, their faces animated with laughter and periodic expressions of excitement.

Back at our table, Josephine sighed and shook her head. "I can't believe I said that in front of your daughter," she admitted sourly. "I swear, sometimes I don't know what comes over me. I just spit out words without thinking."

Landon's lips curled into a smile, his eyes sparkling with amusement. "Oh, don't sell yourself short, Josie," he said in a playful tone. "I've always thought you were more the calculating type."

The corners of Josephine's mouth turned up into a small smile as she let out a soft chuckle. "True. I am calculating. Like a mathlete on steroids."

Why would a mathlete take steroids?

Josephine's smile faded. "I forgot about Evie's issues. The girl's brain sometimes freezes up when she burns spaghetti, but she walks into Ben's place to find him dead on the floor, and she's fine? I don't know that I would have been fine." Josephine held her hands up. "Forgive me for not remembering the girl has a wonky head and heart."

"I don't think anyone's upset with you, Josie. Besides, brain damage is always an odd thing. Everyone's brain is a little unique," Laurie said and then sipped her drink. "Each brain is shaped by a complex combination of genetic and environmental factors. No two brains are exactly alike. None."

"Twins?" Landon asked with a puzzled arch of his eyebrows.

"Nope. Not even twins. So the symptoms and severity of brain damage depend on the extent and location of the damage. The symptoms people show can vary wildly from person to person. Evie, for instance, may have difficulty making dinner but be more than capable of examining a dead body." Laurie smiled, acknowledging the paradox. "I know, it seems weird."

"I didn't know Evie had brain damage," Mario said, his voice low like Evie's condition was a secret. "I knew about the heart defect, but that's it."

"It was her third surgery," I told him. I noticed my voice calmly reflected my acceptance of it all now, but that wasn't always the case. "It was complicated and incredibly long. She was on the heart-lung bypass machine for longer than she'd ever been. Maybe that did it. Maybe not." I shrugged. "When she came out of the surgery, she was different. She couldn't do math anymore. She'd lose track of the steps she'd need to take halfway through doing her laundry. I knew something was wrong, but it would come and go, and there was nothing they could do to check, anyway."

"They wanted an MRI to see what was wrong, but Evie can't have one," Laurie said. Turning to me, she added, "That must have been so frustrating."

"It was," I admitted. "How do you ground a teenager for not taking out the trash when you're not sure whether she blew it off or her brain just deleted that file?"

"You never had an MRI?" Mario frowned. "Why not?"

"She has a pacemaker," Laurie explained. "The strong magnetic fields in the MRI machine can interfere with it, potentially causing it to malfunction. It's just too risky."

"That's not the case anymore, though," I said. "When her pacemaker was changed, we got one that was MRI-safe and then got the MRI. That's when we discovered the small patches of damage from the surgery."

Landon regarded me with a silent but supportive gaze from across the table. I could tell he was itching to say something reassuring, but he kept his thoughts to himself for the time being.

"That poor girl," Josephine said. She rapped her knuckles on the wooden tabletop. "Let's hope and pray she never has to undergo another surgery again."

The room was filled with murmurs and amens meant to display everyone's good intentions and well wishes, and I appreciated it. I did.

Even so, I didn't join their chorus.

I already knew Evie would have to face multiple surgeries. We had been told that her aortic valve would need to be replaced at some point. Many children with heart defects were fortunate to have their heart repairs last a lifetime. But for Evie, like others, the luck lay only in the fact that these surgeries would keep her alive.

"Is that why she still lives with you?" Mario inquired, his tone gentle and understanding. "When I was her age, I was already years out of my parent's house."

I nodded. "She can forget to take her medication.

She can't drive—well, she probably could, but the doctors don't want her to. She gets ocular migraines—"

"What's that?" Landon asked.

"Evie will see flashing lights and zigzag lines for about half an hour. Then she'll get numbness in her hands and have difficulty speaking. It comes on so quickly that if she was behind the wheel of a car, it could be dangerous," I explained. "Because of all this stuff and her periodic difficulty in moving through it, she's more comfortable living with me."

"I had no idea," Mario murmured.

"I'm surprised. Evie's convinced the whole town knows about the brain damage," I told him. "And I think she's less concerned about the actual effects of it and living with it than having everyone know she has it."

I could tell by the look on Mario's face that he was still processing all of this information. He was quiet for a few moments, then finally spoke up.

"That sounds really tough," he said, his voice thick with sympathy. "But Evie shouldn't worry so much about what people think of her. We can't control how others view us, nor should we try, you know? All we can do is focus on ourselves and being the best versions of ourselves."

"Amen." Landon nodded slowly, his gaze locking with mine.

Chapter Four

THE FOLLOWING DAY, I WANDERED INTO EVIE'S room to find her hunched over her laptop, bathed in the early morning light that filtered into her room. She held a steaming cup of coffee in one hand while the other tapped away at the keyboard. "It's six in the morning," I said, surprised. "What are you doing up already?"

"Checking SocialBook, obviously," she replied without looking up, her eyes scanning across the screen. "Did you know Leo Barnett was fired a couple of months ago?" she added, nodding toward the laptop. "You remember that guy, right? He used to check us out at the store before Ben started working there himself. The one with the long hair?"

I felt a pang of sadness at her mention of Ben's name. "Yes, I remember Leo," I said. "I didn't know Ben fired him, though. And unless Leo posted that himself, I'd take it with a grain of salt. There will be all sorts of rumors now, you know."

As I made my way toward the pile of clothes scattered across the floor like fallen leaves and picked each item up one by one, Evie said, "I can handle doing that, you know. I can get up on my own, too. I don't know why you come in here every single morning. I've got an alarm clock."

I paused for a moment and then shrugged. "I suppose it's just become a habit. I've been doing this for nearly twenty-five years. No real reason to stop now, I guess," I said, my hands deftly scooping up a pair of discarded jeans a small cat was sleeping on and tossing them into the hamper quickly.

The adorable little tabby glared at me and then waddled toward the door, its fluffy tail swishing back and forth in annoyance.

Evie smirked, "This is more like an obsession, Mother."

"Motherhood is far from an obsession, my darling daughter," I muttered, irritated at the notion. "But sure. Let's say it's an obsession. You're obsessed with solving murders, and I'm obsessed with clean laundry. I will next be obsessed with breakfast, and hopefully, you will be obsessed with the cat boxes."

"Maybe a magic scooper will show up one day. You know, one that magically cleans the cat boxes?" Evie looked up, spotted my expression, and smiled. "What? One can always hope, right?"

This was my morning ritual. I did a little "dust off and straighten up" before I prepared breakfast and savored the first sip of coffee while watching the sunrise from the second floor balcony.

As I scanned the room, my gaze landed on a fluffy gray ball of fur nestled in the corner. The tiny kitten, only nine weeks old, had bright blue eyes that twinkled with mischief. With its tail held high, the kitten scampered over to me, its eagerness for attention palpable. As I bent down to pet the little one, a smile spread across my face.

It was the small pleasures that made life worth living, really.

Living...

I sighed.

Poor Ben.

Mario had been surprisingly forthcoming with details about the case last night, but it was evident they were already hitting dead ends before they even began. The enigmatic pattern on Ben's back remained a mystery, and the cause of his death was nothing short of brutal. Someone mercilessly held his face down in a pan of honey until he suffocated, a cruel and senseless act that shocked us all.

It was an absurd way to die.

It also seemed an awfully personal way to kill someone.

My mind was lost in thought until Evie's voice interrupted my daydreaming. "Mom, do you need me to make breakfast?" she asked, returning me to reality.

I shook my head and replied, "No need, I've got it covered." Making my way toward the door, I leaned against the jamb. The details of what Mario had shared with us the previous night kept swirling around my head. "I was just thinking about what Mario told us last night."

"Which part?"

"Ben drowning in a pan of honey seems...almost weirdly specific and personal. Someone would have to stand over him and hold him down, or they'd have clocked him on the head until he was unconscious and left his face in the pan. That wasn't an accident. Someone wanted Ben dead."

"I know, right?" Evie said. She turned her computer around to face me and gestured for me to come closer. "There was no denying that someone had wanted him dead. I thought the same thing, and look what I found on JuxtaPorte from a year ago."

I leaned over her shoulder to get a better look.

Nina Coleman, head beekeeper at Buzzing Blossom Farms, had accused Ben of poisoning her bees. According to her post, the bees had become sick and started dying off at an alarming rate — which she suspected was the result of Ben's actions.

And "suspected" felt like too feeble a word to describe the certainty in Nina's post as she leveled the public allegation against Ben.

Nina went on to suggest (and by suggest, I mean accuse) that Ben had done this to ensure that his honey took the title of "Best Honey" at the town fair. Buzzing Blossom Farms had taken first prize for five years running.

Until a year ago.

As Evie scrolled through the comments section of the town's online forum, I couldn't help but notice that Ben had vehemently denied the accusations hurled against him by Nina. His words were defensive, and he'd gone as far as to insinuate that Nina was a subpar beekeeper and that she alone was responsible for the plight of her bees.

"You think Nina killed Ben over issues they had with each other a year ago?" I asked my daughter.

"No. But maybe." Evie shrugged, her expression thoughtful. "I'm not sure. I don't have enough information to make any conclusions just yet," she said, tapping her chin. "But it's definitely suspicious. And it would be interesting to hear what she says about him now that he's gone."

I couldn't argue with that. It was worth talking to Nina to understand what kind of person she was and her relationship with Ben.

"Well, we do need honey for the café since the police have Ben's whole place cordoned off and shut down," I said without thinking. "We could get it from Buzzing Blossom Farms."

A grin spread across Evie's face, and her eyes

sparkled with amusement. "I knew you'd be all over this," she said.

Confused, I arched an eyebrow. "All over what?"

"Investigating the murder," she said.

The slyness in her smile did not escape my notice.

I leveled a firm gaze at Evie, not wanting her to get too ahead of herself. "Let's be clear. We're not investigating anything," I said, hoping to temper her enthusiasm. "We're simply going to Buzzing Blossom Farms to get honey for the café, which we need. No investigation, just satisfying our curiosity."

"Of course."

"And if we happen to come across anything suspicious, we'll inform Mario right away," I added, wanting to ensure we didn't get in over our heads. "Not do anything ourselves."

"Sure thing, Mom," Evie replied, her tone infused with a hint of amusement. With a press of a button, the printer in her room sprang to life, whirring and whizzing as it produced several pages of neatly printed notes. "But before we dive in, I've got a list of questions for Honey about those two individuals — Nina and Leo," she explained, rising from her seat and snatching up the sheets of paper. "I'll head in and chat with him after breakfast."

Despite my attempts to downplay and derail Evie's intentions, it was clear to me that our visit to Buzzing Blossom Farms — and her list of questions for Honey —

were the beginning of something that resembled an armchair investigation.

Following breakfast, as we made our way to the isolation room, Evie attempted to persuade me that we were at the forefront of a burgeoning trend.

"You know, there's this whole new thing where people investigate crimes online and share information," she said. "You heard the term crowdsourcing? People scour publicly available information like news reports and online forums to gather evidence, analyze clues, and form their own theories about what happened in a particular crime."

"And no one in this crowd of cold case busters is concerned about the risks of that?" I asked Evie.

"Well, everyone warns you not to be crazy about it, but not generally, no," she said with a shrug. The gravity of her words was at odds with her laid-back manner. "When's the last time you watched a Dateline about a dead armchair sleuth?" she asked.

I paused, racking my brain to remember the last crime show I had seen. "I'm not sure," I admitted. "But that doesn't mean it's wise to go around playing detective." I couldn't help but wonder how many armchair sleuths were out there, attempting to solve crimes from the safety of their computer screens. "And we're talking about visiting someone connected to the case, so it's not all behind a screen. Just be cautious, Evie. That's all I'm trying to say."

I was only cautioning Evie because if I outright forbade her from pursuing this armchair investigation, she would do it anyway, clandestinely. And then, I wouldn't have any inkling of what she was up to.

Evie truly believed that if the police presented us with a potential feline crime witness, our societal obligation was to follow through since the police couldn't speak to the cat.

While I couldn't disagree with her on principle — after all, working toward the greater good was a noble cause — I honestly didn't anticipate having to act on her view of our community obligation.

Tablerock was a sleepy town where life chugged along at a snail's pace. Crime wasn't something we worried about; the most excitement we saw at the rescue was when someone's cat went missing.

Well.

Until the Blackwell murders turned everything on its head.

"Hello there, Belladonna," Evie greeted the black cat perched just outside the shut door of the isolation room. "Would you like to join us inside?"

Fiona's black cat returned Evie's gaze with a measured blink and waited expectantly for her to open the door.

Stepping behind Evie, I was enveloped by a soothing blend of chamomile and lavender. Belladonna entered with feline grace, her eyes dancing from shadow to shadow.

Unable to contain his displeasure, Honey emitted a low, menacing hiss. His eyes became narrowed slits filled with animosity as they locked onto Belladonna.

Unfazed by his hostility, Belladonna rose to the challenge, her back arching like a drawn bow and her fur rippling into a bristling mane. A retaliatory hiss escaped her lips.

Finally, Honey let out a snarl, and Belladonna responded with a fierce growl.

It seemed the two cats were about to launch at each other at any moment.

"I think we should—"

"It'll be fine, Mom. Look."

Just as suddenly as it had started, the standoff ended.

Honey turned on his heel and stalked away, his tail twitching in annoyance. Meanwhile, Belladonna let out a satisfied yawn and jumped into the cubby hole holding the crystalline plate.

The black cat's disdainful voice sliced through the air with an air of superiority. "Might I assume that your intention is to poke at this gentleman's grief-stricken heart regarding the loss of his beloved owner?" she asked while casting a disapproving look my way. "Perhaps it would be wise to allow him the space and time to grieve in peace."

"This wasn't my idea, you know." I turned to Ellie.

"Why does that cat always sound like a medieval duchess in temporary exile?"

Ellie let out a chuckle. "That's Belladonna for you. If she wants to talk like a duchess, let her talk like a duchess. What's the harm?"

Belladonna let out a bored yawn, her whiskers twitching. "Pray tell, how can one determine that I am not, in fact, a duchess currently in temporary exile? As far as 'letting me,' I am rather curious to know how you plan on thwarting my innate tendencies for greatness," the cat said. Her voice was laced with skepticism.

She had a point, though.

Not about greatness.

About not knowing whether she was a duchess in exile.

I mean, stranger things had already happened.

Despite the cat's appallingly insulting manner, I couldn't help but feel a sense of warmth toward Belladonna. Something about her aloofness was undeniably endearing, and I'd grown used to her haughty demeanor and enigmatic personality.

"Might I inquire as to the source of your amusement?" she asked me, her eyes narrowing in suspicion at the slight smile on my face. "Honey's caretaker is dead, and I fail to see any justification for mirth in such a sorrowful circumstance."

I quickly dropped the smile as I realized how callous I must have seemed. "I'm sorry, Honey. I didn't mean to appear insensitive. It's just that...well, Belladonna seems to make even the bleakest of situations seem a little bit brighter."

Probably because nothing was as black as her sociopathic little heart.

Belladonna blinked, her expression softening ever so slightly. "I see," she murmured as if pondering my words. "Perhaps it is because you are a simpleton," she said with amusement, "that you must find joy even amid sorrow and ignore hard things. How very human."

She didn't mean it as a compliment.

I couldn't help but feel a twinge of irritation at her condescending tone, but I didn't want to start a fight with Belladonna. I ignored her jibe, picked up a feathered cat toy, and dangled it on the floor.

Belladonna froze.

The only thing that moved was her eyes, which followed the toy as it swayed back and forth.

She narrowed them, calculating her approach.

With a quick flick of her tail, she crouched down and wiggled her rear end before launching herself at the toy with a burst of energy.

Checkmate, you puffed-up little grimalkin, I thought.

"There," I told Evie. "Go ahead and move Honey onto the plate."

Belladonna may be a haughty, mysterious cat with a vocabulary that even an Oxford scholar would find pretentious, but at the end of the day?

She was still a cat.

Honey scowled and narrowed his eyes as he stared at the black cat. "I don't like her," he said, his gaze fixed on Belladonna. "Black cats are bad luck."

I frowned at his words, wondering where he had picked up such a superstition. The belief that black cats were bad luck was long-standing, but it was also rooted in ignorance and prejudice. It shocked me a little to find a cat with a bias that originated with humans.

"The belief that black cats are bad luck is a superstition. It's been around for centuries," Evie explained to Honey in a gentle tone. "A superstition is an irrational belief or practice not based on evidence or reason. Belladonna isn't bad luck because her fur is black. That's ridiculous."

"Is it?" Honey looked skeptical, his tail twitching nervously behind him. "Then why is she bad luck?"

"No, that's not what I—she's not bad luck. People aren't bad luck," Evie said.

The orange and white cat looked up at us, stretching out his paws to reveal his sharp claws, then settled back into a comfortable position. He yawned, exposing a row of long, pointed teeth. "She's not people," he rumbled in his low, feline voice.

"What do you mean?"

"She's a cat like me. Cats are not people," he repeated as if stating an indisputable fact. "At least that's what Augusta always told Ben. Cats are not people, so get Honey off the table," he added with a flick of his tail. "Cats are not people. Only people sleep in the bed. No cats. Cats are not people, so who cares what he wants."

"Who's he?" Evie asked.

"Me."

"Augusta?" I asked. "You mean Augusta Walton, the baker?" My mind immediately conjured images of her mouth-watering pastries and cakes. They were so delectable they could tempt even the strictest dieter. She ran a bakery in historic downtown with a Great Dane, Tank, always at her side. "Is that who you're referring to, Honey?"

"I suppose."

Interrogating cats was quite a challenge.

"Is it or isn't it, Honey?" Evie asked.

"Yes. Ben was seeing her until recently. Or maybe it was the week before. Who can keep track of time?" The cat lay across the plate, his fluffy tail swishing back and forth lazily as he surveyed the room with an air of nonchalance. Honey paused to lick his paw before continuing. "She had this enormous, slobbering beast of an animal, all dim-witted howls and ball-chasing manners. She treated him like a person but refused to do the same for me."

It wasn't the politest description, but it sounded like a Great Dane.

"Well, I'm sorry she treated you that way, Honey," Evie said, scratching him behind the ears. "But don't worry, you'll always be a person in our book."

"I may not have been a person to her, but that didn't stop me from knocking her cake off the counter and onto the floor," the orange cat said with a hint of menace. His eyes glinted in the sunlight filtering in through the window.

"Honey, do you know what happened to Ben?" Evie asked.

Honey emitted a low, rumbling meow from deep within his throat, his head shaking side to side in a human-like denial. His bright, golden eyes blinked lazily, as if in slow-motion, while his ears quivered and stood erect.

"I do not. I didn't see anything," Honey said, his whiskers drooping. "Ben was always so kind to me, bringing me treats and toys. He let me on the counter. And the table. And the bed. No one would want to hurt him."

"It's okay, Honey," I said, reaching out to give him a reassuring pat on the head. "The police will find out what happened to Ben and make sure whoever did this is brought to justice."

Honey's ears twitched uncertainly, and his head cocked to the side. The cat seemed tense as if bracing himself for more bad news. "Is this my new home now?" he asked. "Or will I become homeless and be left to fend for myself?"

Evie looked at Honey with a sad expression on her face. "You don't have to worry about that right now, Honey," Evie said. "You can stay here for as long as you need to, and then once you're ready, maybe we can find you a new family."

I winced.

With Ben gone, we had no idea who Honey's rightful owner was. I wished Evie hadn't given him the assurances she did.

I understood why she'd done it.

Honey needed security and stability, especially in this time of turmoil. And yes, it was likely to turn out precisely as Evie said. The sad truth was people rarely fought over animals.

But sometimes, the unexpected happens.

Chapter Five

Evie and I hopped in the shelter's sprinter van and began our journey to Buzzing Blossom Farms, located on the other side of Tablerock. The winding Hill Country roads twisted and turned as we moved closer to town, revealing stunning views of rolling hills and endless greenery that stretched for miles.

When we reached the stoplight on Main Street, I noticed that Evie was wearing more makeup than usual. Her lips were painted with a bright red, glossy hue of color instead of the faintly tinted lip balm she usually wore, and her ordinarily messy bun was twisted with a fancy jeweled hair comb.

I couldn't help but recall how my daughter had been blushing around Matt lately. I suspected her newfound interest in health and beauty had something to do with that, but I didn't want to push her or make her uncomfortable by bringing it up.

If she wanted to tell me why she was all made up, she would.

Obviously, she didn't.

I stepped on the gas and focused on the road ahead, not saying a word — and I'm very proud to say that resolve lasted until the following stoplight.

I turned to Evie as she fiddled with the radio. "So, how are you and Matt doing?" I asked, raising an eyebrow. "I noticed you've been spending a lot of time together."

A faint blush rose on Evie's cheeks, and she laughed nervously. Her eyes darted away and refocused on the radio, but she answered when she settled on a classic rock station playing Fleetwood Mac.

"We're just friends," she said.

I raised an eyebrow skeptically. I knew Evie was not the type of girl to dress up or put makeup on without a good reason. "Come on, spill it," I urged, nudging her playfully. "There's definitely something going on. A mother knows these things."

Evie's cheeks flushed slightly. "Okay, fine," she said. "Matt invited me to a fancy dinner tonight at that new Italian restaurant in Cedar Park, and I wanted to look good for him. Well, this isn't what I will wear tonight, but he's coming to work after class this afternoon. I didn't want him to change his mind last minute after spotting me looking like a shlub."

"You could never look like a shlub. It's a date, then?" I asked.

"Yep," Evie said. She peered out the window, her lips upturned in a joyful grin. "It's a date. It's definitely a date. Only one, but...yeah, anyway. It's a date."

"I think that's great, sweetheart." As the light changed, I stole another glance at my daughter before stepping on the accelerator. "You know, Evie, I've noticed a change in you lately. You seem much more confident than you used to be."

Evie's eyes widened in surprise. "Really?"

"Really."

"I feel a lot more confident than I used to. I used to feel like I couldn't do anything — I didn't drive and couldn't handle school the last time I tried to go. But I helped put someone in jail, Mom. I stopped a crime," she said. Her tone still sounded a little awed. "I was terrified when I heard what was happening to you and Landon at that cabin, but I didn't freeze. I didn't panic. Neither did Darla. I got the recorder going, taped the killer's confession, and she called the police to get you help in time."

"You guys did great," I replied with a hint of pride in my voice.

"We sure did." Evie nodded thoughtfully, her fingers tapping on her lap. "It was a real rush, too. I felt like I was on top of the world. Since then, I've felt like I can do things. I need to make some changes. Take some risks. Life's too short to stay in your comfort zone."

I couldn't help but feel a twinge of guilt at my daughter's words, knowing that my reluctance to take risks with her had likely rubbed off on her.

There was a constant battle between my desire to protect and care for my daughter and my need to let her be her own person. Because of her medical issues, it had been going on for as long as I could remember. I still grappled with it.

To be fair to myself, I think I came by it honestly. The countless hours spent in hospital waiting rooms, the constant worry and fear, and the overwhelming sense of responsibility that came with caring for a child with special needs. There's no handbook, no parenting book that tells you the best way to handle a situation so fraught with peril. There's—

Stop it, Eleanor.

I took a deep breath, glancing at my daughter with pride as I pushed those thoughts aside.

"You're absolutely right, Evie," I said, reaching over to give her hand a reassuring squeeze. "And I couldn't be more proud of you for stepping out of your comfort zone and pursuing your dreams."

"Dreams? Oh my gosh, Mom, it's just dinner," she said and rolled her eyes. "Get a grip. It's not that big of a deal."

"It's not just dinner." It was challenging to let go, to allow my daughter the independence she suddenly decided to reach out for seemingly overnight. But she was a young woman, already in her midtwenties. I knew she needed to spread her wings and discover who she was. "But it's not easy, letting go," I told myself, my voice barely above a whisper.

"I know, Mom," she said, her eyes filled with understanding. "But still — I'm not moving to New York to
pursue a fashion career. I'm just going out to dinner with
a boy in Cedar Park. No big deal."

Tears pricked at the corners of my eyes, and I
reached over to take her hand. "I love you," I said. "And
I'll always be here for you, no matter what."

The corners of Evie's mouth tugged gently upward.
"I know, Mom," she said, squeezing my hand back.

A second later, she pulled away to turn the
volume up.

We pulled into a parking spot, and as I stepped out of
the car, my eyes were immediately drawn to the bustling
activity behind the stand-alone storefront. It was a hive
of activity — no pun intended — with beekeepers in
protective suits hard at work, carefully collecting honey-
combs and tending to the numerous hives stretching for
acres.

Evie closed the car door and blew a low whistle as
she surveyed the sprawling farm before us. "This is a
way bigger operation than Ben's," she said

I nodded.

A huge hand-painted faux rustic sign next to the
storefront proudly declared Buzzing Blossom's award-
winning honey as the best in all of Tablerock for
multiple years running. It was a masterpiece of artistry,

its bright colors almost seeming to leap off. Toward the bottom, it listed all the years their honey had won the town's top prize. The previous year was conspicuously missing.

As we pushed open the door to the quaint storefront, a small bell tinkled overhead, announcing our arrival. The interior was warm and welcoming, with honey-colored wooden shelves lining the walls and filled with jars of honey in every shape and size.

As we made our way deeper into the store, my eyes were drawn to a massive creature lying on the floor. At first, I was taken aback, thinking it was a polar bear that had wandered onto the farm. But as I got closer, I realized it was an entirely white dog — the biggest I had ever seen.

The dog's fur was long and fluffy, and its snout was large and imposing. It looked like it could swallow a watermelon whole. Despite its size, however, the dog appeared asleep, its eyes closed and breathing deep and steady.

"That is one gigantic dog," I said to Evie.

"Great Pyrenees, I think." She nodded, stroking the dog's fur gently. "Isn't he just the cutest thing ever? They're huge."

As we approached the counter, a tall, lanky man with a thick beard and a straw hat emerged from the back room. His eyes crinkled at the corners. "Welcome to Buzzing Blossom's," he said. "I'm Tom, the owner. What can I do for you two lovely ladies today?"

"Hi, Tom," I said, walking up to the counter and putting my purse down. "My name's Ellie. This is my daughter, Evie. We—"

Tom interrupted me with a smile that lit up his face. He emerged from behind the counter, his eyes crinkling even more. "I know exactly who you are," he said. "You two are running that wonderful cat rescue in Fiona's big house on the north side of town. I'd know those names anywhere!"

The enormous white dog sprawled across the floor shifted and raised his head, his gaze locked onto us before he released a deep, resounding bark.

"Quiet, Zeus," Tom commanded, his tone firm yet gentle. "They didn't bring any cats along. Go back to sleep, buddy."

Zeus obeyed, lowering his head back to the floor, but his eyes continued to study us with an inquisitive glint.

"It's nice to meet you, Tom." I looked down at the dog. "And Zeus. Yes, Evie and I are the ones that started the cat rescue in town. You said you're the owner here?"

"Yes, ma'am."

"I was told a woman named Nina owned Buzzing Blossom Farms. Nina...Nina Coleman, I think," I asked, a hint of confusion coloring my voice.

"Oh, she does. Nina's my wife. She's the brains behind this operation, and I'm just the muscle," he said, flexing his biceps playfully. "She's out running some errands right now, so you're stuck with me."

"Gotcha. We're actually former customers of Ben

Tyson," I said, gesturing toward Evie and myself. "We went over there yesterday to pick up our weekly order for the cat café, but we…well, we couldn't." I didn't mention we found Ben, though; between the local newspaper and the gossip in this town, I suspected Tom knew already.

"I imagine you didn't." Tom smiled gently, his pale blue eyes softening as he spoke. "I'd heard that you all were the ones that found him."

Of course, he knew. "Yes, we did."

"That must have been awful for you both." He leaned forward slightly, his body language gentle and open. "Ben and my wife certainly had their dust-ups over the years, but we were sad to hear what happened to him. I'll be happy to get you whatever you need. We keep quite a variety in stock since pure honey does not go bad or spoil. Well, not in the traditional sense."

I handed Tom a list of the items we needed. "Dust-ups? What kind of dust-ups?" I asked, adding quickly, "I'm sure you won't have any trouble filling the order, right? Your operation seems quite a bit bigger than Ben's was."

I frowned.

I asked that out of order, I thought.

I should have discussed the order first, then asked about the dust-ups. Now he's just going to fill the order and not answer. If I'd reversed the order, he might have talked about it more.

Darn it.

I'm not good at this stealthy investigator thing.

Tom shook his head. "Not at all, and we'll be mighty grateful for your business. I'll make sure to give you the non-profit discount, too. Anyway, let me go grab it for you," he said, disappearing into the back room.

See?

Nothing about the dust-up.

"He didn't tell you what the dust-up was," Evie said, her eyes sweeping the place.

"I did notice that," I whispered back. "That could have been my fault, though. I mentioned the order before Tom could answer. I should have talked about the dust-up first."

"Mom," Evie whispered urgently, extending her hand to gesture discreetly toward the corner of the room. My eyes followed her gaze, and I noticed a small black camera lens pointed directly at us.

Just then, Tom emerged from the back room, a wooden crate filled with jars of honey in his arms. "Here you go, ladies. We can set up an account for you and bill you once a month if you'd like," he said, placing the crate on the counter. "That would probably be the easiest thing, I suspect. It's what most of our larger customers do. I've tucked the paperwork for the account in the box. Just fax it back to me."

Fax it? Who still had a fax?

"Sounds good. I can give you a check for this first one. I'm in a little bit of a rush to get back and would rather fill out the paperwork at the rescue."

Before I could pull out my wallet, Tom waved his hand dismissively. "Consider this first order a donation to the cat rescue. Nina and I are big supporters of what you do," he said, a genuine kindness in his eyes.

"Thank you so much, Tom. That's incredibly kind of you," I said.

Tom merely shrugged, a smile on his lips. "It's the least we can do. Your cat rescue is doing some important work, and we're happy to support it in any way we can. Y'all have a good day now," he said before turning to attend to another customer.

Once the crate of honey was nestled safely in the back of the van, I couldn't help but feel a sense of gratitude for the unexpected kindness.

Of course, just because Nina's husband was kind didn't mean she was.

And it didn't mean either of them were innocent.

Evie looked stunning, dressed in a sleek black cocktail dress that hugged her figure gracefully, the hem falling just above her knees. A delicate string of pearls adorned her neck while her hair was swept into an elegant chignon. Her eyes sparkled with anticipation, framed by tasteful makeup accentuating her natural beauty.

She descended the final step of the stairs, the muted click of her black wedge heels echoing against the polished wooden floor. Her posture betrayed a hint of uncertainty as she glanced around, taking in her reflection in the entryway mirrors. "Do I look okay?" she asked, her voice wavering slightly.

Laurie beamed at her. "Honey, you look fantastic."

"Laurie's right. You look great." I studied her appearance, my gaze lingering on the design of her dress. Its high neckline covered her collarbones and part of her neck, concealing the jagged surgery scar — a silent reminder of her multiple open hearts.

A subtle smile graced Evie's lips as she adjusted her dress one last time, her nervous energy giving way to anticipation.

"What time is he coming to pick you up?" Laurie asked.

"Any minute now," Evie said, her eyes flickering toward the mantrap.

No pun intended.

The after hours doorbell chimed as if on cue, announcing Matt's arrival.

Laurie hurried to open the door.

He stood tall in his suit, the tailored cut highlighting his broad shoulders and trim waist. His confident smile and warm gaze made Evie's cheeks pink.

The two of them were adorable.

The kids exchanged small talk with us old fogies about the restaurant and the traffic, making light of their upcoming date. Finally, they bid us farewell casually and stepped out into the evening. Their laughter mingled with the soft rustle of leaves as the door closed on their night together.

"Okay," I announced, snatching my keys from the hook by the door, "let's go."

"Awesome. Where to? How about Mexican food?" Laurie suggested. "I could go for a margarita. A margarita would help this headache. Do you know how loud and long huskies can howl at you over a little tiny shot? One little shot. You would have thought I sawed his paw off."

"We're going to the Italian place in Cedar Park," I informed her, locking the door behind us as we made our way to my car. "Well, not that place exactly, but the restaurant right next to it."

"The one the kids are going to? That place?" Laurie furrowed her brow, her confusion evident. "What restaurant is next to it?"

"I don't know. There's probably something nearby. It doesn't matter what. We'll find something," I said, opening the driver's side door and sliding into my seat.

Laurie settled into the passenger seat, her expression a mixture of confusion and concern as I started the engine.

"Don't give me that look," I said. "I just want to be nearby in case Evie has a problem Matt doesn't know how to handle. It's just a precaution."

"Just a precaution." Laurie's eyes widened, her mouth dropping open in shock. "Oh my God, Eleanor Rockwell, you can't be serious," she breathed, staring at me in horror. "Are we stalking the kids on their date? Did you invite me to come with you to have company while you stalk your daughter?"

"You make it sound so sinister," I said, pressing the accelerator and guiding the car onto the street.

"Sinister? Try criminal. I'm pretty sure stalking is illegal in the state of Texas."

"Oh, don't be so dramatic," I dismissed her concern with a wave.

Laurie grabbed her phone, tapping rapidly on the screen. "Under Texas law, stalking is defined as intentionally or knowingly engaging in conduct that causes someone else to feel harassed, threatened, or in fear of bodily injury or death." She put down her phone. "Now, I know you don't want to hurt or threaten her, but I think she'd have you dead to rights on the harassment thing."

"This is nothing. I just want to make sure she's okay," I insisted, my grip tightening on the steering wheel.

"Ellie, I love you, but this is beyond the pale."

"This is no different from when I used to wait for her outside parties in case she needed to go home. I'm not going into the Italian restaurant," I added defensively, hoping to appease her. "She won't even know I'm nearby, and unless you tell her, she won't even know why we were around."

"Ellie —"

"What if she calls me because she has an issue and needs me? It'll take me forty-five minutes just to help her. That's a lifetime if something happens with her pacemaker."

"How often has something happened with her pacemaker?" Laurie questioned, her tone softening with concern.

I gripped the steering wheel more tightly but didn't answer.

"Ellie, I know that you've had to be the type of mother most of us wake up from nightmares grateful we're not, but even with everything you've been through, I can't believe you think all those excuses you just came up with make what you're doing okay," she replied, shaking her head in disbelief. "Did you ask Evie if she needed you nearby or if she was okay doing this alone?"

I drove silently, my jaw clenched and eyes focused on the road ahead.

"Ellie, did Evie ask you to stay close?" Laurie persisted.

"No," I admitted, my voice barely above a whisper. "But I told you, I'm not going to interfere. I'm just going to be nearby in case she calls."

The car filled with a tense silence as we continued our drive, the weight of our disagreement heavy in the air.

Chapter Six

Nestled beside the Italian eatery, we found ourselves at the South Congress Café in Cedar Park — a quintessential Austin establishment despite our location being neither Austin nor anywhere near South Congress Avenue. Neon signs didn't just illuminate the parking lot; they dazzled like jewel-toned fireflies among an array of quirky decorations that spoke to the heart of Austin's culture. Each colorful accent seemed plucked straight from the psychedelic soul of the city the restaurant wished they could afford to call home.

One exasperated attorney stood right in front of the "Keep Austin Weird" sign.

"Seriously? She called you?"

Josephine's eyes rolled heavenward, thin lips pursed with weary annoyance. It wasn't just an eye roll but a long-suffering sigh in physical form. "You were with her in the car, Ellie. She didn't call me. But she did send me a text, informing me that you might end up in cuffs for stalking your own daughter during her date with that young man. I told Charlie to get his dinner and headed right over."

The gentle breeze carried the aroma of sizzling fajitas and freshly brewed coffee as we stood outside the lively café, the hum of conversation and laughter spilling from its open doors. The subtle creases around Josephine's eyes seemed to deepen as she awaited my response.

"You two just don't get it," I said as we entered the Austin-inspired eatery. "Raising a child with disabilities and unique challenges is worlds apart from your experiences. Laurie, your daughter's a cheerleader, and Josephine, your kids attend Ivy League schools. We're simply different kinds of parents."

The restaurant's lively atmosphere enveloped us, with warm lighting casting a golden glow over the eclectic mix of rustic and modern decor. As we ventured deeper into the buzzing establishment, a waft of succulent barbecue and zesty spices filled the air.

Josephine arched her eyebrow, clearly taking exception to my comment. "You don't think I've ever been tempted to track Connor's phone? Or tail Maxwell when he claimed to be going to the 'library' on a Saturday night wearing enough cologne to choke a horse?" She paused and informed the hostess that our party consisted of three. Turning her attention back to me, she continued without missing a beat.

"Eleanor Rockwell, sometimes you act like you're the first parent to ever have a helicopter urge you had to fight."

The hostess led us to a cozy booth in a quiet corner of the restaurant, away from the hustle and bustle of the main dining area. As we settled into our seats, I noticed the booth was intimate and cozy, with soft lighting casting a warm glow over our faces. It was the perfect setting for a night of good food and company.

Or, you know, a dressing down.

As we settled into the booth, the world outside faded away, replaced by a sense of seclusion. Towering ferns and verdant vines encircled us, their lush foliage creating a living curtain shielding us from the booths to either side.

With a warm smile, the hostess placed a menu in each of our hands and then gestured toward the specials of the evening. "Tonight, we have a slow-cooked brisket, tender and juicy, infused with the rich aroma of smoke. It's served with a side of our famous jalapeño cornbread, baked fresh."

My stomach growled.

Josephine piped up. "Could I get one of those fish-bowl-sized margaritas, please? My friend here" — she pointed at me — "is acting like a lunatic tonight, and I think I'm going to need one."

A soft chuckle escaped the hostess's lips, her eyes crinkling with warmth. "Absolutely, I'll pass that along to your server. They'll be with you in a jiffy." With a final nod and a wave of her hand, she disappeared into the bustling restaurant.

Laurie's eyes flicked up from her menu, meeting mine with gentle firmness. "Listen, Ellie, we understand your concern. We really do. But Evie is all grown up now and more than capable of taking care of herself. She always wears her medical alert bracelet, and you've ensured that every detail a paramedic could need is on her wrist. Matt is aware of Evie's challenges and is more than capable of handling anything that comes up. He's a responsible young man, and you trust him. Don't you?"

"What if they were both in a car accident? Or what if Evie just got overwhelmed and needed to step away from the situation?"

Laurie gestured toward the window, her finger pointing toward Bella Vita's cozy exterior. "See that outdoor seating area? Your daughter could go there anytime she needs fresh air, just like anyone else. It's a safe and quiet spot where she can breathe away from the crowds."

Josephine chimed in. "Plus, she has her phone with her. She can always call a car if she needs to get away. You did link your credit card to her account, didn't you? Just to make sure she had a ride?"

"I saw her do it." Laurie nodded. "Ellie, you've always set her up for independence if she decided to do it. She's decided to go for some of it. That's a good thing."

"Is it?" I asked.

"She'll be okay. You've done everything you can to prepare her for this. Trust her, and trust yourself."

Their words sounded perfectly reasonable.

Even so, they didn't entirely quell the anxious knot that had formed in my stomach when Evie walked out the front door with Matt. It was challenging to let go and trust that my daughter could handle whatever life threw her way, especially considering her unique challenges. I'd spent so much of my life ensuring she knew she had a safety net...

"I get it. I hear you." I drew in a deep breath, unwilling to concede without making my point. "But I don't agree with you that what I did tonight was unreasonable—"

"I didn't say unreasonable," Laurie interrupted, her tone firm but still friendly. "I said stalking, Ellie. Illegally stalking your daughter. You didn't tell her what you would do, which means you knew this was wrong."

Her words stung, but deep down, I knew both of my friends were right.

I let my protective instincts get the better of me, and as a result, I crossed a line. Despite my concerns, I had to acknowledge that my daughter was growing up, and she deserved the chance to navigate her own life without me constantly hovering in the background, afraid that she would fail.

It was time to loosen the reins, however reluctantly, and trust that she could handle whatever challenges came her way.

"Fine. I screwed up. Happy?" I admitted, picking up my menu with a sigh. "Let's order dinner. Turns out, being a terrible mother works up quite the appetite."

As we discussed the menu, the conversation shifted to lighter topics as we eagerly awaited our meals.

And then they lectured me again after the appetizers.

"My point is, you don't have to be perfect, Ellie, that's all."

Josephine nodded in agreement with Laurie as she dug into her zesty avocado salad, taking a moment to wash down the spice with a sip from a margarita Barbie could do laps in. "Dr. Doolittle is right. You have to be willing to learn and grow and adapt to the ever-changing landscape of your daughter's life—"

Our conversation momentarily halted as a woman's voice pierced through the leafy barrier from the booth next to ours. "What the hell do you mean I have to meet with the police tomorrow?" she practically shouted, her agitation palpable. "I have three cake orders to fill tomorrow, and none of my staff know how to ice a cake without screwing it up. I don't have time for this!"

We exchanged curious glances, the woman's distress capturing our attention.

Laurie's eyes widened suddenly, a look of recognition crossing her face. She leaned in closer, her voice dropping to a hushed whisper. "I know that voice. It sounds like Augusta Walton."

At the mention of the name, I froze, my mind racing back to what Honey had told me about the woman who hadn't treated him like a person. A mixture of curiosity and concern washed over me. What are the chances we'd both go to dinner two towns away?

Josephine leaned in closer, her voice dropping to a whisper. "Excuse me, but who's Augusta Walton again?" she asked, her eyes darting between Laurie and me with a look of confusion.

"She owns that high-end bakery in Tablerock," I whispered back, careful to keep my voice low.

"The one on Main," Laurie added, looking around cautiously before lowering her voice further. "She was the one that made that incredible towering cake made to look like city hall for the mayor's picnic last July 4th. Maybe one of her employees finally pressed charges against her."

"Why would you say that?" Josephine asked.

"I heard she doesn't always treat her employees well. I heard she doesn't treat anyone well, but she supposedly hit an employee."

"When Evie and I talked to Honey with the plate tray thing, he mentioned her," I said, glancing toward the foliage that separated us from the next booth to make sure no one from the other booth was listening.

"He did?" Josephine leaned in. "What did he say?"

I recounted Honey's words, keeping my voice

hushed. "It sounded to me like she and Ben Tyson were dating and were at the stay-at-each-other-place stage. She favored the dog, treated his cat kind of crappy from the cat's perspective." I glanced around cautiously. "Honey said the dog was a Great Dane, I believe?"

"Yep, I know her. Were they dating when Ben died?" Laurie whispered.

I shook my head. "The cat said they broke up a week or two ago."

"What do I pay you for if you can't get me out of talking to the police about an ex-boyfriend I'd rather forget ever existed?" Augusta's shrill voice cut through the restaurant's ambient noise, making it impossible not to eavesdrop.

"She's talking to her lawyer," Josephine deduced confidently.

Laurie let out a sarcastic chuckle. "Yeah, no kidding."

"That complete moron." Augusta's voice was deceptively even, but rage swirled beneath the surface. "I paid him to make sure whatever happened at Ben's wouldn't involve me, and yet the police want to question me tomorrow. Not talk to me—question me. I know a threat when I hear it. Isn't there anything you can do about it?"

"Why, honey, I couldn't even keep my son from being arrested, though that was more the county's fault. The county, Fiona, and that wretched woman with all the cats." The familiarity of the new voice sent a jolt of recognition through me.

I knew that voice anywhere. It was Tablerock's mayor, Jessa Winthrop.

And in case you were wondering? I was the wretched woman with all the cats.

"I still haven't met her," Augusta said dismissively. (She had, by the way.) "How is Joel doing? Do they have a date for his trial?"

"He pleaded guilty. I managed to keep it quiet in town, which was a challenge. But people were more obsessed with that woman inheriting Fiona's piles of money and the house than with Joel and what he did."

"That's just because no one in town cared about the Blackwells getting killed, Jessa. That's the key to getting away with murder, you know. Kill people no one likes."

"Well, that clearly didn't work for Joel," Jessa pointed out.

"That cat woman liked Fiona for some reason. Can't fault her for it. It clearly paid off."

We exchanged astonished looks as we listened to the conversation unfolding in the next booth. The casual way they spoke about serious matters like murder and death sent a shiver down my spine.

"Did people like Ben?" Laurie whispered the question hesitantly, her voice barely audible as she sought to maintain our cover as eavesdroppers. "Was he a nice guy?"

"I didn't know him very well." I thought for a moment before adding in a similarly hushed tone, "It's hard to say. He had his share of friends, but he also had a reputation for being a bit... difficult. I guess it depends on who you ask."

Our eyes met in a moment of shared contemplation as we silently considered the implications of Ben's standing in the community and how it might relate to the drama we were overhearing. The loud conversation between Augusta and Jessa continued to unfold, revealing a web of judgments and resentments that left us feeling increasingly uneasy.

Josephine gasped dramatically as Augusta and Jessa finally exited the restaurant. "Finally," she said. "I thought those two would never stop talking. Who knew two single women could gossip so much in one night? I swear they covered every inch of town with their scandalous complaining."

Laurie and I exchanged amused glances.

"Don't start with that look, Miss Sass. First, I'm not single. Second, we're not gossiping. We're investigating. There's a difference." Josephine defended herself and then pointed at me. "She already stalked her daughter. Do you really want her to break her promise to Evie that we would investigate cases that cats brought to us, too?"

Laurie's head shook slightly, a small smile tugging at the corners of her mouth. "I suppose not, but we should be careful about it, don't you think? We don't want to attract any more attention than we already have. And you remember what happened to Ellie, don't you? She ended up staring down the barrel of a gun."

"Oh, she never would have gotten hurt." Josephine waved off the concern. "Landon would have thrown his big, burly body in front of her and taken an automatic weapon's cascade of bullets to keep her safe."

"He wouldn't do that," I said.

"He absolutely would," Laurie countered with a grin.

"Charlie told me that he was helping Waldo Monroe with some paperwork for his race against Mayor Mouthy earlier today, and Waldo told Charlie that Landon was planning on taking another run at Miss Thing over here," Josephine revealed, hitching her thumb toward me. "That man told everybody in that martial arts group they got going on in the park. Told them the whole gun thing made him realize he knows what he wants, and what he wants is the crazy cat lady."

My cheeks flushed at the mention of Landon's interest.

"You're blushing," Josephine pointed out.

I shook my head. "It's the tequila."

"You didn't have any tequila, Ellie. You drove."

My companions shared a knowing look; their eyes lit up with amusement, relishing the thought of a budding romance amid our amateur investigations.

"Stop it. Both of you. I can't get involved with anyone—"

"If you start telling me that Evie needs you too much

for you to have a life of your own, I swear I will throw this margarita right in your face, Eleanor," Josephine threatened, reaching out for the huge glass. "Now, look here. You're right. None of us know what it's like to be the momma of a little one who faced so much adversity, but at some point, you'll have to realize your girl overcame it. Maybe not unscathed, but well enough for a life of her own."

"She's the same age you were when you had her. When is it time for you to have a life of your own?" Laurie asked gently, her eyes filled with genuine concern.

I hesitated, feeling the weight of their words. It was true that I'd devoted so much of my life to caring for Evie, and my friends might be right—maybe it was time for me to consider my own happiness as well Evie's.

But that didn't necessarily mean running out and finding a man.

And I told them so.

Josephine nearly doubled over, roaring with laughter. "Eleanor, you don't have to go anywhere! Your man comes to your house and builds shelves for your cats!" She snorted. "Run out. Are you kidding me? He even brings his own tools."

I couldn't help but snicker, feeling the tension ease from my shoulders. Just as I was about to say something, I looked up and spotted the kids. "Look!" I pointed toward the window. "The kids are done with dinner."

The three of us looked out at the neighboring eatery,

our attention drawn to Matt and Evie emerging from the double doors of Bella Vita. The warm illumination from the interior cast a gentle amber hue upon the pair.

"They really are sweet," Laurie said, her voice filled with warmth.

Josephine nodded in agreement, adding, "I know Evie could have chosen far worse, but as for finding someone better? I doubt it's possible. That young man's a good egg."

Evie turned to Matt, her eyes sparkling with excitement.

In response, Matt placed his hands gently on her shoulders. His lips moved, forming words we couldn't hear, and Evie replied, her head tilting slightly as she listened intently. He smiled. She smiled.

"Oh, my gosh, is he going to kiss her?" I asked, surprised.

"Be quiet and watch, Eleanor," Josephine whispered.

Oh, really?

I couldn't help but wonder what had happened to the two friends who had previously scolded me for my intrusive surveillance of my daughter. It seemed like a pair of hopeless romantics had entirely taken over their bodies.

Hypocrites.

Slowly, Matt closed the distance between them and tenderly, with more than a touch of romance, pressed his lips against my daughter's.

"Now, that's what I'm talking about," Josephine said.

"How sweet," Laurie said.

As the kiss ended, Evie stepped back from her date, her cheeks seemingly flushed with excitement and bashfulness. She turned — a radiant smile on her lips — and began walking across the dimly lit parking lot toward Matt's car. Her eyes drifted casually toward our restaurant, scanning the scene...

Uh oh.

And then, suddenly, they found their way to the wide window, peering into the cozy booth where we sat...

Uh oh.

I tried to duck out of sight, hoping to disappear into the booth beneath the window. However, before I could manage the evasive maneuver, our eyes locked.

In that instant, her beaming smile transformed into a fiery glare.

"Mom!"

Her voice was a potent mix of disbelief and indignation that could be heard even from across the parking lot, so potent it seemed to reverberate off the thick glass windows between us.

"Uh oh," I said out loud.

Josephine quickly tried to offer some consolation. "Don't worry," she said with a reassuring smile. "This story will be much funnier when you tell it to the grandchildren in thirty years."

Chapter Seven

"I can't believe you," Evie said. Her footsteps tapping angrily against the asphalt filled the evening air as she paced back and forth in front of my car. Laurie, Josephine, and Matt stood awkwardly on the other side of the parking lot, trying to appear uninterested in the confrontation unfolding before them. "How could you spy on my date?"

Her words stung, and I could feel the weight of her disappointment as she glared at me, her hands on her hips and her brow furrowed. "I understand that my well-intentioned —"

"Well-intentioned?"

"— monitoring crossed a line," I said. "Remember how you always asked me to wait outside parties and school dances in case you wanted to leave, Evie? I suppose I continued with that because I've grown used to it." I looked up. "I didn't think it through."

Evie shook her head. "You didn't think it through? I'm not a child anymore, Mom. I'm in my midtwenties. I can take care of myself."

"I know you can," I said, sounding reasonable. "But I just worry. You're my only child, and I love you more than anything. You know that, right?"

As I poured my heart out, expressing the love and concern that had driven me to act as I had, I noticed a subtle shift in Evie's demeanor. The hardness in her eyes began to soften, and the tension in her shoulders seemed to lessen just a bit.

"I do," Evie said, her voice softening. "I do know that. But you have to let me be independent, Mom. You can't always be there to protect me."

In my mind, I stubbornly thought, "Of course, I can." After all, this argument stemmed from her frustration at my proving I would always be there to protect her, whether she wanted me to or not. It brought a sense of resolve, but I also recognized the importance of giving Evie the space and freedom she needed to grow and make her own choices.

As I stood there, the evening breeze rustling the leaves in nearby trees, I knew I had to strike a delicate balance between being a loving, protective parent and respecting her independence.

It was a difficult lesson to learn

I took a deep breath and said, "You're right, and I'm sorry for spying on your date. I promise not to do it again."

My daughter studied me for a moment as if trying to gauge the sincerity of my words. Finally, she gave me a small smile. "Thank you, Mom," she said. "I appreciate that."

We stood in the parking lot for a few more moments, the tension between us gradually dissipating. Eventually, Evie sighed resignedly and said, "Well, we should probably get going. I'd like to finish my date, if that's all right with you. We were about to go to the Grackle Tavern for a drink."

I nodded. "Go ahead, have fun," I said, smiling. "Just remember not to drink any alcohol. Dr. Johnson said—"

"Mom!" Evie interrupted, her expression a mix of amusement and exasperation. "I know I can't have alcohol with my medication. Just because I'm on a date doesn't mean I'll drink anything besides a Shirley Temple." She stepped forward and wrapped me in a warm, reassuring embrace. "I know you care. But I got it, okay? Back off."

"Okay." I released her, and she took a step back. "Josie, Laurie, and I will return to the house to talk. You won't believe who wound up in the booth next to us."

"Who?" Evie asked.

"Jessa Winthrop and Augusta Walton."

As Evie walked toward Matt, she said in disbelief, "The mayor and the baker?"

"The mayor and Ben Tyson's ex-girlfriend," I corrected while walking beside her.

Evie's eyes widen in surprise at the unexpected pairing.

"Augusta was yelling at her lawyer because they didn't get her out of talking to the police tomorrow, and she was asking the mayor if she could do anything to help her get out of it."

"She's the baker with the big dog, right? The cake place that makes all the wedding cakes? The one on Main Street?"

"Yep, that's the one," I said. "The two of them were talking about Ben's murder, and Jessa seemed to be trying to calm Augusta down, but it didn't sound like she was having much luck."

Evie shook her head in disbelief. "Wow. I never would have thought those two would be hanging out." Suddenly, her eyes sparkled, and she looked at me slyly. "You know, I've always wanted to try her cakes. Maybe we should swing by her bakery tomorrow and pick something up."

"Are you plotting already, young lady?" Josephine asked as we joined the group, her tone a mix of sternness and playfulness.

"Yep," Evie responded with a grin. "I am, indeed."

Josephine smiled in return. "Good girl."

"Mrs. Reynolds and Dr. Gray have been filling me in on what they heard," Matt told Evie. "Would you rather we go back home and talk about the murder?" He glanced down at his phone. "Darla says she has grenadine and can fix you a Shirley Temple, no problem. She also says Landon and Mario are there now repairing that cat tree that Digby broke, too."

"We could ask Mario about what the baker said." Evie considered the proposal for a moment, weighing her options as she decided how she wanted to spend the rest of her evening. The prospect of discussing the murder case while sipping on a refreshing mocktail with her date was apparently too good a combination to pass up. She looked at Matt. "Are you sure you're okay with doing that?"

Matt nodded, offering her a reassuring smile. "Of course. I'm just happy to spend time with you, Evie. Whatever we do, I'm in."

Josephine and I exchanged an amused glance.

I dug my keys out of my pocket and led Laurie and Josephine to my car while Matt and Evie walked off in the opposite direction toward his.

We arrived back at the house — which doubled as the rescue — around the same time. The rescue's lower café area filled up with people, and it dawned on me that most of them knew about the magic table tray we had upstairs.

Almost all, in fact.

All except Officer Mario Lopez. He remained blissfully unaware of our cat communicado ability...and that could make for a tricky evening.

"How was dinner?" Landon asked, wiping the sweat off his brow. He inadvertently left a streak of sawdust on his forehead. Before I could respond, he added with a teasing grin, "I heard from Darla that you got caught watching Evie's date from across the parking lot."

"I didn't 'watch' Evie's date from across the parking lot," I told him while petting a black and white cat named Sylvester. "I watched the place where Evie's date was happening while eating barbecue. And, just so you know, I've already been lectured by Laurie and Josie, so there's no need to pile on."

"It's lucky Ellie decided to go all Inspector Clouseau on Evie, actually," Josie said, addressing Landon. "We never would have overheard Mayor Prissy yapping with Baker Snooty about the murder of Ben Tyson if Ellie hadn't decided to stalk her own daughter like she'd seen Matt on 48 Hours last week."

"Who's' Inspector Clouseau?" Evie asked.

"You don't know who Inspector Clouseau is?" Matt asked incredulously.

Evie shook her head, a sheepish smile on her face.

"He's a character in a movie franchise," Josephine explained. "He's a bumbling, incompetent detective that somehow manages to solve the case in the end."

I was a bit insulted.

"I know she's not exactly a nice person, but I don't think it's likely that Augusta killed Ben or even hired someone else to kill him," Laurie argued. "Whatever else she is, she's always been an upstanding citizen — why would she do something so terrible?"

Landon nodded in agreement and added, "Besides, if Augusta did have something to do with the murder, then why would she say something in public like that? It doesn't make sense. If I'd killed someone, I wouldn't discuss it in a Cedar Park restaurant."

"Good to know," Mario told him and clapped him on the back.

Landon nodded once. "No problem."

"Maybe Augusta didn't actually have anything to do with the murder," Evie said, "but I have to admit, someone talking the way she talked in a public place with Jessa Winthrop? It makes me instantly suspicious."

"That's because you still think she had something to do with Fiona's murder," Josephine pointed out.

"I sure do. You don't?"

Matt crossed his arms and leaned back against the wall behind him. "So you overheard people talking about murder like it was no big deal. That's not much to go on." He looked up at the isolation room. "Maybe we should ask someone else about the baker?"

Evie glanced at Mario, who was sitting quietly and listening.

Matt nodded. "Right. Later, I mean."

"Why later?" Mario asked. "Who are you talking about?"

"No one." Matt's head shook in a dismissive gesture. "It's nothing."

"Nothing, huh?" Mario's surveying gaze rested on each person in the room as he spoke. "Why are you all so concerned with who killed Ben Tyson?" His eyes darted from one face to another, studying their expressions.

"What do you mean, Mario?" Josephine asked innocently.

"I mean, I can see why Evie and Ellie would be interested since they're the ones who stumbled upon the poor guy," Mario continued, nodding toward us. "But Matt? The two of you?" Mario swiveled around to face the petite woman behind the café counter. "Darla? What's your interest?"

Darla's cheeks flushed a subtle shade of pink as she paused wiping down the gleaming counter. Her eyes flicked up to meet Mario's, and she nervously tucked a stray strand of hair behind her ear. "I don't know what you mean, Officer Lopez. We're just all talking here. It's a small town, and we just like to gossip."

Mario looked at the faces surrounding him, his expression unreadable. After a few moments of silence, he finally said, "Gossip, huh?"

Well, that didn't sound like he believed us at all.

Landon's body pivoted toward Mario. "What is the reason behind this sudden interrogation, friend?" he asked in a low voice. His words came out with a slow, viscous quality, as if dripping from a spoonful of molasses.

"Call it a hunch," he said slowly, his dark eyes searching Landon's face for any hint of deception. "I suddenly feel like everyone in this place is hiding something from me."

Landon didn't seem to know what to say to that.

Mario wasn't wrong — we all were hiding something from him. Just not, I suspected, what he thought.

"I don't know what you're talking about," Josephine, ever the lawyer, told the officer. "Mario Lopez, your job is making you paranoid."

"Is it?" he asked her.

Our eyes fixed on each other in tense silence.

From his perch atop the bookshelf, the black and white Sylvester let out an abrupt sneeze, momentarily shattering the silence. His whiskers twitched, and for a fleeting moment, it almost seemed as if he were laughing.

Landon held his friend's gaze. "I'm not sure how to help you here."

"Look... I'm just doing my job. I have to investigate any leads I can find in this case, no matter how small they seem. You all say you'll talk to someone, and I just want to know who that is."

None of us said a word.

"Unbelievable. I want to get to the bottom of this murder as much as anyone else here — and if you all know something that could help me with that, then I need to know about it." He finished firmly, emphasizing the last word with a sharp look at each person standing before him. "Well?"

As Mario stormed out of the front door, the bell jingled violently in his wake, and a pang of guilt twisted in my chest. The decision to keep the secret of the magical cat plate from him had seemed straightforward...

...until the moment he sensed our deception and was clearly hurt by it.

It wasn't that we didn't trust Mario. We had simply let the secret slip to too many people already. The more we divulged, the more vulnerable the magical plate became, and we couldn't risk exposing it any further.

"I feel awful," I admitted quietly, my voice barely more than a whisper.

"Of course you do, Ellie. That's your modus operandi. Do things, then feel bad about them. You'll be fine tomorrow morning," Josephine teased, attempting to lighten the mood. Her words were playful, but there was an unmistakable hint of empathy in her eyes, reflecting the shared understanding of the difficult situation we had found ourselves in. "Trust is a deep well, you know. I get that the man doesn't trust people because his job exposes him to all sorts of nastiness, but so does mine. I didn't storm out."

"But you know about the plate," Laurie pointed out.

"Of course I know about the plate," Josephine declared, her tone matter-of-fact. "I never would have left until I'd managed to drag the truth out of you people. Mario doesn't know because he gives up too easily." She paused for a moment, her eyes narrowing. "I wouldn't have stormed out like that. He should have stood his ground instead of running off because he was butt-hurt."

"Yes, we know. You're perfect," Laurie said. She rolled her eyes playfully, a smirk tugging at the corners of her mouth as she, too, tried to inject some levity into the tense atmosphere.

Josephine looked at her. "I want it clearly noted for the record that I didn't say it."

"Mario's under a lot of pressure right now. Remember, the towns don't have detectives," Landon reminded us. "Markham is deputy for the county and detective for the town — when we call him in. Mario told me we haven't called Markham in, so he's trying to piece together what's happening without the resources he needs to solve the case. He's just stressed."

"Why haven't they called in the county?" I asked.

Landon shrugged. "No idea."

"I know he needs to cool off, Landon, but this isn't something we can just tell him — too many people already know about it," Josephine said.

"For being the last one to find out about it, Josie, you sure have a lot of opinions on why no one else should know," Laurie said. She turned to me with a raised eyebrow. "Can you believe her?"

Frequently, no.

But I didn't say anything about it.

"Maybe we should tell him about the plate," I said — even though I was doing an about-face from my previous position. I hated that Mario left here believing we were hiding something from him. "He's our friend and trying to solve this case. If we could give him any information that might help, shouldn't we?"

"I understand the urge, Mom. I do," Evie said, her expression somber. "But we need to think about the bigger picture. We have no idea what would happen if word gets out about the plate. There has to be a reason Fiona kept it secret. We've already shared the secret with too many people."

"I resemble that remark, young lady," Josephine said.

"Would you focus?" Laurie said to Josie. "I have to agree with Evie here. Even though Mario is our friend, I don't think it's worth the potential consequences of telling him."

"What potential consequences?" I asked.

"Isn't that the point?" Evie looked at me. "We don't know."

"I hear what you're saying," Matt told her, nodding solemnly. "And it's a good point. But Mario's the only one in our social group that doesn't know. Doesn't it make sense to tell him? Sooner or later, one of us is going to slip up."

"So every time we make a new friend, we tell them?" Evie asked.

A heavy silence descended upon the room as we all contemplated the weight of our decision. We needed to strike a balance between our loyalty to Mario and our duty to protect the magical plate and the feline inhabitants that relied on it.

It was a difficult choice that we couldn't take lightly.

Finally, Josephine broke the silence. "Maybe we can help Mario solve the case without exposing the plate's existence. We can use Honey's information to point him in the right direction without disclosing how we obtained it. That's what Evie had planned to do, right?"

"So you want to do what we were doing already?" Josie nodded. "If we were already doing that anyway, did we resolve anything?" I asked.

"Yes. We weren't taking it that seriously and now we know that Mario needs our help," Evie said. "We need to buckle down and focus on helping him from the shadows instead of just stumbling around like Inspector Clouseau."

The group nodded in agreement.

However, I couldn't shake the feeling that nothing had really changed.

Chapter Eight

THE LINGERING SENSE OF GUILT CONTINUED TO gnaw at me the next morning as I prepared the cat rescue for another day. The air was filled with the soft sound of purring and the gentle rustle of leaves from the indoor trees, but not even the heavy lavender calming scent could keep my mind from returning to the feeling of guilt that had settled in my stomach like a stone.

The day the magic tray entered my life was a turning point in a line of turning points, and it opened up a connection I had never imagined possible. Being able to communicate with cats, to understand their unique personalities and quirks, had been a gift beyond measure.

It allowed me to connect with the feline residents of the rescue in ways I'd never dreamed of.

But as much as I enjoyed my newfound access to the

inner world of cats, Evie and I were left with many unanswered questions about the tray's origins.

How had Fiona, our late benefactor, gotten her hands on such a magical item?

Why did she leave it to us, along with her substantial fortune?

What would happen if people knew of it?

I couldn't help but be concerned about the possible ramifications if word got out that we possessed something so extraordinary. In the wrong hands, the magic tray could become a tool of exploitation or...worse.

As I filled the food dishes with fresh kibble and replaced water bowls, the cats approached me with their tails high in greeting. Some brushed against my legs, purring contentedly, while others reached out with tentative paw taps.

I turned, and to my surprise, I found Honey sitting in the main room next to a regal-looking Belladonna. The orange and white cat should have been in the isolation room since he was still in his quarantine period.

"What are you two doing out here?" I asked.

Of course, no one answered me.

Belladonna might have somehow discovered how to open the door to the cat room. The entitled cat had always been a little too smart for her own good, her golden eyes gleaming with intelligence and mischief.

Or maybe the magic tray had other capabilities only the cats knew.

"Okay, little one, back upstairs for you." Gently, I

scooped Honey into my arms and walked upstairs toward the isolation room. "One more day, you can come out and play with everyone else."

Belladonna followed closely behind, her eyes never leaving her orange and white companion. The bond between them was kind of impressive, considering their vastly different personalities.

We spotted Evie emerging from her bedroom as we reached the second floor landing. She stopped abruptly, a look of surprise crossing her face. "Is that Honey?" she asked, pointing at the bundle in my arms.

"He escaped," I explained to Evie, "I'm not sure how Belladonna managed to pull it off, but I found the two of them downstairs."

"Huh. No kidding."

I carried Honey into the isolation room and gently placed him on the bed. "Just one more day, little guy," I told him, scratching him behind the ears. "Although I have to say, I'm surprised to see you hanging around with Belladonna. You two didn't seem all that fond of each other at first."

Honey meowed in response.

Belladonna began lecturing me the moment her feet touched the plate. "Ignore him. I assure you, I had no involvement whatsoever in the escape of that insufferable ginger-colored buffoon from the confining quarters you find it acceptable to detain us."

"Well, someone's in a grumpy mood," Evie said.

"Grumpy because they got caught," I said.

"Belladonna, don't help your friend leave this room, please. He really needs to stay in here for a little longer."

"It is highly offensive to me that you persist in placing blame upon my person for the subpar craftsmanship exhibited by the doors in question."

"Landon did just fine with the doors." I let out an exasperated sigh as I looked at Belladonna. It was clear that she wasn't going to admit any responsibility anytime soon.

"It is quite evident he did not adequately construct these doors, as they are entirely ineffective for their intended purpose." She paused and blinked. "Which is to contain us within this chamber." Belladonna sniffed. "Which it cannot do. Obviously."

"I've been wondering, did you and Fiona watch Downton Abbey a lot before she passed away?" I asked. "I mean, your accent is spot-on. You'd have it in the bag if you were auditioning for a walk-on part in Bridgerton. But it's got to be exhausting to keep up that posh act all the time."

"Your current discourse bears an uncomfortable air of insult toward my person," Belladonna replied snootily from her cubby.

"Yeah, that's the one," I told her.

Evie arched her eyebrow, clearly skeptical. "Uncomfortable for who, exactly?" she asked, a hint of amusement in her voice. She knew all too well about Belladonna's love of melodrama.

Belladonna let out an annoyed huff and turned her

back to us. "I am dismayed by the manner in which you and your associates seem to always underestimate and undervalue my contributions and presence in this establishment," she declared, her voice dripping with disdain. "Filled with dismay, in fact."

I couldn't help but roll my eyes at her theatrics. "Oh, you're filled with something, all right," I said, unable to resist making a joke.

Evie chuckled.

I couldn't help but raise an eyebrow as Josephine strolled into the bustling cat café behind Matt. "Don't you have a job?" I asked half-jokingly.

Matt nodded in my direction and made a beeline for Evie, who was busy brewing coffee behind the counter. I watched as they exchanged a quick greeting before he settled in at the counter and pulled out his laptop.

The café was alive with the gentle meows of cats lounging on comfortable cushions and playful visitors engaging with them. The sound of chatter filled the air, creating a warm and welcoming atmosphere.

Josephine raised an eyebrow, a hint of amusement dancing in her eyes. "Who needs a job when you have a cat café to hang out in?" she replied. "Part of my job is this rescue, isn't it?" She offered a nonchalant smile before continuing, "As for my day job, I'm a lawyer. I have a paralegal to handle most of the heavy lifting. I just hired a new one. His name's Billy Fordham and he's great."

"You have a male paralegal?" I asked, my eyebrows raised in surprise.

"Eleanor Rockwell, is that a hint of sexism I detect in your voice? What's wrong with having a male paralegal?"

"You're right. There's nothing wrong with it," I said, my cheeks coloring slightly. "I was just surprised, that's all. You never struck me as all that forward-thinking."

"Well, that was offensive." Josephine grinned, her eyes twinkling with amusement as she patted my shoulder reassuringly. "No harm done, Ellie. It's just a reminder that we all have our preconceived notions, even when we think we've moved past them. Billy's been a godsend. He's quick, efficient, and incredibly organized. It's a nice change of pace from being the only person with a brain in my office."

Suddenly, Evie sprinted toward us with a burst of energy, her eyes alight with excitement. "Mom, you won't believe it!" she exclaimed. "Matt just told me he's a licensed private investigator now!"

Josephine's eyebrows shot up in surprise, and she blew a low whistle. "Well, well, well," she said wryly. "It looks like you're officially joining the ranks of the not-so-amateur sleuths. Congratulations."

"Not licensed quite yet," he admitted. "But my card should be on its way."

I turned to Matt, a hint of surprise in my voice. "I

didn't even know that was something you were interested in," I said, trying to keep up with the rapidly-
changing relationship status and career choices of my
daughter and her...boyfriend, I think?

Matt flashed a sheepish grin. "Honestly, I wasn't
sure if I was up for it," he admitted. "But my uncle runs
a security company in Austin, Lodestar Investigations
and Recovery. I told him a few things about what we're
dealing with up here, leaving out the gory details. And
he sponsored me."

Evie's eyes drifted toward the isolation room. "He's
being modest. Matt's uncle had been trying to recruit
him for years, but he wasn't sold on the idea until we
discussed it over dinner last night. With all the craziness
going on," she gestured toward the ominous room, "we
figured it was time to take the plunge."

Clearly, they were boyfriend and girlfriend.

Why else would Evie suddenly be using 'we?'

"Private investigation firms have access to databases,
public records, and surveillance equipment that aren't
available to regular folks," Matt explained. "Since I
offered to help him with some work he needed to do in
Tablerock, he granted me access to all that. Just in case
we need it."

My eyebrows shot up in surprise. "Hold on a minute,
you two talked about this at dinner last night, and now
you're a private investigator?" I asked. "It can't be that
easy."

"In Texas, pretty much," Matt replied with a shrug.

Josephine stepped forward to lawyer-splain things, her tone matter-of-fact. "In Texas, to become a private investigator, you must be at least eighteen and have a clean criminal record. Fill out the necessary paperwork and get your fingerprints taken. That's it. Although Matt is still waiting for his license, he can work with his Uncle Javier's firm and its resources in the meantime."

Matt's eyes widened in surprise. "Hold up, you know my Uncle Javier?"

Josephine nodded. "I trust Lodestar Investigations and Recovery implicitly. Your grandmother introduced me to the company when I first started practicing law, and I've been working with them ever since for the...uh, less savory tasks that come up." She gave a wry smile as if she had some juicy secrets tucked away. "I am some of the work in Tablerock, young man."

Suddenly, a deep voice interrupted with a polite, "Excuse me?"

As if on cue, a vaguely familiar man appeared just a few steps away. He was dressed in what could only be described as beekeeper gear, with a wide-brimmed hat and a protective mesh veil hanging around his neck. His clothes were slightly disheveled as if he had been working hard all day (even though it was still morning.)

I scrutinized the man's features, racking my brain to recall where our paths had crossed previously. He shifted awkwardly on his feet, clearly uncomfortable with my critical eye.

"Leo Barnett?" I said slowly. "Are you Leo Barnett?"

Josephine's eyes widened with recognition as soon as the name left my lips. "Oh, you're the one who used to work at Ben's honey farm," she exclaimed. Her expression shifted, and I could see a flicker of distress cross her face before she quickly recovered and leaned in with a friendly smile. "What brings you here?"

The man's expression remained tight and guarded as he spoke. "I came to check on Ben's cat, Honey. The police told me she was brought here when Ben... when he was found."

I noticed something odd about his statement — he had referred to Honey as "she." It was a minor inconsistency, but one that caught my attention.

Most people who cared about animals enough to check on their well-being in a shelter would likely know that animal's gender. Honey was a male, and this man, who claimed to have worked with Ben, had misgendered him.

"Actually," I corrected gently but firmly, "Honey is a male cat. He's been doing well here, and he's made friends with another cat. Would you like to see him?"

The man hesitated momentarily, his eyes darting around the room nervously before shaking his head. "No, that's not necessary. I just want to make sure Honey's safe until whoever Ben left him to comes to pick him up." He stepped closer, his tone low and conspiratorial. "Have the police told you anything about who's getting Ben's stuff? You know, like the cat?"

"I wouldn't know," I said, my tone guarded as I eyed

the man warily. I couldn't help but wonder about his true intentions. Was he genuinely concerned about Honey's well-being, or did his interest in the cat have to do with the ongoing investigation into Ben Tyson's case? "I forget — how long ago did you stop working for Ben, Leo?"

I noticed a subtle flicker of tension in the man's face as he answered, "Six months ago, I guess."

He came by to check on a cat he hadn't seen for six months?

Not likely.

Evie leaned in, her voice friendly. "So, where are you working now? At Buzzing Blossom Farms?"

"Excuse me?" The man's tone shifted from wary to subtly hostile, and Matt leaned in closer to Evie as if to protect her. I noticed some of the cats seemed to sense the change in Leo's mood, their ears perking up and tails twitching in unison as they watched him.

"I said—"

"Why would you ask that?" the man demanded, his eyes narrowing.

Evie pointed to her head and neck, her voice steady despite the man's sudden antagonistic shift. "The outfit."

Realizing his beekeeping attire was a giveaway, the man's expression softened slightly. "Oh, right. No, not there. Just working around. You know, in the area."

I couldn't help but notice how guarded the man remained through the rest of the conversation, his eyes darting around the room nervously and his posture tense.

It was as if he was ready to bolt at any moment.

As the peculiar man left through the front door, Josephine furrowed her brow, a thoughtful expression on her face. "Being a lawyer has made me quite perceptive," she remarked. "I can't shake the feeling that something's off about that young man."

"I don't think you have to be a lawyer to pick up on that," I remarked. It was clear that Leo had come in without ordering anything, and his concern for Honey's welfare seemed questionable at best, just an excuse at worst. "He always seemed like a nice enough young man when I chatted with him at Ben's while picking up my order, but today he appeared... frazzled."

Evie's eyes widened with curiosity as she turned toward me. "Mom, do you remember why he left Ben's shop six months ago? Did Leo quit, or was he fired?"

I paused, searching the depths of my memory for any details. "I'm not entirely sure," I admitted, feeling a twinge of frustration. "Honestly, I was just friendly with Ben, not friends. I don't remember that he said much about it. I remember Ben telling me that he had to let Leo go for some reason, but he didn't say why. He seemed genuinely upset about the whole ordeal."

Josephine turned her gaze toward me, her eyes

narrowing as she mulled over the puzzle. "It just doesn't add up," she said, her voice laced with skepticism. "Why would he barge in here, supposedly to check on Honey, and then not even bother to see how he's doing?"

"Maybe he was trying to dig up some information on who was taking over Ben's property now that he's... gone," Evie suggested, her voice faltering ever so slightly. "But for whatever reason, he didn't want to go to the police to find out."

"That's a bit suspicious." I said.

Evie's eyes lit up with realization. "And another thing — he had beekeeping stuff on, but he got fired from Ben's place and said he doesn't work at Buzzing Blossom Farms." She turned to Matt as if seeking his confirmation. "Those are the only two honey farms in Tablerock. If he wasn't getting honey from the hives at either of those places, why was he wearing the net thing around his neck?"

Matt's brow creased as he frowned, lost in thought. "What if he's working for a competitor from out of town?" he speculated, a hint of uncertainty in his voice. "Someone who wants to swoop in and take over Ben's shop now that he's no longer around? They could have hired Leo and sent him back here to snoop around and gather intel."

Josephine shook her head dismissively and tapped her finger on the counter. "That's quite the imaginative theory, but I think it's a bit of a stretch," she said, her voice laced with skepticism. "Don't get me wrong — I'm not saying he isn't a viable suspect in Ben's murder. The guy's obviously got some shady vibes, and his supposed 'cat checkup' charade only adds to that impression. But spinning this elaborate conspiracy, out-of-town honey conglomerates swooping in to get Ben's little operation? I don't buy it. People just aren't that complicated."

She crossed her arms as if to emphasize her point.

"We're already digging into the baker ex-girlfriend angle," Evie interjected, sidelong glancing at Matt. She seemed eager to get to the bottom of the mystery, her eyes flashing with determination. "Why don't Matt and I head upstairs with our laptops and see what else we can dig up on this guy? Where he works, what went down when he left Ben's, all that."

She leaned forward as if anticipating our agreement.

"Sounds good," I chimed in, feeling compelled to remind everyone of another aspect of the case. I leaned forward, my eyes scanning each of their faces. "I hate to complicate this, but let's not forget the feud between Buzzing Blossom Farms and Ben's place. Sure, maybe it was just a social media spat, but something about that whole situation keeps gnawing at me."

"Sounds like bad sushi," Josephine said.

I wished. "From two weeks ago?"

In addition to the lingering guilt I felt about Mario, which hung like an oppressive cloud over my thoughts, the feud between Buzzing Blossom Farms and Ben's place made me uneasy.

Evie's sudden transformation from anxious and

struggling young woman to superwoman added another layer of unease to the already complex emotional cocktail brewing inside me.

As I watched her and Matt disappear up the stairs, their determination palpable, I couldn't help but feel a twinge of worry. Evie had always been strong-willed, but this new intensity and confidence was... something else entirely.

The weight of unanswered questions and mounting suspicions grew stickier by the minute.

Chapter Nine

Time seemed to fly by as the day progressed.
The café was a hive of activity, with patrons coming and going, their animated conversations filling the air with a pleasant buzz. The cats, each one more adorable than the last, pranced and played, delighting the now-regular café patrons and newcomers alike with their charming antics.

If the town was concerned about Ben's unsolved murder, you'd never know it from the crowd in the café.

The kids remained sequestered in the isolation room, accompanied by Honey and Belladonna, who presumably assisted with information and opinions as Matt and Evie worked on their laptops to dig up information.

By midday, as I made my way to the isolation room, the sound of furious and incessant typing grew audible from behind the closed door. When I knocked tentatively, Evie's muffled response was barely audible. "Not now, Mom. We're in the middle of something."

"But Evie —"

"Not now, Mom!"

I dropped my hand and turned, feeling worried as I walked away.

At the end of the day, I realized it felt almost shameful to admit that Evie's "dramatic improvement" was starting to unsettle me. I knew it wasn't something a parent should typically feel, but this nagging doubt followed me like a dark shadow as I made my way back down the hallway.

But I did feel it.

Evie's practically overnight change bothered me.

The neurologists had warned me years ago that Evie would always grapple with some lingering challenges. They'd cautioned she would need to ensure a solid foundation beneath her feet each time she took a step forward, and they advised those steps should be slow and steady. Her brain could forge new pathways to compensate for those she'd lost, but it would be a gradual process that required a lot of time and a lot of patience.

And yet her newfound confidence defied those predictions, emerging swiftly and without warning, an unexpected flash transformation that left me feeling a mixture of pride and unease. I tried to reconcile the image of my daughter as I'd known her with the person she was rapidly becoming without being alarmed, but it wasn't easy.

"Mrs. Rockwell, the last customer just left the café." Amber Grove, a bright-eyed seventeen-year-old who recently joined our team, snapped me out of my worrisome thoughts. "Should I go ahead and lock the front door, then start serving the cats their —"

"Don't say it —"

" —dinner?"

No sooner had the word "dinner" left her lips than a chorus of feline whines and meows erupted throughout the café like the wailing undead in a low-budget horror flick. Eager for their evening meal, the cats made their anticipation and hunger known, their voices mingling into a band of discordant bellyaching that brought a smile to my face (despite my annoyance at being called Mrs. Rockwell.)

"I have a feeling that if you don't, you might face a mini-stampede of pint-sized lions," I replied, grinning. "Do you need any help with that?"

She shook her head confidently. "No, ma'am. I've got it."

Amber came out from behind the café counter and walked toward the door, her hand reaching for the lock. Just as she was about to secure it, the door swung open to reveal Landon on the other side, his arrival impeccably timed.

"Hello, Miss Grove." Landon greeted her with a warm, friendly smile as his steel-toed boots thudded across the hardwood floor. He didn't get five steps in before the calico that was particularly fond of him rubbed against his leg. "Hello, there. Aren't you a pretty girl, Sundae," he cooed, bending down to scratch behind her ears.

"You're going to adopt that cat, you know," I told him. "She's pretty sure of it." No matter how tired Landon was after a long day, he never failed to give any feline in the place his full attention if they gave theirs to him.

"We'll see. How's it going, Ellie?" Landon asked, making his way to the counter where I sat on a stool.

"It's been a very long day." I smiled, glancing at the array of handcrafted scratching posts and climbing structures Landon had built for the café. "The kitties loved that new sisal scratcher you put together, by the way. I had to refill it with catnip twice, and Jojo tried to drag it up the stairs."

He let out a chuckle, his eyes crinkling at the corners. "Happy to be of service." Landon brushed cat hair off his hands before sitting next to me. "I hate to bring this up, but we've got to figure out what to do about Mario. He cornered me at lunch today at the diner, full of questions about Ben's death. He knows everyone's hiding something from him and is determined to find out what it is. He thinks it has to do with the case."

I knew there had to be a reason I felt a nagging sense of guilt and a perpetual concern about him all day. Mario was too astute at detecting lies and evasions, and I suspected he wouldn't let it go. "What exactly did he ask you?"

"Everything under the sun. If we know who saw Ben last, who we were going to talk to, and why. Like he said last night, Mario's convinced there's more going on than people are letting on." Landon ran a hand over his face, worry etched into his features. "I tried to shrug it off as best I could, but you know I've never been able to fool him. He's like a dog with a bone, and he won't stop digging until he finds answers."

I bit my lip, thinking of the magical cat plate hidden in the cubby upstairs. "Even if we did tell him, Landon, we'd put him in a terrible position. We can't have him write about it in a police report. I don't want to ask him to keep our secret yet..." I trailed off, shaking my head. "I can't believe Fiona kept this secret for so many years. How on earth did she do it?"

"Fiona hated everyone."

I rolled my eyes. "She didn't hate—"

"Okay, she strongly disliked most people. Better?" Landon sighed. "I don't think Fiona cared what people thought after that mayor thing. I know what you mean, though. I hate deceiving him, but protecting him from that knowledge seems like the thing for us to do at this point. For him, for us, and the cats."

I turned to Landon, hoping to reassure him with a confident tone. "Don't worry," I said, trying to inject more certainty into my voice than I felt. "We'll think of something."

"I hope you're right."

So did I.

Evie and Matt came thundering down the stairs. Their faces were alight with excitement, and their steps echoed their eagerness.

"Mom, we found something big," Evie said. She looked at Matt. "Matt, tell her."

"You should tell her," Matt responded.

"No, Matt, you —"

"Someone just tell me, will you?" I asked, exasperated.

"Sorry, Ms. Rockwell." Matt held up a sheaf of papers. "I was searching online court records and found a defamation lawsuit Ben filed a few months ago. Against Nina Coleman from Buzzing Blossom Farms."

"Defamation?" Landon scratched his head. "What was that all about?"

Before Matt could respond, the front door chimed, signaling the arrival of Laurie and Josephine. The two women seemed engrossed in a lively conversation as they stepped inside. They made their way toward us, with Josephine casually adjusting the strap of her laptop bag as they approached.

"Hush up. The kids were just about to tell us something," I said.

"Don't hush me, lady," she winked. Josephine's piercing gaze took in the papers in Matt's hand. "What have you got there?" she asked, her voice laced with curiosity.

Evie quickly filled her in on the latest thing they had found, detailing Ben's defamation lawsuit against Nina Coleman.

Josephine took in the information with a sharp focus, and when Evie finished speaking, she leaned forward. "It's certainly a possibility that this has something to do with Ben's murder," she said, her voice measured. "But we can't jump to conclusions just yet. Matt, hand me those papers, would you?"

Matt handed Josephine the documents.

"Ruining someone's livelihood and name in a small town like this is no small thing. Money and appearances mean a lot to some people," Laurie said as Josephine scanned the pages. "Nothing provokes a person to violence more than threatening what they hold dear."

"Where'd you learn that, Psych 101 in college?" Josephine asked her without looking up.

"I read a lot of bad-boy romance," Laurie answered.

The lawyer's eyes raised. "Please tell me you're making a joke," she said.

"I am not." Laurie shrugged indifferently and flashed a mischievous smirk. "Romance novels can offer insights into relationships and people," she said with a hint of amusement. "The guys are also really hot."

Josephine shook her head and went back to reading the documents.

I poured two more decaf coffees and passed them to Laurie and Josephine as they settled around the counter. Despite Laurie making a bit of a joke out of her bad-boy romance insights, I thought she was right. Anger, greed, wounded pride — any one of those could drive someone to kill if they were pushed far enough.

Landon cleared his throat. "There's something else Mario mentioned to me at lunch. He said there was some kind of confrontation between Nina and Ben at the farmers' market last weekend. In full view of everyone."

"A confrontation?" Josephine's eyebrow rose. "About what exactly?"

"Nina accused Ben of trying to hire away some of her employees. She makes all her employees sign a non-compete so no one can take the secrets of her honey to a competitor, and Ben can't even talk to them. Being competition and all."

"You mean they can't talk to Ben," Evie pointed out. "The contracts would be on the employees, not Ben. Ben could talk to whoever he wants."

"Are you serious? The 'secrets' of her honey?" I raised an eyebrow. "She doesn't make the honey. The bees make the honey. What secrets could she possibly have?"

"I don't know, but I'm guessing she thinks she's got some." Landon sighed. "Mario said the other farmers had to break it up because it looked like things would get physical. Nina was hollering like a tornado siren at midnight, calling Ben all kinds of names children should not have heard."

"I know Nina a little bit from the Tablerock

Economic Development group. She's pretty stubborn," Laurie said. "Try telling her something once she gets an idea into her head, and you won't get very far."

"No doubt," Josephine said, looking up from the papers. "Her response to this lawsuit? Calling it unhinged would be generous — she didn't hire a lawyer, just responded herself. My guess is no lawyer would put their name to papers like this." She tapped her chin thoughtfully. "A confrontation like that at the farmers' market the week before Ben's murder seems an unlikely coincidence. We may need to chat with the self-crowned queen of Tablerock's apiaries."

Laurie nodded. "She seems to have a motive and a volatile enough temperament to do it."

"Did Ben have an attorney?" I asked.

Josephine shook her head. "No, it doesn't appear so. Ben most likely intended to represent himself. Filing a suit pro se for defamation is risky, but not unheard of." She flipped through the pages. "This poor judge. This looked like a circus."

"Do you think Nina's accusations about Ben poaching her employees have any merit?" Laurie asked.

"I don't think she'd have a leg to stand on," Josephine replied. "Non-compete clauses are difficult to enforce, and methods of honey production aren't exactly a trade secret." She leaned back, regarding us over the rim of her coffee mug. "The picture emerging here is not a pretty one. I'm surprised Mario hasn't picked her up yet."

"So what now?" Landon asked. "Do we call Mario?"

"I think that may be premature," Josephine said. "We have suspicions and theories but little in the way of hard evidence. Mario and the other officers are aware of Nina's quarrel with Ben and must be aware of this lawsuit." She sighed. "As difficult as it is, the best thing we can do now is to wait and dig. Let the facts and more concrete clues, come to light."

"Besides, I think we should look more into Leo," I said.

"Leo?" Landon's voice held a note of surprise as he echoed the name.

He leaned back in his chair and listened intently as I related the man's earlier visit. Though others added observations and filled in forgotten words when I missed something, Landon's gaze remained focused on me.

As the kids retreated back upstairs, Laurie and Josephine made a hasty exit from the cat café with such a sense of urgency that I wondered if their rear ends were ablaze.

Landon slid onto a stool closer to me, a grin tugging at his lips. "Well, will you look at this? Finally got you all to myself."

"Landon, we were alone just a few minutes ago before the others came in."

"Were we? Maybe so, but not like this." He winked, taking a sip of his coffee. "I meant without everyone else underfoot. It feels like it's been ages since we've had a chance to talk without worrying about interruptions, you and me."

A flutter of warmth stirred in my chest at his words, but it was tempered by a dose of apprehension. I could sense the conversation Landon seemed to be angling for, and I wasn't sure I was ready to have it.

If I could sense the conversation, he seemed to sense my hesitation.

Landon reached across the counter to squeeze my hand. "Ellie, you know how I feel about you. How I've felt for a long time now." His eyes were earnest, willing me to accept his words. "And the last time we talked about this, you were insistent that you couldn't give us a try because of Evie."

"There were other reasons."

"I'm sure there were. I'm sure. I can't help but notice Evie and Matt are dating now. Maybe you've thought some more about what we discussed and are willing to give this — give us — a chance."

I ducked my head and cleaned an already clean glass, emotions warring within me. Landon had been patient, waiting for me to move past the need to give all of myself to my daughter — even though I told him it would never happen. His polite persistence was impressive.

And the truth was a part of me longed to give up and try. I recognized in Landon a caring soul who had always been there for me.

I drew in a steadying breath, meeting Landon's gaze

with a sad smile. "You're a good friend, Landon. And I really do like you a lot. I like spending time with you. But as for the rest..." I shook my head. "I know to everyone else it looks like Evie's jumped into adult life with both feet, but... the thought of not being there for her when she needs me, terrifies me. If I wasn't there for her because of you, Landon, I'd never forgive myself, and I'd never forgive you. It's just not fair to you."

A hint of disappointment flashed across Landon's face, but he didn't push. "I get it, Ellie. I'm not trying to pressure you. I just want you to know I'm here for you, no matter how long it takes." He squeezed my hand once again, his eyes gentle and warm. "And can I say something without coming off as pushy?"

"That depends on what you say," I told him.

"Any man worth your time would be there for you and your daughter when she needs it, no questions asked."

I couldn't help but smile at Landon's sincerity. It was one of the things that drew me to him in the first place. With his rugged good looks and laid-back charm, he could have any woman in this town he wanted, and why he seemed to like me, I could not fathom. "Thank you. For your patience, kindness, and being a good friend."

Landon lifted my hand to his lips, kissing my knuckles tenderly. "Always."

Our eyes held for a long moment.

As if sensing I was about to pull my hand away, Landon dropped it gently.

"Now," he said, the intimate tone gone from his voice. "How about you and me go out to dinner at Pepper Jalisco's? I may have heard that Nina and her husband will be there tonight." He winked. "I'm sure they'll want to be seen being friendly with the non-profit cat lady."

"I'll get my bag," I said with a nod.

I knew I was holding back to protect my heart, and I couldn't give Landon the answer he wanted.

Not yet.

Maybe one day, I could let go of the fear that held me back and embrace what Landon had to offer. But for now, I took comfort in knowing that he was willing to wait for me, no matter how long it took.

Chapter Ten

As Landon and I stepped inside Pepper Jalisco's, the tantalizing scent of spices and grilled meat wafted toward us, making my stomach rumble. The restaurant was a local favorite, especially on Tuesdays when the taco plates were half off, and it seemed like the entire town had the same idea for dinner.

"There's Augusta and Mayor Winthrop," Landon murmured, angling his head discreetly to the right. "Mario told me she was questioned this morning, and it didn't go all that well."

I glanced at Augusta and noticed the tell-tale signs of exhaustion on her face. Her eyes were rimmed with red, and dark shadows smudged underneath them. In contrast, the mayor's eyes gleamed with malicious amusement as she leaned over the table, whispering something that made Augusta flinch.

I felt slightly sorry for the baker.

Dealing with Jessa Winthrop was like tangling with a thorny rosebush.

"Hello, you two." We looked up from the menus to find Mario Lopez beside our table. He glanced at the nearby table, his expression darkening as he spotted the mayor and her stressed-out dinner companion. "Well, now. This feels like one heck of a coincidence," he said quietly.

I smiled. "See, I would have thought the opposite—"

"Mario's being sarcastic," Landon interrupted me, nodding to a chair at our table. "You want to join us, or do you lecture better from a standing position?"

"I'm not going to lecture you, Landon. I wasted my breath at lunch, which didn't get me anywhere. I'm not ruining my dinner, too." Mario gazed intently at us. "Unless you two are going to tell me what you're hiding?"

The sound of a lively mariachi guitar filled the air, the upbeat melody starkly contrasting with the tense silence at our table. The candles flickered softly, casting a warm glow on Landon's tanned face and accentuating the creases of his weathered expression.

"Nothing to tell," Landon lied.

"That's what I thought. You two have a good night now." Mario turned and stepped deeper into the restaurant, hands shoved in his pockets. "When you remember what it is, you let me know."

"You're stubborn, Lopez," Landon called after him.

"Uh huh," Lopez said dismissively, tossing the word over his shoulder.

I watched him go feeling a sense of frustration. "I hate not being able to tell him. Honestly, it's not surprising he's suspicious. It's literally his job to uncover secrets." I picked up a crispy tortilla chip and dipped it into the tangy salsa, a futile attempt to distract myself with a spicy crunch.

Landon furrowed his brow. "He's not a detective."

"Well, that's the silliest thing you've said in a while," I told him. "I know this is difficult, Landon, but you can't be upset with Mario for trying to do his job well. And he may as well be a detective since Tablerock doesn't have any."

Landon grunted, and for a moment, I wasn't sure how to interpret the sound. Was it an agreeable grunt or a disagreeable one?

I looked over at him, trying to read his expression. His stubbornness could be endearing at times, but right now, it only reminded me of the precarious position we found ourselves in.

"Landon, I don't want this to come between you and Mario's friendship," I said. "There's a voice in my mind telling me so many people know already. What's one more person? Will it really matter?"

"As you pointed out before, he's a cop," Landon pointed out, his voice carrying a hint of reluctance. "How would he explain the information he gets?"

"We haven't gotten any information from Honey so

far. And he's our friend," I countered, my eyes meeting his. "This is a small town. I'm sure he's driven drunk teenagers home without arresting them, or overlooked things because it was better for him or the town to do it. You don't think he'd do it for us?"

"You don't like people mad at you," Landon teased me, a playful glint in his eyes that momentarily cut through the tension.

"You're right, I don't," I admitted as a warm flush rose in my cheeks. "But I especially don't like friends feeling like I don't trust them. I got to know Mario when he worked with you at the rescue, and I like him." I sighed, running a hand through my hair as I glanced back at Mario's table. He was still watching us intently. "The longer this goes on, the less I like this."

"You may be the toughest squishy woman I've ever known," Landon said with a hint of admiration.

I rolled my eyes. "I'm not tough."

I was squishy.

Couldn't argue that.

"Eleanor Rockwell, you sell yourself short." He leaned in closer, the warm scent of his aftershave mingling with the aroma of the restaurant. "You saw Evie through three open-heart surgeries, pacemaker surgeries, brain damage from her last open-heart surgery, and an ex-husband who decided paying child support for his critically ill daughter needing expensive medical care was optional." Landon's eyes were filled with sincerity and warmth as he spoke. "You really don't think you're tough?"

Landon's words made me pause. I couldn't help but reflect on my challenges and the resilience I had been forced to cultivate.

I had navigated through some of life's most daunting storms, but it had never occurred to me that I might be considered tough for doing it. It's not like someone gave me a choice about any of it.

When you're caught in a storm, what choice do you have but to hunker down and make it through?

Halfway through my meal, savoring the rich flavors of my cheese enchilada, the restaurant's front door banged open with a jarring crash. The lively atmosphere was momentarily disrupted, and all eyes turned toward the entrance.

Nina Coleman walked in dragging her husband Tom behind her like a reluctant anchor. The clatter of silverware and laughter seemed to pause, replaced by a collective intake of breath as everyone braced for the impending confrontation they sensed was coming.

Nina's eyes darted around the restaurant, her face reddening with anger as she zeroed in on Augusta. I couldn't help but notice the way her chest heaved with each breath, like a bull ready to charge.

"Wow," Landon whispered.

"Quiet," I whispered. No one had spoken yet, but I didn't want a single sound to derail whatever was about to happen.

Even the mariachi band stopped playing.

Nina's heels clicked ominously on the tiled floor as she approached the mayor and Augusta, her face set in a scowl. But before she could reach them, Tom stepped forward, grabbing her arm to halt her progress.

He leaned in close, his expression a mix of concern and embarrassment as he murmured something in her ear.

Nina's voice hissed like a snake, loud enough for nearby tables to hear. "Don't tell me to calm down!" she spat. "That little tart thinks she can bat her eyes and point the police to my doorstep for something she did? She's got another thing coming!"

Tom guided Nina forcefully toward the bar, his grip firm and unyielding. As they moved away from the center of attention, he cast an apologetic glance at the room, silently pleading for understanding in the face of his wife's outburst.

"So, Augusta talked to the police this morning and must have pointed the finger at Nina," I whispered to Landon. I glanced at the corner table where Mario and the three other police officers sat, observing with keen interest. "I wonder why none of them bothered to get up and stop that," I asked Landon under my breath.

Landon looked over at them. "They watched the whole thing closely, but Tom had Nina under control. I guess they wanted to know what Nina and Augusta would say to each other." He gestured toward Mario's table and the half-empty glasses filled with vibrant green liquid. "Besides, those are margaritas on the table. They're off duty."

The restaurant's din slowly returned to normal as Nina and Tom settled onto the barstools. Even as the lively chatter and laughter resumed, a palpable sense of unease lingered, like a low hum beneath the festive music.

As we finished our meal, our plates speckled with the remnants of rich sauces and stray tortilla bits, Tom approached our table. His eyes creased with a mix of relief and lingering tension. "Evening, folks. I wanted to apologize again for the, uh, commotion earlier. My wife's been under a lot of stress lately," he explained.

"No need to apologize," Landon said. "We understand these things happen."

Landon's reassurance seemed to do the trick as Tom's shoulders visibly relaxed. "Since you're new customers at the farm, I figured proper introductions were in order," he said, gesturing toward Nina, who stood a few paces behind him with a rigid posture. "This is my wife, Nina. Nina, this is Ellie Rockwell. She runs the cat café."

Nina's lips pressed into a thin line as if she were

holding back a torrent of emotions. "Nice to meet you both," she said, her coolly polite tone contrasting her earlier outburst. Though she had managed to regain her composure, at least for the moment, a subtle flicker in her eyes betrayed the angry storm that still brewed beneath the surface.

An awkward silence fell over the table, the atmosphere thick with unspoken thoughts and lingering tension. Sensing the discomfort, Tom patted Nina's shoulder gently. "Nina, love, why don't you join these nice folks? I'll get our coffee."

I cringed inwardly at the prospect.

As Tom strode off toward the bar with purpose in his steps, Nina sighed, her shoulders sagging slightly. She seemed resigned to joining us, her posture stiff and defensive as she took the empty seat beside me. Though I had little desire to share a table with Nina, it did present an opportunity to ask her about her anger toward Augusta.

"I'm Ellie Rockwell. We haven't officially met, though I did meet your husband when the café set up an account with Buzzing Blossom Farms." Hoping to defuse lingering hostility, I offered a warm smile. "It's nice to meet you."

Nina's expression softened slightly, the hard edges of her anger giving way to a hint of vulnerability. "The cat lady, yes. I've seen you at the market." She glanced away, clearly embarrassed, a faint pink blush tinting her cheeks. "I'm...sorry you had to witness my anger issues

on full display. It's just been a stressful week. I think it
was Ben's final insult to me, dying in such a way that
people think I did it."

I bit back a sarcastic retort that threatened to slip out
—Yes, no doubt Ben plotted his own murder just to get
you. What a pill this woman was.

Instead, I opted for a more diplomatic approach.

"Don't worry about it," I said, doing my best to
sound understanding and empathetic. "Emotions often
get the better of us. I'm not sure I understand what
Augusta has to do with that, though?"

I looked at Nina expectantly, hoping she would take
the opportunity I had given her to share the real story
behind her anger. The candlelight flickered on the table,
casting a warm glow on her face. It softened her hard
features as she considered whether and how to respond
to my question.

Landon sat quietly, watching.

"I'm afraid I let an old rivalry get the best of me
tonight." Nina rubbed the back of her neck, staring
down into her lap. "The way she looked at me, so smug,
like she'd finally won twice over...I couldn't bear it."

Landon looked puzzled. "Won what?"

Nina gave him an odd look. "Ben, obviously," she
replied.

I gasped. "You and Ben were romantically
involved?"

Nina opened her mouth to answer when Tom reap-
peared with two mugs of coffee. Settling into his seat, he

slid an arm around Nina's shoulders. "There now, let's start over. We were just getting acquainted properly, weren't we, dear?"

At the sight of her husband, Nina's mouth snapped shut.

As soon as we were alone again, Mario strode over to our table, his expression unreadable. "Evening once again, folks. Mind if I join you for a minute?" he asked.

"Of course, have a seat," Landon said. Mario slid into the chair beside him, his gaze flicking toward Nina and Tom, who sat huddled together across the room.

"I saw Tom and Nina over here with the two of you. Did they say anything I should know about?" Mario's question sounded casual, but the intensity in his gaze told me this was more than just polite interest.

Landon and I exchanged a hesitant glance.

"Really? You're not going to tell me what they said to you when I saw with my own eyes that the four of you talked minutes after Nina had a meltdown in the middle of the restaurant?" Mario's voice held a note of frustration, his eyebrows furrowing as he sought answers.

"She didn't have a meltdown, Mario," I said. "Nina was upset, but she managed to regain her composure."

"I'm not interested in her emotional state, Ellie. I want to know if she said anything I should know." I could see Mario's jaw clench.

Did we really want to tell Mario about Nina's admission of a long-standing feud with Augusta that seemed to stem from a honey-drenched love triangle? I wondered if it was too soon to be handing over pieces to a puzzle we had just begun fitting together. After all, Nina's words could have meant something else entirely.

Okay, she probably didn't mean something else entirely.

But she could have.

Mario's expression softened. "Look, I know you two are investigating, and I also know you're hiding something from me. But in case I wasn't clear before, anything that relates to my murder case, I need to know about. No exceptions."

"Nina seemed genuinely remorseful about causing a scene tonight, but there was more to what she did, I think, than just Ben's murder and what Augusta said accusing Nina of being a suspect," I told Mario what Nina said regarding her rivalry with Augusta.

Mario listened closely, then nodded. "This helps provide some context, though I wish I'd heard it directly from Nina." He shook his head. "The way folks in this town avoid airing their dirty laundry, you'd think they were guarding national secrets."

His comment hit too close to the mark, and I felt my cheeks warm.

Mario studied me for a long moment. "You look like the cat that ate the canary, Ellie. I'm going to ask you again. Anything I should know about? Because if it relates to my case in any way..." He let the implication hang, waiting.

Landon looked at me.

I looked at Landon.

I turned back toward Mario, carefully choosing my words. "There are confidences we've been entrusted with that could impact people's safety and well-being if mishandled. Please trust that you'll have it if we come across any information directly relevant to your investigation that we think you need." I hoped my promise would be enough to assuage him for now.

Mario frowned, clearly unsatisfied but recognizing he wouldn't get more from us tonight. He stood. "All right, we'll leave it at that — for now. You two be careful. A killer is still on the loose, and they may not take kindly to anyone poking around in their business."

With a final searching glance at each of us, Mario strode out of Pepper Jalisco's, the chime of bells above the door signaling his departure into the night.

I released a breath I hadn't realized I was holding. "I hate this," I muttered, the frustration evident in my voice.

"You know, at some point, we're all going to have to commit to this crime-fighting cat thing," Landon said, his voice filled with determination and uncertainty. "And if we do that, having a cop who knows about what we have access to might be better than not having one."

"You realize we're going back and forth like pendulums on whether to tell Mario about the cat plate, right?"

I said, highlighting the constant oscillation of our opinions on the matter. "Two hours ago, you were sure we shouldn't tell him."

Landon nodded. "I know. It's not easy."

No, it wasn't.

Secrets can be a burden, I thought. They have a way of creating distance between people, even those closest to us. Carrying them can be exhausting, and the fear of being discovered can consume us.

I glanced over at Nina, and the chasm between her and her husband, Tom, was almost visible. He chattered cheerfully, animatedly engaging with a couple at the next table while she sat sullen and ignored, her expression grim.

As I watched them, a sense of unease washed over me, a nagging reminder of the damage that secrets and mistrust could inflict on even the strongest relationships.

Chapter Eleven

I FLOPPED IN BED LIKE A BEACHED FISH, BUT SLEEP
remained elusive.

My mind was consumed by a labyrinth of theories
and suspicions sparked by the eventful dinner. The
weight of my worries and responsibilities felt as tangled
as a ball of yarn left to the mercy of mischievous
kittens.

A gentle tap on my cheek suddenly jolted me from
my sleepless reverie.

I opened my eyes to find Belladonna's angular face
suspended mere inches above my own, her piercing eyes
shining in the dark. For a brief moment, I couldn't quite
shake off the fog of confusion, and I wondered if I was
still trapped in my restless thoughts.

My senses gradually focused, and I realized
Belladonna was really there, her paw resting gently on
my face — though "gently" may be a slight misclassifica-

tion, as her unsheathed claws were hovering perilously close to my delicate skin.

"What is it?" I whispered. "How did you even get in here?"

The black cat meowed insistently in response, her tail swishing with impatience.

I stifled an exasperated sigh. "Can't this wait until morning?"

Belladonna meowed again, more urgently this time, padding in tight circles around me until I threw back the covers in resignation.

"All right, all right, I'm coming."

Stepping onto the second floor veranda, the old wooden planks groaned under my feet. The air was crisp, and the moon illuminated everything through the windows with a silvery glow. A faint meowing emanated from within as I walked toward the isolation room.

The door was slightly ajar, and I pushed it open.

Belladonna sat waiting on the table next to the cat house with the magic plate cubby, gazing at me expectantly. I took a seat across from her.

"Okay, here I am. What's got you so eager to talk in the dead of night?"

The black cat stared at me, her golden eyes unblinking.

"I thought you needed to tell me something important?"

Belladonna remained silent and then began grooming her paw nonchalantly.

I rubbed my eyes, wondering if exhaustion and an overactive imagination were playing tricks on me. Maybe she didn't want me to follow her, and I should have just stayed in bed. But no — I was sure she had wanted me to follow her in here, insistent I get up. Wasn't she?

"Were you just trying to get me out of bed for your amusement?" I asked.

The cat yawned, giving no indication whatsoever my accusation was off base.

"All right, you've had your fun. I'm returning to bed — some of us need to sleep." I stood, stretching muscles gone stiff, and approached the doorway.

"I am not one to be characterized by impatience," Belladonna's haughty faux-British voice snapped just before my hand reached the doorknob.

I turned. "Bella, I don't even know what that means."

"It means you have formed an erroneous impression of my temperament."

"And what erroneous impression would that be?"

Belladonna peered down her nose at me with an indignant sniff. "You seem to think I dragged you from your bed in the dead of night merely to satisfy some feline fancy for tricks or amusement. I assure you, my reasons are far more serious."

"Okay, like I said — you have my attention." I walked across the room and settled back into my seat. "What's so urgent that it couldn't wait until morning?"

Belladonna cast a withering glance across the room to where Honey, Ben's orange tabby, slept curled in his bed. The orange tabby appeared oblivious to the commotion unfolding in the isolation room. "It seems Honey has been withholding pertinent information regarding your murder victim. His foolish attempt to protect certain parties has gone on long enough."

"Long enough? This very moment, in the middle of the night?" I asked.

"Yes."

Honey's eyes snapped open as Belladonna's answer rang out. Hackles rising, his orange fur bristling along the ridge of his spine, Honey launched himself at Belladonna. He collided with her like a snarling, spitting furry missile, knocking her off the enchanted plate with a resounding crash. "How dare you! I have done no such thing, you arrogant furball!"

"No need for name calling," I chided gently as Honey glared at Belladonna, his back arched and tail whipping against the plate. Turning to Belladonna, I asked, "What information do you think Honey is withholding?"

Belladonna stalked back toward the enchanted plate, snarling ominously at Honey, who shrank back with an affronted hiss and vacated the cubby so Belladonna could commune through the plate unimpeded. "Our friend Honey overheard Ben arguing quite heatedly with someone the day of the murder. Isn't that right, Honey?"

Honey meowed in protest.

"Oh, be quiet," Belladonna told him, her ebony tail swishing arrogantly. "I have been deprived of my treats this evening, you lamentable interloper — this one" — she glared at me — "was out dining, while the other one was idly tapping upon a book devoid of pages throughout the night. Both forgot their duties to me, and I won't have it."

"I'm sorry we missed that. You could've come downstairs and eaten the soft food that all the cats get at dinner, Bella," I told her. "I know it's not your super-fancy canned stuff, but it's good food."

"You want me to eat what the peasants eat?" The black cat's sides heaved, and she retched as if struggling to expel an enormous hairball lodged in her throat. After several anguished moments, her body stilled, and she raised her head, an indignant gleam in her golden eyes. "If you, marmalade face, possess knowledge that may end this situation for me, you will step forward and make yourself useful," Belladonna told the orange cat. "Tell her about the fight that happened."

I turned to him. "What fight that happened?"

The orange tabby fidgeted uncomfortably under my probing stare and Belladonna's self-satisfied gaze. After several moments, Honey heaved a surrendering sigh, his resentment palpable. Sullen but compliant, the cat slunk over to the enchanted cubby and clambered onto the magic plate as Belladonna left the area. "All right, it's true. I didn't want to say, but it's too late now." Honey peered up at me, golden-yellow eyes filled with regret. "Ben was arguing with Augusta the day he died. It sounded as though she accused him of being unfaithful. Whatever that is."

Honey's revelation caught me off guard, and I felt a flurry of thoughts swirling inside my head. My prime suspect list, which had been a muddled mess, suddenly narrowed down to one — and that one made me groan inwardly.

I did not look forward to tangling with someone in Jessa Winthrop's orbit again.

But I might have to.

Augusta and Ben had argued on the day of his murder, and a possible motive emerged from the pages of a familiar tragic play. Jealousy, that "green-eyed monster," may have reared its ugly head; this time, it seemed, the beekeeper could not escape its bitter sting.

As I opened the cat café, my morning routine felt slower than usual, my thoughts churning with the previous night's revelations. Honey's middle of the night disclosure firmly pointed the finger of suspicion at Augusta, who now had a clear motive and opportunity.

Well, if the cat was to be believed.

Even with Honey's revelation, something about the whole scenario felt off, like a picture that had been hung slightly off-kilter.

Augusta claimed Nina had murdered Ben (according to Nina's own outraged account), but Nina vehemently denied that accusation and pointed an accusatory finger of her own directly back at Augusta. Nina's antagonistic history with Ben suggested a long-term simmering resentment rather than passionate fury, and yet the woman seemed to all but admit to engaging in a clandestine romantic relationship with Ben just last night.

Nina also had a habit of attacking Ben's character, using malicious gossip and outright lies to discredit her business rival whenever possible. Could this just be more of the same? Some odd posthumous character assassination?

What was I missing?

The claim of an affair could be another attempt by Nina to deflect suspicion onto Augusta. Honestly, though, I didn't see the reason — the baker and the beekeeper broke up recently. Surely no one needed to pile on more reasons to look at Augusta, especially untrue ones.

But...was it true?

Did Nina and Ben have an affair?

And if so, would Augusta be so angry at Ben that she would kill him?

Jealousy was a twisted, powerful emotion, and heaven knew what it might drive someone to do when it festered, poisoning every thought.

I rubbed at my temples, feeling a tension headache

forming as another memory poked through. I'd heard
Augusta talking about Ben at the restaurant the night I'd
stalked — um, followed Evie. The baker had hardly
sounded bothered by Ben's death at all.

Which, I suppose, was a clue all by itself.

The cheerful jingle of bells announced the arrival of
Evie and Matt, interrupting my troubled musings.

"Matt took me out for donuts at Dale's this morning," Evie said, holding up a brown paper bag laden with
tantalizing scents. "I got you a cream Bismark. Even
though that thing alone is probably taking you five giant
leaps closer to full-blown diabetes and an early grave."

I took the bag of donuts from her outstretched hands,
feeling the warmth through the thin paper as my fingers
gripped the sides. The sweet, tempting aroma of fried
dough and sugar tickled my nose. "Thanks. I really do
love these things. And I could use the sugar jolt, to be
honest. Belladonna got me up in the middle of the
night."

"She did? Why?"

I dug into the bag to retrieve a donut and recounted
the details of Honey and Belladonna's late-night revelations and the strange encounter with the Colemans at
Pepper Jalisco's.

Evie frowned. "That does make Augusta seem the
most likely suspect. But Nina and Ben having an affair?
Matt and I scoured the internet we never saw a single
mention of them being romantically linked." Evie
reached into the paper bag and fished around. With a

satisfied "aha!" she extracted a single donut hole, round and plump, its golden fried surface dusted with a flurry of powdered sugar. "Though someone did post that they saw Tom Coleman yelling at Ben in front of the hardware store a couple weeks ago. Said they almost came to blows."

Tom, Nina's husband, arguing with Ben as well?

This case was becoming more complicated by the hour.

"What on earth is going on in this town?" I asked her.

"In small towns, secrets have a way of festering under the surface," Matt said, then popped one of the powdered donut holes into his mouth. A few stray flecks of powdered sugar escaped, dusting his lips and chin like snow. After swallowing, he added, "Everyone knows everyone else's business. Except when they don't."

"I swear, those have to be laced with something. There's no way simple donuts should be that addictive," Evie said as her hand plunged again into the bag, fishing out a second donut hole to prove her point.

I chuckled, lifting my own half-eaten treat in a mock toast. "If that's the case, I hope they never find a cure. An addiction to Don's Donuts seems like one worth cultivating."

She lifted her donut in response, and we tapped them together before polishing off our respective treats. "I agree with Matt, though. I didn't know about Fiona's husband having a years-long affair with the mayor until he got killed," Evie said. "No one knew about the mayor's son. This town? It knows how to keep secrets."

I sighed. "True. And those secrets are proving dangerous. We need to figure out what happened — before the killer decides, no one else can be trusted with the truth. Considering our talk last night, Honey's mourning period is over enough for us to ask some serious questions."

In a town full of simmering rivalries, betrayals, and long-buried motives waiting to be unearthed, knowing where to begin searching posed a mystery.

Honey bounded across the isolation room in two effortless strides, his lithe orange body gliding through the air with feline grace before he landed on the enchanted cat plate. His soft belly fur shimmered and rippled briefly as his paws came into contact with the plate's glowing crystalline surface.

I crouched down so I was at eye level with the tabby. "Honey, we're trying to figure out who killed Ben. We know this will be difficult for you, but we think you may be the only one who knows about Ben's relationships. Would you mind if we asked you some questions about them?"

Belladonna came careening into the isolation room in a streak of inky black, colliding with Honey and knocking him bodily from the enchanted cubby with a resonant thud. Honey yowled in protest, landing in an ungainly sprawl of orange fur and flailing limbs on the floor below. From her perch atop the plate, Belladonna scoffed, peering down her nose at Honey's form with contempt. "Oh, please. I find it difficult to believe that the insipid ginger fur ball possesses anything of substance within the confines of his empty head."

"Hush, you," I told her. "Go sit over there."

She sniffed but did as I asked.

Honey sighed and returned to the talking perch, his ears back as he hissed at Belladonna. "Must you always arrive unannounced and unwelcome, you vainglorious harpy?" Turning to me, he said, "It's true. Ben did confide in me at times. We lived together for years, after all."

"What can you tell us about Nina?" Evie asked gently. "Were she and Ben romantically involved?"

"Nina?" The tabby shook his head. "No, that's not true at all. Nina and Ben were rival beekeepers. She resented his success, but there was no affair."

I exchanged a glance with Evie. One suspicion down, at least. "What about Augusta, the baker? How did Ben feel about her?"

"Augusta was...possessive of Ben," Honey said carefully. "Their relationship was passionate but tempestuous. They were always fighting or making up, on and off again like a merry-go-round. Ben said she could be jealous and controlling. Honestly, I think he was considering permanently ending things with her."

"Because of her jealousy?" Matt asked.

Honey dragged his rough, pink tongue slowly over his lips. "Partly. And because Ben felt Augusta didn't trust him and was trying to dictate who he spent time with. The argument with Tom you mentioned started because Augusta saw Ben talking to Nina and accused him of flirting with her."

Evie looked confused. "I don't understand. How did Tom find out that Augusta thought Ben was flirting? Were Augusta and Tom talking?"

Before Honey could respond to Evie's question, the isolation room door banged open behind us, and Honey leaped upward from the glowing cat plate with an alarmed yowl. Landing unsteadily, he spun quickly, searching for the source of his terror.

We, meanwhile, had already turned to find Mario in the doorway staring at the glowing cat plate. I hoped that he hadn't heard anything yet—

Hopes that were dashed when Honey spied the unexpected intruder.

The cat leaped up again with an alarmed yowl, fur bristling in consternation, and began cursing at Mario in a jumble of meows, yowls, and distressingly human profanities that seemed utterly bizarre and unnatural coming from a small tabby cat.

Mario's eyes went wide as saucers. "Is that cat...talking?"

Slowly the puffiness subsided from Honey's coat, and his ears regained their usual expressive tilt. "Jerk," the cat muttered, then set to grooming his disheveled fur with a vengeance.

In our haste to question Honey, we had neglected to lock the isolation room door. There could be no explaining this away as some trick of the light or a radio left playing. Mario had witnessed too much already — an ordinary cat conversing freely, illuminated by the impossible glow of enchanted magic.

Mario now knew the truth about the cat plate, and there was no unseeing what he had stumbled upon. The time had come to roll the dice on our ability to trust him and hope they fell in our favor.

Chapter Twelve

Mario's eyes stretched wide, a look of shock plastered across his face. His gaze moved frantically between Honey and Belladonna, and his jaw fell slack. "They can talk. The cats...they can actually talk?" he asked, his voice a little breathless. He pointed a trembling finger at the two felines, looking from one to the other with wonderment and confusion.

Evie slowly reached out and grasped Mario's trembling hand, giving it a gentle, reassuring squeeze. "Mario, please, just try to stay calm. We can explain everything," she said.

"We can," Matt agreed with her.

But Mario, his head swimming with disbelief, wasn't ready to listen.

"Explain?" Mario burst out, disbelief and hurt in his tone. He then took a deep, steadying breath and let it out slowly. "How long has this been happening? How long have you known about this?" His gaze swept the room. "Does everyone else know? Everyone but me?"

My gaze dropped momentarily as I thought of how to explain it to him without causing further turmoil. He deserved the truth, as difficult as it was, yet protecting him was also a concern. I lifted my eyes to him, hoping he could see their sincerity. "Mario, we didn't tell you because we weren't sure how you'd react, considering your position as a police officer. We didn't want to put you in a difficult situation."

"Is that your reasoning? Really?" Distress creased his features. "How could you not tell me about something like this?"

"We were trying to protect you, Mario," I said gently. "This isn't an easy secret to keep, and it certainly wasn't easy keeping it from you. But under the circumstances, we didn't see any other choice."

Running a hand through his hair, Mario let out a long, unsteady breath. His eyes were fixed on Honey and Belladonna. "Talking cats. This is... unbelievable. So, all this time, you two could understand us? And communicate with each other?"

Honey meowed apologetically before leaping onto the plate, which glowed a soft pink hue. "Obviously, we can communicate with each other," he huffed, displaying feline pride. "We're cats. We don't need this ridiculous plate to talk to each other. And we can always understand you. You're just too dim-witted a species to understand us without tools."

Mario blinked. "Did that cat just call me stupid?"

"You get used to it," Matt told him.

"Mario, I really am sorry for not telling you," I repeated. "It wasn't easy for us to keep it from you. You're our friend."

Honey huffed indignantly, his tail flicking in irritation. "Well," he retorted, "you're not my friend. After you slammed the door and scared me, you'll probably never be."

A mixture of amazement and disbelief washed over Mario as he stared at the feline duo, grappling with the stunning revelation that turned his understanding of the world upside down. "Talking cats," he whispered, the disbelief mixed with awe. "This town never ceases to surprise me." He gazed at the glowing platter, his brow furrowed in confusion. "How does this thing even work?" he asked.

I shrugged helplessly. "We don't really know. Fiona sent the platter to us with Belladonna when she was arrested for Beau's murder. She promised to explain everything but was gone before she could."

"Right," Mario said, nodding thoughtfully. "So, has Honey given you any useful information since he's been talking?"

Honey hissed in annoyance, his fur bristling. "I'm sitting right here, you oaf. It's rude to talk about me as if I can't hear you."

Mario blinked at the cat's outburst, then grimaced. "My apologies. I didn't mean to offend."

With a dismissive sniff, Honey replied, "As if I care about your fragile human emotions. To answer your question, no, I don't know anything about the origins or mechanics of the magic platter. I can speak with you dim-witted humans when I step onto it. That's all I know."

"There's no need for insults," I chided gently.

Honey merely meowed in response, licking his paw nonchalantly.

"Is he always like this?" Mario mumbled under his breath.

I chuckled, glancing at Mario. "You did give him a bit of a scare, Mario, so I think he's a little spicy now. It's Belladonna that's got healthy self-esteem in comparison to everyone else in the world." At the mention of her name, Belladonna meowed and brushed against my leg, purring. I reached down to scratch behind her ears. "No one believes you're that sweet, dear."

Belladonna hissed, her momentary sweetness replaced by a flash of feline indignation. Her golden eyes narrowed as she looked up at me, clearly not appreciating my comment.

"This is unbelievable," Mario said, shaking his head. "Talking cats, magic platters, and another murder in our small town...I feel like I've stepped into some kind of movie."

"Tablerock's always been a little dramatic," Matt said wryly.

Mario studied Honey. "So, Honey could answer

questions about what he saw the day Ben was murdered?"

I nodded, my gaze shifting between Honey and Belladonna, who were busy grooming themselves without a care in the world. "Yeah. Landon sound-proofed this room, see? That way, we can chat with any feline witnesses without being overheard."

"Landon's in on this too?" Mario raised an eyebrow. Another nod from me.

"I see." He frowned, lost in thought, mulling over the staggering reality of a talking cat witness in his murder case. After an eternity, he let out a heavy sigh, rubbing his weary eyes. "This is... a lot. Chatty cats, enchanted platters."

"We get it," I reassured him, my voice gentle. "Not every day something comes along and flips your entire understanding of the world upside down."

Mario burst through the isolation room door, a gleam in his eye that betrayed his typically calm demeanor. "This might just be the break we needed," he announced, excitement lacing his hushed voice. "Honey said—"

Evie's eyes widened in alarm, and she frantically gestured for Mario to quiet down, pointing at the patrons mingling in the cat café beneath the veranda.

Catching Mario's gaze, Matt subtly nodded toward the door leading to my upstairs office.

We filed in, shutting the door behind us. Mario ran a hand through his hair, letting out a deep breath. "Apologies. I didn't consider the risk of eavesdroppers."

"I have a quick question before you get to that. If the information Honey gave you leads somewhere, how will you explain where you got it?" I asked.

Mario's brow furrowed as a frown creased his face. He sighed, shaking his head slightly as he contemplated the situation. "You know, I wish Josephine was in the loop," he said. "Having a lawyer involved might give me some much-needed cover."

"Say no more, Officer." I whipped out my phone and dialed Josephine's number. It rang a few times before she answered. "Josephine, it's Ellie. You're on speaker with Evie, Matt, and Mario. So, uh, Mario found out about the whole cat plate situation. He caught us in the act this morning."

"Did he now?"

Mario froze in place, cringing at the icy tone in Josephine's voice as it came through the phone. Her usual sassy manner had vanished, replaced by a frigid, barracuda-like aggression.

"Did you have a search warrant?" The question was punctuated by a weighty pause as she waited for his response, and when he could muster no answer, she spoke again, each word clipped and sharp as a blade. "There's no law against having a magic item, Officer Lopez."

"I think we're — look, here's why they called you," he

said. "I need information that only cats — specifically Honey — might know. But I can't very well put in my police report or tell my captain I got confidential information from a talking cat." He paused. When she didn't answer, he said, "Do you see my predicament?"

"Oh, I see it, all right." I could practically hear the knowing smirk in Josephine's voice, a hint of sassy amusement tempering her earlier ire. "You want a legal loophole so you can use fantastical evidence from a feline informant without ending up in a padded cell." Her tone was dry, hinting at thinly veiled amusement. "Luckily, you've come to the right lawyer, Officer. Finding loopholes is my specialty."

"Well, wait a second," I said. "Do we even need to find a loophole? You're the shelter's lawyer, so technically, that would make you the cat's lawyer, too, wouldn't it?"

"Ellie?" Josephine asked.

"Yes?"

Josephine's smirk was almost audible. "That's a loophole."

Oh.

Right.

"As your legal counsel, any information you provide me in confidence cannot be disclosed without your permission. That includes the identity of any unnamed informants. And what's more, I have a contract with Matt's private investigation firm, so anything he finds would fall under the same privilege." Her tone turned conspiratorial. "Surely, as an officer of the law, you understand the need to protect the anonymity of confidential informants, right, Mario?"

Mario barked out a laugh. "Why Ms. Reynolds, if I didn't know better, I'd say you're suggesting we bend a few rules here for the greater good."

"Perish the thought, Officer," Josephine replied, mock offense infusing her voice. "I would never suggest subverting proper legal procedure. I'm simply advising you of the broad protections of attorney-client privilege."

"Yes, ma'am."

"Any information an official with the shelter or the investigative firm I contract with provides to me would be covered under that umbrella of privilege. If I think you need it, I will pass it on to you. Naturally, how you came by that information would be known only to me. And legally, if I were directed to not pass on who gave me that information, I could not do so."

Mario nodded. "Okay, how is this going to work?"

"I just explained that. Again, I will provide you with any information I obtain related to criminal activity in Tablerock that I think you should know." Josephine's voice through the speaker turned stern. "You must not, under any circumstances, speak with the cats directly regarding this case."

Mario's face fell. "But—"

"And the rest of you," Josephine said, her tone brooking no argument, "will not speak to Officer Lopez directly about any statements obtained from cats. All information will pass through me to avoid compromising the confidential informant's identity. Is that clear?"

This seemed super sketchy, but we nodded, murmuring our agreement.

Frustration rippled across Mario's face as he ran a hand through his hair, exhaling deeply. His eyes strayed toward the isolation room. "It's clear," he conceded, releasing a heavy sigh.

There was a heartbeat of silence, and when Josephine spoke again, her tone had softened. "Officer Lopez, while I understand your enthusiasm, you must continue to refrain from speaking with Honey or any other cat in a way that could compromise this case. We're walking a precariously fine line here as it is." Josephine's voice took on a sly, conspiratorial note once more. "However, that does not preclude you from a casual social conversation with shelter cats, so long as you keep your questions focused on subjects other than Ben Tyson's murder. Discuss the weather, comment on conditions at the shelter...get them talking and comfortable. People often let slip useful details when they feel at ease."

Mario blinked, then barked out a laugh as her meaning struck home. "Why, Counselor, are you advising me to interrogate cats on the sly?"

"Absolutely not!" Josephine chided, her tone indignant. "I would never suggest deception, Officer. I'm merely pointing out that while you should avoid discussing sensitive case details with Honey, there's no

harm in having a casual conversation with other
Tablerock cats to lighten your mood. Just be mindful of
what you say."

Mario exhaled, his eyes wandering back to the isolation room. "I just wish..." His voice trailed off as he
pinched the bridge of his nose. "How am I supposed to
catch a killer with these restrictions?"

Josephine's voice softened. "By proceeding with care
and integrity, as you always do. The road ahead may be
uncertain, but if we persist, justice will prevail. Trust the
process, Officer Lopez, no matter how slow or winding it
may appear. The truth will be revealed. If you'll excuse
me, I have other calls to attend to. Keep up the good
work, Officer. Tablerock is counting on you."

Mario stood up straighter, adjusting his uniform. "
Catch you later, Counselor."

"Goodbye, Officer Lopez."

Mario's face hardened with resolve as he marched out of
the room, the door clicking shut behind him.

Evie's eyes gleamed as she faced Matt. "This could
be the breakthrough we've been hoping for. Honey's
testimony, channeled through Josephine, might open
this case."

"But we haven't gotten much useful information
from Honey," I reminded her. "Most of what we've
learned came from eavesdropping. And Honey ruled out

Ben and Nina's romantic involvement, so that theory's dead in the water."

"Mom, we've come a long way in just a few days. Don't be such a downer." Evie's eyes sparkled with excitement, chasing away the dark circles that had formed from countless nights spent combing through the community's shared secrets and anonymous accusations. "We should revisit our information and look for any connections we might've missed."

"I'll make a fresh pot of coffee," Matt offered, planting a swift kiss on her temple before darting out the door.

"Evie, you're looking worn out. Remember Dr. Johnson's warning about too much caffeine. You can't—"

"Mom, I'm fine," she interrupted, waving off my concerns as she followed Matt. "I can handle it."

The door shut behind her.

"You can handle it," I echoed softly, even though she was gone. "And if you couldn't, would you admit it? Of course not."

The room fell silent, the soft ticking of the wall clock the only sound. I slumped into my desk chair, reflecting on the morning's startling developments. Chatty felines, secret informants, legal technicalities — my once-quiet life had veered wildly into the bizarre and unexpected.

A knock at the door jolted me from my thoughts. I straightened, regaining my composure. "Come in."

Waldo Monroe, local martial arts instructor and mayoral candidate (thanks to a hefty sum left him by

Belladonna's previous owner Fiona) stepped into the room. His weathered face broke into a smile. "Morning, Ellie. Hope I'm not interrupting." He glanced around, noting the vacant chairs and disarray of files.

"Not at all. What can I do for you, Waldo?" I asked.

Upon entering, he closed the door behind him. "I wanted to check on Honey and see how the little guy is settling in." Waldo's expression shifted to a somber one. "Poor Ben. I still can't believe he's gone."

"Did you know Ben well?"

Waldo shrugged. "As well as most, I suppose. He'd been taking private self-defense lessons from me for the past few months. He said he was worried someone had it out for him and wanted to ensure he could defend himself."

Well, that's a story I hadn't heard before. "Did Ben say who he was worried about?"

"No, only that life had a habit of creating complications." Waldo sighed, shaking his head. "I should have pressed for more details, but Ben was a private man. Still, I mentioned his concerns to Officer Lopez. Just in case there was something to it." He rolled his eyes. "Well, obviously, there was something to it. I mean...he's dead."

"That's certainly troubling." I frowned, sorting through this new information. "He really didn't seem particularly worried about anyone in particular? Man or woman? Someone from his present or his past?"

Waldo stroked his stubbled chin thoughtfully as he

spoke, eyes narrowing in recollection. "Ben didn't say anything specific to me, but there was that nasty scene at the farmers' market just last week. Augusta came tearing into Ben's booth, yelling at the top of her lungs about how he was flirting with Nina and didn't pay Augusta any attention anymore."

"Oh?"

"Yep." He shook his shaggy head, tsking at the memory of such a public altercation. "It must've been the final straw for Ben because he broke it off with her right then and there, in front of the whole town. Told her he wouldn't be treated like that, and he was through letting her make a fool of him."

My eyes widened. "Their breakup happened in public?"

Waldo nodded. "She seemed convinced he was cheating, though Ben denied it. Told her she was acting crazy, and he wanted nothing more to do with her." He shook his head sadly. "It was an ugly moment, I'm afraid. The kind that might fester. It wouldn't surprise me to find out Augusta killed him."

Augusta's name had repeatedly come up in relation to Ben's murder, and it appeared she had the motive, opportunity, and an obvious reason to seek vengeance. The whole setup felt almost too tidy, though. "Or someone murdered him, knowing Augusta would be the prime suspect due to their very public clash at the market," I said.

Waldo's eyes widened with alarm. "You really think so?"

I waved a hand dismissively. "Maybe I've read too many mystery novels, but it seems a possibility worth exploring. Who else witnessed the altercation at the farmers' market?"

Waldo rubbed his stubbled chin, his gaze drifting out the window as he searched his memory. "Well, all the local farmers were there, of course. Setting up their stalls and getting ready for the day."

My eyebrow arched slightly. "Nina as well?"

He shook his head, eyes still distant. "No, Nina wasn't there. But Tom, her husband, was in the booth beside Ben's."

Tom.

Nina's mild-mannered and congenial husband.

The same Tom who had dragged his wife bodily to the side of the restaurant to silence her. The Tom whose return to our table at Pepper Jalisco's had caused Nina's mouth to snap shut mid-sentence.

"How well do you know Tom Coleman?" I kept my tone casual, but Waldo didn't miss a beat.

"Don't you mean, how well did Ben know Tom?"

I spread my hands, conceding the point. "Either way. Both seem relevant, given the connections between Nina, Ben, and Augusta." I leaned forward, clasping my hands on the desk. "Can you tell me more about Tom? His personality, his relationship with Nina, his connection to Ben? Anything?"

Waldo settled into the chair across from me. "Tom Coleman is a quiet man who keeps to himself. Opposite of his wife in every way. While Nina is loud, abrasive, and quick to pick fights, Tom avoids confrontation at all costs." He paused, scratching at the stubble along his jaw. "Come to think of it, Ben and Tom were friendly for years. Or civil, if not friends. They often chatted at the farmers' market, commiserating over beekeeping."

A usually peaceful man, embarrassed by his wife's actions. A man friendly with the victim for years, who avoided conflict whenever possible—until tensions between Nina and Ben brought long-simmering issues to a boil? "Huh," I said. "The quiet ones often shock us the most, don't they?"

"Oh, come on." Waldo's eyes widened in surprise. "You think Tom could be involved?"

I shrugged. "A facade of gentleness may hide darker secrets beneath."

Waldo rubbed his chin, seeming troubled by the turn in our conversation. "You make a fair point. But Tom? I can't fathom it. He's always been so soft-spoken, so quick to defuse tension and keep the peace."

"Maybe you're right."

And yet, at the restaurant, he hauled Nina bodily away from Augusta's table to silence her. A kind, gentle man does not manhandle his wife.

Chapter Thirteen

THE FOLLOWING SATURDAY MORNING, AS I MADE MY
way down the dirt path toward the farmers' market, the
sun filtered through the broad oak trees casting dappled
shadows on the ground. I hadn't told anyone where I was
going because, to be honest, I didn't want to admit the
truth to myself: that I was there to investigate.

I justified my solo trip by claiming I was simply
running out to grab something at the store. Sure, the
farmers' market wasn't a traditional store, but it still
counted, didn't it? And if my brief excursion involved a
casual chat with some folks at the market about Ben
Tyson, that was purely coincidental.

A pang of loss hit me as I strolled by Ben's vacant
stand. The once lively display was now reduced to an
empty table, wedged between Leo Barnett's undeco-
rated honey stand and Tom Coleman's sprawling three-
table area for Buzzing Blossom Farms.

As I approached, Leo looked up and offered a weak, "Morning, Ms. Rockwell."

"Good morning," I replied, returning the smile and hoping to put him at ease. "How are you doing today?"

He responded with a grunt.

I couldn't help but notice that Leo didn't ask about Honey, the cat he had come to see just a few days ago. It struck me as peculiar, but I didn't want to push the issue. Instead, I waited for him to speak.

Instead of using his words, Leo anxiously fidgeted with a strange contraption, twisting and turning it in his rough, callused hands. It appeared to be a handheld tool, but its purpose eluded me. One end featured a wooden handle, worn smooth from frequent use, while a cylinder made of wire mesh jutted out at a right angle, like a short paint roller. However, instead of fabric nap, the cylinder was covered in sharp, menacing spikes that glinted in the morning sunlight.

"What brings you out today?" he asked finally, not looking directly at me. "I heard you started an account with Buzzing Blossom, so I doubt you need any honey."

"I just needed a few things and decided to come here instead of HEB. I needed to get out of the café for a bit and clear my head. It's a beautiful day, after all," I explained, eyeing his meager offerings of honey and beeswax candles. They were a far cry from the vibrant displays that Ben had always put together or that Buzzing Blossom displayed two stalls away. "How have sales been?"

Leo shrugged, still avoiding my gaze. "Well, you know. Better. Most folks know I used to work for Ben, so I've picked up a few more customers than usual. Ben's honey was always more popular. I don't have to worry about that now."

His table was almost bare, except for a few honey jars and a handwritten sign displaying their prices. The jars themselves looked nearly forgotten, their labels peeling and the honey inside crystallized. He had two boxes behind him, each marked twenty-four quarts. I didn't know if he'd sold a lot of honey or just never brought much to sell.

"I'm glad to hear it," I replied, my gaze wandering over to the jars of honey behind him as I searched for another neutral conversation topic. From the corner of my eye, I noticed Tom Coleman observing us from his booth. He looked away when I turned, but my curiosity was piqued. "I do have a question, actually. Where are your beehives? I wasn't aware there were more hives in Tablerock besides Buzzing Blossom's and Ben's."

Leo's eyes narrowed, his body tensing. "Why do you want to know about my hives?"

"Well, I just... I thought beekeepers had to register their hives and get permits, and I wasn't aware of any other places besides the two I mentioned. That's all." His sudden shift in demeanor caught me off guard, and I stumbled over my words as I searched for a reasonable explanation. "Isn't that the case?"

"The crazy cat lady is correct," Mayor Jessa Winthrop's haughty voice rang out as she strode over to Leo's table, arms crossed over her chest. "According to city ordinances, any apiary with over five hives must be properly permitted. And as far as I'm aware, Mr. Barnett, you have no such permit."

"Good morning, Mayor," I greeted her in a friendly tone.

Jessa Winthrop ignored me.

"I didn't say I had five hives," Leo protested, his face paling as his eyes darted nervously between Jessa and me. "And I... I've only just started since Ben let me go. I haven't had a chance to file the paperwork yet. But I will when I have five hives or more."

Jessa's eyes gleamed with suspicion as she leaned in, placing her hands on the rough wooden plank of Leo's counter. "I'm sure you've registered with the state as a honey manufacturer, too, right?"

Leo stared at her, his nostrils flaring.

Jessa picked up a jar of honey. "Because none of these jars say who they were produced and packaged by, do they? There are regulations regarding the cleanliness of the processing area and equipment and the handling and storage of the honey." She slammed the jar on the table and straightened, brushing imaginary dust from her impeccably tailored jacket. Then, she pointed her manicured talon at Leo's face. "Consider this your first warning, Mr. Barnett. Get your paperwork in order immediately, or you'll be forced to cease operations. Am I clear?"

"Y-yes, ma'am. Understood." Leo swallowed hard, his Adam's apple bobbing.

With a curt nod, Jessa spun on her heel and marched off down the row of stalls. An awkward silence fell between Leo and me, punctuated only by the soft buzzing of bees hovering near the crystallized honey jars.

Leo refused to meet my gaze, fiddling nervously with the jars on his table. I felt a twinge of guilt, realizing that my question had caused trouble for the hapless beekeeper — if he was just a hapless beekeeper.

"Leo, I'm sorry," I said, "I didn't mean to cause problems. I was just..."

"It's fine," Leo said, his jaw tightening as he finally glanced up. His eyes were shadowed with frustration. "You were just curious, I get it. But maybe in the future, satisfy your curiosity by minding your own business."

What he said made no sense.

No one could satisfy their curiosity by minding their own business.

While Leo's words were difficult to parse, his tone wasn't. The abrupt warning in his voice took me aback. I opened my mouth to respond, but I thought better of it and gave a quick nod.

"Message received," I said. "Again, I apologize."

Without waiting for Leo's reply, I turned and made

my way up the dirt path as quickly as possible, still a little shaken by the encounter. My trip to the farmers' market had been even more illuminating than anticipated, and now I feared I was squarely on Leo Barnett's bad side — which, if he was the murderer, was probably not a good thing.

The familiar lavender sign of the Rockside Café came into view, a welcome sight. I hurried inside, the little bell above the door tinkling to announce my arrival for our standing Saturday morning breakfast. Going to another café when we had one back at the shelter seemed silly, but this standing date with Laurie and Josephine had become a weekly tradition.

Distracted by thoughts of fresh coffee and warm pastries, I nearly tripped over the threshold in my haste. Righting myself, I glanced up — and stumbled to an abrupt halt, struck speechless at the sight before me. "Those busybody biddies," I thought. "With friends like these, I don't need enemies or a matchmaker."

Landon was sitting at our usual table with Laurie and Josephine. His familiar smile faltered into a look of concern as I gaped at them like a fish out of water.

"Ellie, what's wrong?" Landon rose halfway from his seat, his concerned expression etched into the familiar lines of his face.

I waved a hand and shook my head. "I'm fine, just had an interesting encounter at the farmers' market, that's all." I pulled myself up into the fourth chair. "Is anyone else coming for breakfast, or is it just us and him?" I asked.

"Just us," Josephine replied, arching an eyebrow. "Do tell us about the market."

I recounted my conversation with Leo and Jessa's untimely interference. By the end of my tale, Laurie was frowning, and Josephine was scribbling notes on a napkin.

Landon raked a hand through his hair, scowling. "You shouldn't have gone by yourself. What if Leo had reacted badly? He could be dangerous. There's no telling what he might be capable of if provoked."

"I didn't provoke him." His implication that I couldn't defend myself ignited a spark of indignation. "Besides, I'm perfectly capable of handling myself," I said. "And I was in a public place. I hardly think Leo would have tried anything, even if he is the murderer."

"Still." Landon's jaw clenched, emphasizing the lines life had etched there. "After everything that's happened, none of us should take chances until we find out who killed Ben and why. We are poking around a murder investigation, Ellie."

Landon's patronizing tone irked me, as did his attempt to set limits on my actions. However, I detected genuine concern for my well-being beneath his stern words. Despite my independent spirit resisting the idea of depending on someone else's protection, I couldn't deny that Landon's warnings had merit.

"I hate to admit it, but Landon's right," Laurie agreed. "We should try to travel in pairs when doing anything like that until this situation with Ben's murder is resolved. There's safety in numbers."

"When doing anything like what? Shopping for tomatoes at the farmers' market?" I retorted with a touch more sass than intended. I sighed, acknowledging the wisdom in their words despite my wounded pride. "Fine. You're probably right. I'll be more cautious in the future." I glanced at Josephine, who was scrutinizing her notes with pursed lips. "What's on your mind, Josie?"

Josephine looked up, pushing her glasses further up the bridge of her nose. "I'm thinking about our friend Mayor Winthrop. She may have unintentionally helped us," she said, her eyes gleaming with curiosity. "Barnett has been selling 'local' Tablerock honey at the market since he left Ben's employ. Tell me, how many jars did he have on his table?"

"Forty? Maybe Fifty?" I said. "It wasn't that much."

Josephine tapped on her phone. "One quart of honey weighs about three pounds, and one hive of bees can produce up to ten pounds of honey during peak season, which in Central Texas is..." She scanned the screen. "...mid-March to mid-June, with the highest production usually occurring in April and May. So, say he really does have less than five hives. Let's say four."

She looked up. "Being generous, that's only twelve jars a week, not forty or fifty jars."

"So he has more hives than he's claiming?" Laurie said, shrugging. "He wouldn't be the first startup to cut corners or try and avoid taxes."

"Or he has no hives at all," Landon pointed out. "His excessively defensive reaction could signify a guilty conscience."

"Guilty of what? It was probably just annoyance at Jessa's bullying and my questions," I said.

"Maybe," Landon said, shifting in his seat and crossing his arms over his chest. "Or Barnett could be purchasing honey from outside the area and misrepresenting it as local to hike the price."

I took a sip of coffee and asked, "Wouldn't it just be easier to steal it from other beekeepers?"

"Now, that's a thought, isn't it?" Laurie frowned, tapping a finger against her coffee mug. "Leo used to work for Ben. He'd know Ben's hives inside and out, how to extract the honey. They're not fenced off. What if Ben caught him stealing from the hives? That could've led to a physical confrontation."

"You think Ben might've threatened to report Leo to the police?" Josephine asked. "It would certainly provide a motive for murder, particularly if Leo relied on reselling the stolen honey as a significant portion of his income."

Laurie nodded thoughtfully. "That's right. Local honey sells for about $12 to $25 per quart. If Leo sold fifty jars weekly, that would translate to $4800 to $10,000 in monthly revenue. For a small-scale operation, that's a lot of money."

"Felony theft is $2,500 or more," Josephine pointed out. "If he stayed in the third-degree felony range, we're still talking 2 to 10 years in prison. If he stole enough to make it a second-degree felony, we're talking 2 to 20 years."

The theory seemed plausible and could explain Leo's jumpiness at my questions — as well as his threatening tone. If he'd been caught red-handed stealing from Ben and resorted to murder to silence him and protect his illegal operation, anyone asking too many questions might pose a threat.

The midday sun beat down on the gravel parking lot of the Rockside Café as I walked toward my car. Throughout brunch, I managed to maintain a friendly demeanor. Now, alone among the dusty vehicles of patrons savoring the café's comforting dishes, my irritation bubbled closer to the surface.

How could Laurie and Josephine ambush me like that by inviting Landon to our girls' breakfast? Their meddling had complicated an already awkward situation, and I didn't appreciate them manipulating the dynamic of our friendship.

Footsteps crunched on the loose gravel behind me as

I fished my keys from my bag. I didn't have to turn to know Landon hurried to catch up, his familiar gait and the scent of his woodsy cologne preceding him.

"Ellie, wait." He grasped my arm, stopping me in my tracks. "Are you mad at me? Josephine just thought it would be—"

I shrugged off his touch and turned to face him, my expression stern. "I'm just irritated that our so-called friends keep meddling where they don't belong."

His brow furrowed, concern evident in his eyes. "Did I do something to upset you?"

Exhaling deeply, I ran a hand through my hair, the frustration mounting. "You didn't do anything wrong. No one is doing anything wrong. Everyone means well, I'm sure. It's just that Laurie and Josephine seem to have made it their personal mission to pair us up, and you appear to be fine taking advantage of that."

"Taking advantage?" Landon's eyes widened in surprise. "Ellie, no. I only came because of everything happening with Ben's case. Josephine thought an extra perspective that's in the know might help figure things out. I didn't come to — to pursue anything or manipulate something." A faint blush tinted his cheeks as he nervously ran a hand through his hair. "I would never attempt to manipulate you in that way."

I observed his expression while a gentle breeze rustled the oaks encircling the parking lot, bringing the aroma of wildflowers from the hillside and stirring his silver hair. I scrutinized his familiar yet guarded features, seeking any sign of dishonesty but finding none. His visible unease and hesitant denial, emphasized by the clenching of his jaw as his eyes locked on mine, all conveyed a sense of genuine sincerity.

"I'm sorry," I said finally, mostly meaning it. "I shouldn't have accused you. I just—"

"It's all right." Landon dismissed my apology with a wave. "I understand why you might think that. But I promise, I'm here as a friend to help however I can. Nothing more, unless or until you say otherwise."

For a fleeting, serene moment, we were enveloped by the tranquil sounds and scents of a perfect summer day in the Texas Hill Country, and I nodded, a smile spreading across my lips. "Thank you."

While Josephine's meddling remained annoying, I couldn't deny that having Landon's help usually proved valuable, even if his closeness was a distraction I could ill afford.

Landon smiled as my phone rang, piercing the peaceful bubble surrounding us.

"Hello?"

"Is this Ms. Ellie Rockwell?"

Finally, someone called me Ms. Instead of Mrs. "Yes."

"This is Nurse Jenkins calling from Tablerock Regional Hospital. I don't want to alarm you, but I'm calling about Evie. She's been brought into the emergency room after a fainting spell. There's a very nice young man with her."

My breath caught in my throat, my heart hammering against my ribs. "Is she all right? What happened?" I gripped the phone with white knuckles, panic threatening to overwhelm me as Landon stepped closer, a look of concern on his face.

The nurse's voice remained calm and reassuring. "Just the passing out so far. Her vital signs are stable for now, but the doctor is running some tests to determine whether we need to be concerned about the cause of her collapse. We need you to come to the hospital to fill out paperwork and speak with the attending physician about her medical history and condition."

"Of course, I'm on my way." I ended the call with a shaking hand, my entire body numb with fear.

"Ellie?" Landon grasped my shoulders, his eyes dark with concern. "Ellie, what's wrong?"

"It's Evie," I choked out, swallowing hard as I fought back the tears. "She collapsed. They've rushed her to the emergency room." Panic seeped into my voice, my mind racing with all the potential dire explanations for her sudden collapse. "I don't even know where she was or what she was doing. I didn't ask. I—"

"Take a breath, Ellie." Landon pulled me into a comforting embrace, one hand rubbing slow circles on my back. "Deep breaths." His calm, steady voice helped slow my racing pulse. "I'll drive you to the hospital right away. Tablerock Regional?"

I nodded against his chest, clinging to his reassurance like a lifeline.

"Okay, let's go to my truck. It's right here." Landon gathered me close and led me to his truck, helping me inside before hurrying to the driver's side.

As we sped down the twisting, hilly country roads, lush green landscape whipping past in a blur, the world felt unbalanced and off-kilter, as if the earth had tilted on its very axis.

Chapter Fourteen

THE ANTISEPTIC SCENT OF THE EMERGENCY ROOM did little to help the panic coursing through my veins as Landon, and I hurried through the automatic doors. My gaze darted around the sterile waiting area, quickly locating Evie lying on a hospital bed in a bay behind the reception area, an IV needle protruding from her arm.

"Mom, I'm fine," Evie called upon spotting me. Her wan complexion and the dark circles under her eyes told a different story.

Matt stood a few feet away, fidgety and avoiding my gaze.

I'd deal with him later.

Nurse Jenkins, I presumed, was checking the IV bag while Dr. Cooper reviewed Evie's chart. He'd treated Evie during previous emergencies and understood the complexities of her condition. His familiar face brought a small measure of comfort.

"What happened?" I asked, rushing to Evie's side.

"Dehydration and low blood pressure," Dr. Cooper explained. "Evie passed out while she and Matt were hiking. The heat and activity likely caused her to become dehydrated, and her blood pressure dropped too low, which led to the fainting episode."

I squeezed Evie's hand, her skin clammy. "You haven't been drinking enough water in this heat. You know better." My reprimand came out sharper than intended, resulting from the panic still coursing through me.

Evie's eyes welled up. "I know, Mom. I'm sorry. I was just busy and not paying attention, and now look—"

"Shh, don't cry." I squeezed her hand again in reassurance. "You scared me, but the doctor said you'll be okay now that you're getting fluids." I took a steadying breath, forcing my raging emotions into temporary submission. Losing my composure would only make the situation worse. Suddenly, I stopped and turned to look at Dr. Cooper. "Wait a minute. I thought Evie's pacemaker would prevent fainting. You said her blood pressure dropped too low, but she's got full heart block. That's literally the purpose of the pacemaker — to prevent that."

Evie's congenital heart defect was complicated by complete heart block following her last open-heart surgery, meaning her heart couldn't keep a steady beat. A pacemaker had been implanted to help control her heart rate, the device sending electrical impulses to stimulate her heart when it slowed too much.

Dr. Cooper nodded. "You're right. With Evie's pacemaker, fainting spells shouldn't happen often, so I've called Dr. Chen, the electro-cardiologist, to take a closer look at the pacemaker and make sure everything is functioning properly. Just in case."

My throat tightened, dread stirring in my gut. "You said it was just dehydration."

"Ellie, it likely is," Dr. Cooper reassured me, "but we won't take any chances with Evie's complex condition. Fainting with a pacemaker isn't common but not unheard of, either. I simply want Dr. Chen to double-check that the pacemaker settings are optimal and do a quick diagnostic to rule out device issues. Just as a precaution."

I swallowed hard, grasping Evie's hand as much for my own comfort as for hers. She looked up at me with an embarrassed expression, her cheeks pink, and at that moment, I saw the little girl she'd been when open-heart surgeries were a frequent ordeal, and each new complication felt like the world dropping out from under our feet.

Dr. Chen strode in then, interrupting my descent into old memories. With reassurance and caution, he greeted Evie warmly and handed her something that looked like a wired mouse. Tapping on a tablet as he checked the settings, he searched for any indication of malfunction.

After an agonizing few minutes, Dr. Chen stepped back with a satisfied smile. "The pacemaker appears to be functioning perfectly well. Your fainting spell seems to have been due to overheating and dehydration. I recommend drinking plenty of fluids and avoiding overexertion in the heat over the next few days, but the pacemaker itself is working as intended."

Relief flooded through me, alleviating the tightness in my chest. Evie smiled up at the doctors, the panic in her eyes replaced with gratitude. "Thank you both."

Dr. Cooper nodded, satisfied. "Once that IV hydrates you, we should be able to discharge you, Evie."

"The bag still has about half an hour left to infuse," Nurse Jenkins added, checking Evie's IV.

"Remember, staying properly hydrated and avoiding overheating for the next few days is key," Dr. Chen reminded Evie. He patted my arm reassuringly on his way out. "Call me if you have any other concerns."

With the doctors gone, the four of us were left in the relative privacy of the emergency room bay. Evie slumped back against the hospital bed, emotionally and physically spent. "Man, that was scary."

Matt shifted his weight, shoving his hands into his pockets. "I'm really sorry, Evie. I should've made sure you were drinking enough water. I feel like this is my fault —"

"Stop it." Evie shook her head. "Don't blame yourself. I'm an adult. Keeping myself hydrated is my own responsibility." Still, her tone held a hint of annoyance, a sign Matt's regret had provoked something in her. "This has nothing to do with you. At all."

An awkward silence descended, interrupted only by the steady beep of Evie's heart monitor. I busied myself gathering magazines and a blanket, needing to do something to combat the last dregs of anxiety and adrenaline lingering in my system.

"Matt, come help me get everyone's drinks from the vending machine."

He nodded, shoving off from where he leaned against the wall, and followed me out of the bay and down the hall.

We'd barely made it halfway to the vending area before Matt burst out, "Ellie, I'm so sorry. I should have made sure Evie was drinking water. I feel terrible that this happened. I don't know what I was thinking. I should have—"

I held up a hand, stopping him mid-babble. A quick glance around located an empty consultation room, and I pulled Matt inside, closing the door for privacy.

Honestly, I wanted to rip Matt a new one.

It was a hot day, and the two of them went hiking? How could he take her out into the Texas heat without having water? My simmering anger was probably a mask for the fear still pounding through me, and I knew that. I also knew that as much as I wanted to hold Matt responsible, it wasn't his fault. It was Evie's.

I bit my tongue.

Losing my temper wouldn't undo the damage already done.

"Matt, listen to me." I reached up to clasp his shoulders, forcing him to meet my gaze. "These things are going to happen. Evie has a complex medical condition, and there will always be complications and periodic scares. That's just part of having her in your life. You can't blame yourself whenever she ends up in the emergency room."

He swallowed hard, eyes shining with emotion. "But if I had just made sure she drank enough water, she wouldn't be here now. I should've known better."

I glanced at Matt, my heart catching in my throat as I recognized the expression on his face. I'd seen it in the mirror more times than I could count.

Fear.

Fear of the unknown and uncontrollable. Fear of loss and helplessness. Fear that loving someone so fragile meant always waiting for the other shoe to drop.

At that moment, seeing my fears reflected in Matt's eyes, my anger at his mistake melted away. He was as new to this world of congenital heart disease as Evie was to love — stumbling through blindly, afraid of saying or doing wrong. Fearful that the temporary joy they'd found might be ripped away without warning at any moment.

Loving my daughter was the most terrifying and rewarding experience of my life. And now Matt had willingly embarked on that same harrowing and wondrous journey.

I sighed.

He deserved patience and guidance, not condemnation.

"Matt, how much have you and Evie talked about the specifics of her heart condition? How much do you really understand what living with her condition entails?"

Matt's gaze dropped to the floor, cheeks flushing. "Not as much as I should. Evie doesn't like talking about it. It's hard for her, so I don't push." He sighed, raking a hand through his hair. "I want to understand better to support her, but I also want to respect her boundaries."

"That's very considerate of you, Matt, but Evie's health issues aren't something either of you can avoid discussing if you want this relationship to work long-term." I hesitated, unsure of betraying Evie's confidence and knowing Matt needed the truth. "Living with her issues is a daily struggle. There will be good days but frequent bad days, complications, and hospital visits. If you're in this for the long haul, you must fully under-stand what you're signing up for."

She'd been doing so well lately.

Yet, the fact that we found ourselves in this hospital served as a stark reminder that things couldn't change overnight, no matter how much she wished to believe they had.

Matt's expression turned somber, pale eyes shadowed. But beneath the fear and regret, I glimpsed determination. "I want to understand. I want to support Evie through all of it, good and bad. I just wish I'd insisted we talk about this sooner." He rubbed his eyes. "I want her to feel like she can come to me when she's not feeling well instead of suffering silently."

I let out a loud, uproarious laugh, unable to contain my amusement.

The situation was just too absurd.

Evie hid her suffering well, hiding the burden of her medical issues as a point of pride. Admitting weakness felt like defeat to her, confiding in others a forfeiture of the rigid control that kept her world in order in her mind. Poor Matt wished for something I hadn't gotten after twenty-five years.

Matt peered at me in confusion, clearly taken aback by my sudden outburst. "What's so funny?" he asked, raising an eyebrow.

I shook my head, grasping for the right words to convey what I'd learned through painful experience.

"Matt, Evie has always been private about her health issues. She hides how much she's going through to avoid being treated like 'the sick girl.' I only know if she's not feeling well if I notice her color is off or her nail bed color is off or I catch her suddenly stilling, breath held as she waits for her heart rhythm to right itself." I leaned against the wall. "The brain stuff? It comes and goes. She's feeling confident lately, which has allowed her to push through and deal with it more easily. It may always be like that from now on," I admitted, hope springing eternal. "The more likely scenario is that she'll hit a wall at some point, and she won't be able to navigate around it."

Matt swallowed hard, realization dawning. The road ahead would be long, and my heart ached at his innocence, soon to be stripped away by the brutal lessons loving Evie would teach.

"It may take time, but just keep the lines of communication open and be there for her when she does want to talk. That's the best advice I can give you right now. That, and ask me any questions you think you need to know whether she wants you to know or not."

His eyes narrowed in determination, and he nodded. "Thank you. I don't give up easily. However long it takes, I'll be here. I will prove to Evie I don't scare away easily."

Perhaps with Matt's stubborn perseverance to aid my own, we stood a chance of convincing Evie she could show her weaknesses without feeling weak. "I'm sure you don't. Let's get those drinks before Evie and Landon send out a search party."

Matt nodded, wiping his eyes before following me out of the room and down the hall.

His heart was in the right place. Now I had to help

Evie find the courage to use her words before her silence tore them apart.

Matt and I returned to the emergency bay, but as soon as we entered, Evie gestured frantically for us to be quiet. Frowning, I traced her gaze to see Landon leaning against the far wall, his ear pressed against it, furiously jotting down notes with a pencil.

"What's going on?" I mouthed at Evie.

She rolled her eyes in response, pointing at Landon.

Landon glanced up then, noticing us watching him. "Shh!" He waved the notepad and whispered, "I'm eavesdropping."

"On what, pray tell?" I asked, keeping my voice low.

He raised a finger, urging me to wait, and then resumed listening intently against the wall, his pencil racing across the page. Moments later, he stepped back, flipping to a fresh sheet on the notepad with an air of triumph.

"I've been listening in on the nurses' station next door. Did you know that Leo Barnett showed up here the day after Ben was murdered with a gash on his neck?"

I gaped at him. "How could you possibly know that just from eavesdropping?"

He shrugged. "Because the nurses talk extremely loud."

I shook my head in disbelief. "We shouldn't know any of that. There are rules.'

"Probably not, and you're right; there are rules. Just not concerning the nurses' voice volume, apparently. If I can hear it, I'm supposed to know it." Landon said, unrepentant. He strode over to Matt and took a can of Coca-Cola from him, clapping him on the shoulder. "Thanks for that, young man. Hope that trip to the vending machine wasn't too tough on you."

Matt nodded, the men exchanging a glance of understanding that left me faintly disquieted. A silent signal had passed between them; the forging of an alliance I wasn't sure boded well for me. I arched an eyebrow at Landon in silent warning as Dr. Cooper strode back in, discharge papers in hand.

Landon's eyes widened with faux innocence. "What? That hike to the vending machine can be a real —"

"Okay, enough," I told him, shaking my head and turning my focus back to Dr. Cooper and escaping from this place as Nurse Jenkins swiftly removed Evie's IV.

Dr. Cooper smiled, handing me the discharge papers to sign. "Everything looks good. Make sure Evie continues to rest, stay hydrated, and follow up with me in a week."

I nodded, scrawling my signature on the dotted line.

Matt shifted beside me, clearing his throat. "I can take Evie if one of you will get my car?" He held out his keys expectantly.

"Landon and I can go grab it," I told him.

Landon nodded, taking the keys from Matt's outstretched hand.

Matt helped Evie into the waiting wheelchair, carefully tucking a blanket around her legs before wheeling her from the bay and down the hall toward the front entrance. Landon fell into step beside me, unusually subdued. I glanced at him, noticing a furrow between his brows.

"What's wrong?"

He sighed. "All jokes aside, I heard disturbing things while eavesdropping earlier."

I took his arm, slowing our pace to distance us from Evie and Matt. "Tell me."

Landon grimaced. "The nurses were discussing Leo Barnett, who came into the ER the day after Ben's murder with a nasty gash on his neck. They couldn't believe the police haven't considered him a serious suspect, especially given his creepy nature and Ben firing him a few months ago." He shook his head. "They seem to think the cops are too busy focusing on Augusta to properly investigate other leads. The hospital reported the thing as a possible knife wound, but no one showed up to investigate."

We exited through the sliding front doors, the midday sun beating down. I spotted Matt's car in the parking lot and pointed. "There. You head over and get the car. I'll go help Matt get Evie settled."

Landon nodded, jogging off across the lot as I

approached where Matt stood behind Evie. Her face flushed upon seeing me.

"You know, I can get in a car alone," Evie snapped. "You don't need to hover over me like I'm some kind of invalid."

At that moment, all I wanted was to whisk her away from this place and tuck her safely into her own bed, enveloped by the familiar comforts of home. I knew her sour attitude was merely a facade, masking the sense of helplessness she experienced whenever we found ourselves in a hospital.

I knew it wasn't really that she was angry at me.

But it still hurt.

"Everything all right?" Matt asked, frowning.

I forced a smile, patting his arm. I said, "We're all fine, Matt," but Matt should get to know that tone. Someday, she'll be pointing it in his direction, I thought as Landon eased Matt's car into the hospital driveway roundabout.

Matt took the keys from Landon and nodded, helping Evie ease into the passenger seat before shutting the door. I waited until Landon pulled up his truck and went to the passenger side.

Matt looked back and called, "You'll follow us?"

"Yes. Drive safe."

I waved them off, my mind focusing on Landon's words about Leo Barnett to distract myself from Evie's attitude. Yes, Leo Barnett had motive and means, a connection to Ben the police seemed determined to overlook. An unsettling thought occurred — had they dismissed him precisely because, as a male suspect, he didn't fit their preconceived narrative?

Landon honked the horn, summoning me from my troubled thoughts. I slid into the passenger seat, buckling in before facing him.

"We need to go see Mario."

He arched an eyebrow but didn't argue, putting the car in gear and pulling out of the hospital lot to follow after Matt and Evie.

Chapter Fifteen

LANDON AND I MADE OUR WAY TOWARD THE
isolation room, where we found Evie and Matt waiting
inside. Evie was sitting cross-legged on the floor
surrounded by Belladonna and Honey, their soft fur
vibrating with rumbly purrs of contentment as she
scratched behind their tufted ears.

As soon as she heard us enter, Evie's gaze flew up to
meet mine, her expression defensive. No doubt she
assumed I was going to scold them for their recklessness.
She paused her hands mid-scratch, bracing herself for
my private reaction in the soundproofed room.

But instead of reprimanding her, I asked, "How are
you feeling?" as I knelt beside her.

Evie blinked, caught off guard by my question.
"Fine," she replied hesitantly. "Look, Mom, now that
we're alone, we can tell you what happened. We were
just —"

Before she could finish her sentence, I held up my hand to stop her. "Going hiking in the Texas heat with no water?" I asked and then stood up. "Sweetheart, you know better than that. That was very reckless, you know."

"We were investigating Ben's case," Matt said, shifting his weight as he stood beside Evie. He shoved his hands into his pockets, his expression sheepish. "We spotted Nina's husband, Tom, walking onto the hike and bike trail carrying a large garbage bag. So, we decided to follow him."

"You decided to follow him." I shook my head in disbelief. "What were you two thinking, trailing someone linked to a murder investigation without informing anyone?" I threw my hands up in exasperation. "Did you have any clue how dangerous that could be?"

"It worked for you a few months ago," Evie said, a smug smirk curling her lips. She leaned back against the wall and crossed her arms over her chest, eyeing me with a self-satisfied glint in her eyes. "And it clearly worked better for me. I didn't have a gun pointed at me." Her smirk widened as she jerked her chin at Matt, who stood shifting his weight from foot to foot. "Nothing happened to us."

Right.

Nothing except a Saturday morning jaunt to the emergency room.

My heart clenched at the thought of what could

have transpired to not just Evie but Matt, too, if Tom was the murderer and caught the kids tailing him. Beside me, Landon placed a comforting hand on my shoulder, giving it a gentle squeeze.

"Did it dawn on either of you that you might have been shadowing an actual murderer?" Landon asked, frowning at them.

Evie exchanged a glance with Matt. "Well, obviously, that possibility crossed our minds. We wouldn't have been sneaking after him otherwise," Evie said. She fiddled with Honey's fur, avoiding meeting our eyes directly. "We didn't fully consider—"

"That's right, you didn't consider carefully enough," I said. "Evie, your heart—"

"I'm fine, Mom," Evie insisted, her voice shaky but determined. "We were careful."

Matt scratched the back of his neck, guilt etched on his face. "We were as careful as we could be, given the circumstances," he said, trying to explain. "I know it sounds like an excuse, especially coming from the ER, but we weren't too far into the trail. I don't think it was the hike itself that did it. Evie just hadn't had enough to drink."

Evie shot him an exasperated look. "Dude, really?" she said, her tone edging into annoyance.

"I'm just trying to be upfront, Evie," he said.

She glowered at him.

Matt gazed down at her, his expression apologetic.

"You and I will have words later, Matt. And look,

I'm sorry for worrying you, Mom," Evie said, turning her attention to me. "Matt's right. I didn't drink enough water, and we were out in the heat. This is on me."

"I don't care whose fault this is," I replied. "I know you want to help, but promise me you'll be more careful from now on. And check with me first before doing anything dangerous."

Evie nodded, her expression contrite. "I promise, Mom," she said.

Landon raked a hand through his hair with a wry chuckle. "Now that we've pried an oath from you two detectives, wanna share why exactly you tailed our suspect, Sherlock, and Watson?"

"Who's Sherlock?" Evie asked.

Matt's cheeks flushed crimson as he discovered a sudden fascination with his shoelaces. "There's no way I'm answering that." He glanced at Landon through a curtain of dark hair. "Evie and I were going out for brunch at Pepper Jalisco's — their chilaquiles are life-changing. Anyhow, on the drive home, Evie spotted Tom lugging this massive contractor bag into the trail-head. Not your typical accessory for a nature hike." Matt chanced a look at Evie, who shrugged.

"It seemed odd," Evie added. "Plus, he wasn't dressed for hiking. He was wearing work boots, not trail shoes."

"So you thought following him was a good idea?" I asked.

Evie shrugged. "We thought he might lead us to

something related to Ben's murder. And we were right —
he went straight to the abandoned barn past the Miller
farm. Dropped that bag in there and left. We took a look
inside after he was gone."

The old Miller farmstead had been empty for ages,
left to crumble into the wildflower fields it had once
tamed. Though some developers had snapped up the
land with big plans after the old man passed, those
dreams dried up quick as rain in high summer after the
recession hit.

The Tablerock hike and bike trail passed right by the
old Miller property, and the barn was just a two-minute
hike off the path. The Tablerock trail might skirt the
property line, but that barn hid in plain sight, paint
peeling like sunburned skin and rafters sagging under
the weight of more owl families than anyone could
count.

The perfect place to hide stolen goods, I thought to
myself. Or to hide evidence of a murder.

"And?" Landon's eyes narrowed.

Matt glanced at me, hesitating.

"They didn't go inside the barn," I said, assuming.

"No, we did. Beekeeping equipment," Matt said.
"Smoker, hive tool, empty honey jars. Well, in the barn.
Evie passed out before we could find the bag."

I took a sharp breath as realization hit me. My gaze
shot to Evie. "You went inside the barn? Do you have
any idea how dangerous that was? What if Tom came
back?"

"Do all human mothers have a tendency to repeat themselves ad nauseam?" Belladonna's tone was snide. "What do you hope to achieve? No wonder the girl is always fainting, with you nattering at her day and night."

I whirled to face the cat. "Belladonna?"

Her lamp-like eyes widened at my expression. She opened her mouth as the glow slightly brightened beneath her, no doubt another scathing retort at the ready, but I held up a hand.

"Fine," the cat answered. "You seem to have enough on your plate."

"I have to agree with Mom on this one. Let's stay on topic, shall we?" Evie said, rolling her eyes at the cat's antics. "We were careful, Mom. And it paid off. Didn't it?"

Well, we were about to find out.

The summer sun filtered through the leafy canopy as Landon and I made our way up the hiking trail. Cicadas pulsed a steady, droning hum around us in the stillness.

When the barn came into view, my steps slowed. The old building seemed to crouch in a state of decay, as though it had grown out of the landscape itself and been left to crumble back into the earth. Doors hung askew on rusted hinges, and shingles littered the ground like broken teeth.

Landon let out a low whistle. "If Tom stashed anything in there, he must've been truly desperate." He shook his head, coming to a stop beside me. "This place looks like it's barely holding itself together. Should we even go inside?"

I chewed my lip, gazing at the barn. It looked like it could collapse at any second. An uneasy feeling stirred in my gut as I took in the peeling red paint, the rotting wooden beams.

But we had come this far.

"We'll be careful," I said at last. My gaze drifted to the surrounding fields, overgrown and desolate. "They don't cut the grass out here. There's got to be a million ticks in the grass. Who would come here casually? The whole place is creepy."

"We're here. The kids were here." Landon shot me a wry look. "Speaking of the two of us being here, it's a little hypocritical, don't you think? You just finished scolding Evie for coming out here, and now here we are."

"We didn't follow a suspected murderer up the hike and bike trail." I swatted at a mosquito buzzing by my ear. "I assume your point is what kind of example am I setting, lecturing Evie on safety and then charging in without backup?"

"A little bit."

"I suppose you never told your kids one thing and did another?"

"Well, we weren't talking about me, were we? And I'm your backup." Landon placed his hand on my back.

"I get it, Ellie. You don't like to admit you can be hypo-critical. Not a problem. I understand."

I raised an eyebrow at Landon's assessment, mustering as much dignity as I could manage. "Well, aren't we perceptive today?" I asked wryly.

"I'm perceptive every day." Landon's mouth quirked. "Ellie, as I see it, hypocrisy is practically a parental rite of passage. Like your kid losing their baby teeth or you developing a tolerance for black coffee because your kid drank all the milk."

"You're hysterical." I rolled my eyes, but I couldn't restrain a chuckle. I took a step toward the barn, eyeing the sagging doorway. "I say we quickly look around and see if we spot anything useful. If it seems dangerous, we'll call Mario on the way out."

Landon nodded. "Fair enough. But any sign of trouble, we call for backup right away. I don't want to have to make two ER runs in one day."

Our laughter faded, leaving smiles in its wake.

The moment I crossed the threshold into the barn, a wave of sweltering heat enveloped me like the unwelcome embrace of an overzealous relative. I could understand why Evie overheated when she entered — this wasn't merely "hot." This was flesh-melting, blood-simmering hot. The type of hot that made you wonder if you'd accidentally wandered into one of Dante's lesser-known circles of hell.

Dust motes swirled in the beams of sunlight streaming through holes in the wood, and the air felt heavy and oppressively still. Within seconds, beads of sweat had broken out on my forehead.

"Could it be any hotter in here?" I muttered. I swatted in vain at the flies buzzing around my face, their insistent droning adding to my growing discomfort.

Landon fanned himself behind me, whistling low under his breath. "Sweet hellfire, you could roast a turkey in here. How has this place not gone up in flames yet?"

I eyed the rotting wooden walls with no small amount of concern. "Don't give it any ideas. At this point, I think even a spark would set the whole thing alight."

The temperature here must have been over a hundred degrees, and combined with the humidity, it felt suffocating. I paused momentarily to catch my breath in the shade of a rusted tractor, suddenly understanding why abandoned places like this were left to slowly decay into ruins. It was hard to imagine anything — or anyone — surviving here for long in this heat.

I wiped the sweat from my face, preparing to venture further into the stifling barn when Landon touched my arm. "There, in the back corner. Isn't that the equipment Matt described?"

I followed his pointing finger and squinted into the dimness. It took me a moment to spot them, but sure enough, there were two white hive boxes, a smoker, and other tools used for maintaining beehives. My pulse kicked up a notch.

"That's definitely beekeeping equipment," I said. I started down the aisle toward the back of the barn, Landon close behind me. Each step kicked up small clouds of pollen and dust that clung to the perspiration on my skin. My gaze roamed the cluttered workbench nearby, catching on empty mason jars and a handwritten label that read "Tyson Apiary."

"What would supplies from Ben's place be doing here?" Landon wondered aloud, his eyes scanning the table in front of us. He picked up the smoker, turning it over in his hands. "Looks recently used, too."

I noticed a dark reddish-brown stain on the rough wooden surface as I approached the workbench. It looked horribly like old, dried blood. I couldn't believe what I was seeing. Had Evie and Matt's reckless actions actually led us to a solid piece of evidence?

"That's not blood, is it?" I asked.

Landon pulled out his phone, nodding grimly. "I'm not prepared to bet you it ain't." He tapped the screen. "I'll call Mario."

As I stood surveying the grim contents of the workbench, I felt as limp and parboiled as a noodle left too long in boiling water. Evie and Matt's impulsiveness could have gotten them into trouble, I thought, but it may well have led us directly to the person responsible for Ben's death.

I said a silent prayer of thanks that the kids were safe and that we had made this discovery before the murderer could cover their tracks for good.

"Is this a Hellmouth? I may die of heat stroke in protest. What an infuriatingly miserable place." Mario scrutinized the contents of the workbench, his expression grim. "I can't confirm without testing, but this appears more like paint to me." He paused, clearing his throat. "What led you out to this place?"

Landon shifted his weight. "Evie and Matt tailed Tom Coleman here today. They saw him lugging a huge black garbage bag into this barn. When Evie passed out from the heat, Matt rushed her to the ER—that's where Ellie and I came from, by way of the cat shelter. We thought we should inspect their lead."

"Apparently, they were onto something," I added with a glance at the beekeeping tools. "This equipment belonged to Ben. Why is it here?"

Mario sighed, rubbing his hand down his face. "Beats me. Those kids could've ended up in a world of trouble tracking someone like that." He shook his head. "Some might call that stalking."

"Those kids aren't much younger than you. And Matt's a private eye now," Landon said.

"Ah, of course." Mario nodded, a wry smile flickering across his lips. "Well, that's not stalking, then. That's working. Did they find the black garbage bag? Or did you?"

"No. And I gave Evie an earful about it already," I said. "Believe me, she won't be repeating that mistake."

"Let's hope not." Mario eyed the ominous stain on the workbench again. "Still, this is suspicious enough that I'll have forensics test that stain and dust the tools for prints. If it all doesn't melt in the meantime, anyway." He wiped his brow. "Something in here has to be on fire somewhere."

"We didn't see any smoke. And I think testing it is a good thing. The sooner you catch Ben's killer, the better." Landon pivoted to face Mario. "Speaking of which, the nurses mentioned Ben's ex-employee, Leo Barnett."

"The nurses? At the hospital?" Mario cocked an eyebrow.

I nodded. "Apparently, Leo turned up at the ER with a cut on his neck that looked like it was from a knife," I said. "The day after Ben was killed."

Mario held up a hand. "While that's interesting, the captain brought Augusta Walton in about an hour ago."

"You all arrested her?" Landon asked.

"Not yet, but it wouldn't surprise me if it happened by the time I return."

I stared at him in disbelief. "Augusta? Do you really think she killed Ben and left him face down in a honey pan because he broke up with her? Come on."

"I don't. The captain does." Mario shrugged. "I can't blame him, though. It's still early, but her fingerprints are all over the alleged murder weapon. I'd say there's a good chance we found our culprit."

Landon and I shared a knowing look.

"What alleged murder weapon?" Landon asked.

Mario held our gaze. "The captain says it was a manual honey extractor. The coroner confirmed those marks all over Ben's back match the pattern. Augusta's prints were on the handle." Mario slapped an invisible book shut in his hands. "Case closed, I guess."

I gaped at him in disbelief. A honey extractor?

"A honey extractor?" Landon echoed my thoughts. "Are you sure about that?"

Mario shrugged again. "As sure as we ever are at this point. The captain seems convinced, and forensics backs it up. We think Ben dumped her, and she just snapped."

My mind was reeling as I tried to process this latest bombshell. Augusta and Ben? I never would have imagined it. And a crime of passion seemed so out of character for her usual calm, rational demeanor.

As improbable as it seemed, was she possibly Ben's killer? If her fingerprints were truly all over the alleged murder weapon, what other explanation could there be? Maybe the simplest explanation is the right one.

Maybe.

"I hope they have the right person for everyone's sake," I said finally.

Landon nodded. "You and me both. After everything that's happened, I'd hate to see them be wrong on this." His brow furrowed. "But if her prints really are on the weapon..."

"Then it looks like we got our killer." Mario scratched his head. "I know it seems far-fetched, but the evidence doesn't lie. I'm as shocked as anyone, but facts are facts."

I sighed. Whether or not all our questions had been answered remained to be seen. As improbable as Augusta seemed, could we argue with hard evidence?

For now, at least, it appeared Ben's case had finally been solved.

Chapter Sixteen

AFTER BEING IN THAT ABANDONED OVEN OF A BARN for so long, I was parched. I poured another tall glass of iced tea from the pitcher in my office fridge and gulped it down greedily, savoring the sweetness on my tongue as the chilled liquid soothed my dry throat.

I frowned.

"I know that look. You don't buy that Augusta did it, do you?" he asked, gazing at me intently with those bright eyes that seemed to miss nothing.

Landon sat across from me at the weathered wooden table in my office, his brow furrowed with concentration. Diffused golden light flooded through the windows, catching the glints of silver in Landon's hair. I was so distracted I didn't even notice how handsome he looked despite the sweaty hell we'd just been through.

He was right.

I didn't think Ben's case had been solved; my instincts told me there were still too many unanswered questions and details that didn't add up.

Call it a gut feeling.

But as I sat in the quiet of my office with Landon, doubts nagged at me, persistent whispers hinting the truth remained hidden beneath layers of assumptions and misdirection.

I shook my head. "No. I don't. Not for a minute," I said, setting down my empty glass. "Nothing about this adds up to her being the killer. There has to be something else going on here."

"Why's that?" Landon asked, studying me closely. "Mario said the police seem pretty convinced."

"Mario didn't sound very convinced to me," I said.

Landon paused, mulling this over, and then nodded slowly in agreement. "No, that's true. He didn't."

"And come on — a honey extractor as the murder weapon?" I said incredulously, shaking my head in disbelief. "That doesn't make any sense. Augusta's a baker, not a beekeeper. Not to sound misogynistic, because I believe women can do anything men can do, up to and including murder, but she's a slight woman who eats too many of her pastries. On the other hand, Ben was a strong man who did a fair amount of manual labor for his job. Does she even have the strength to beat a man Ben's size to death?"

Landon considered this, nodding slowly. "You have a

point there. And we still don't know why Tom Coleman was out at that abandoned place."

"And we didn't find the trash bag he was carrying."

"We also don't know why Ben's jars were there."

"Exactly. There are too many loose ends for me to believe they've solved this already, and none of those ends have a single thing to do with Augusta Walton." I refilled my glass again, the tea doing little to quench my thirst that sprung from the memory of the oppressive heat. "The police are still searching the Miller place?"

"That's right." Landon leaned forward, his eyes meeting mine. "Ellie, I know you want answers. I do too. But promise me you won't go snooping around on your own. Let the police handle this."

I contemplated Landon's words, tapping my fingers on the desk.

He was right that I wanted answers, but sitting still while the police wrapped up an innocent woman with a bow as the murderer would be difficult. My leg bounced with restless energy as my mind raced, trying to piece together the fragments of clues we had into something that made sense.

It had to be one of the Colemans.

Or Leo Barnett.

There was far more circumstantial evidence pointing at any of those three than at Augusta Walton. At least as far as I knew. Why had the male-dominated police department laser-focus on her?

What were we missing?

Landon noticed the concern on my face and raised a warning finger, his eyes glinting with affectionate amusement. "I can see it in your eyes," he said. "That 'I'm going to solve this case no matter what' look. But I mean it, Ellie. Don't go rushing into danger half-cocked on your own again. Last time you had that look, you got a gun pointed at your forehead."

Landon brought up that gun pointed at my face like it had gone off and I'd spent ten years in a coma. Yes, someone pointed a gun at me — but then he gave up. Case closed. Technically, it was a wholly successful and traumatically uneventful outing.

Besides, I couldn't just sit back and do nothing.

A small smile crept across my face as I looked at Landon. "I'm not by myself," I said. "I have you."

Landon looked at me, startled. Then he sighed, his eyes crinkling at the corners. "Ellie, don't you bat those big brown eyes at me. You won't manipulate my emotions by giving me that 'save me, you're my knight in shining armor' look."

"Landon Rogers, I'm a 50-year-old woman. I would never." I gasped in mock offense, planting my hands on my hips.

He shook his head, fighting a smile. "Mm-hmm. Your age tells me you've had more time to perfect those wiley ways, Ellie Rockwell. And you know darn well one little wobble of that lower lip, and I'd be volunteering to charge headfirst into a dragon's lair for you."

"My hero. But don't you worry, I'll save the damsel in distress act for when we really need it." I winked.

He opened his mouth to respond as my cell phone rang, shattering the quiet. At the same instant, Josephine strode into my office without knocking, her brows knitted in concern.

I held up my finger toward Josephine and answered the call, putting it on speaker. "This is Ellie."

"Ellie, it's Laurie," came the familiar voice of our veterinarian, crisp and professional as always. Josephine and Landon leaned in instinctively. "Are they there with you?

"They, who?"

"Landon and Josephine."

"Yes, Josephine and Landon are here. What's going on?"

"I need you three to meet me at the loading dock in the back of the shelter in ten minutes," Laurie said, a note of urgency and insistence in her usual calm tone. "And bring the talking plate thing."

The line went dead before we had a chance to ask any questions.

I met Landon's questioning gaze, and we both knew what the other was thinking. What could be so important that Laurie would want us to meet her where no one could see us?

Josephine stood up, brushing invisible dust from her blouse with practiced movements of her hands. "Should we get Evie and Matt?" she asked.

"No," I told her. "Let her rest."

Landon and I followed Josephine out the door, making our way across the creaky second floor to the isolation room to retrieve the talking plate.

As we walked, my mind raced with unanswered questions. What could Laurie want to tell us that was urgent and required such secrecy? Why did it have to be private, away from prying eyes and listening ears?

What awaited us in the meeting with Laurie, I wondered.

And did I even want to know?

Laurie's spay and neuter mobile clinic van backed up slowly to the loading dock, its metal frame groaning and shuddering in protest like a living thing as it settled into place.

As the rumbling engine finally quieted down, she swung open the driver's side door with a creak and hopped out, her rubber-soled shoes echoing loudly on the concrete as she hurried around to meet us. Her usually cheerful face was drawn and serious, her smile replaced by a grim line as she approached.

"I'm not sure this is gonna work," she admitted, her brow furrowed deeply with consternation and worry as she glanced at the duffel bag hanging off my shoulder, "but I think it's worth a shot."

"You're not sure what is going to work?" Landon

asked, voicing the burning question that was on our minds at that moment.

Josephine squinted at Laurie, her eyes narrowed, and one eyebrow arched in suspicion. "All right, Laurie, spill the beans. What are you up to?"

Laurie sidestepped the question, her attention zeroing in again on the duffel bag I clutched tightly. "That's what I asked you to bring, right?"

I nodded, hoisting the bag that safeguarded our inherited feline communication gadget.

A relieved sigh escaped Laurie's lips. "Thank heavens. Time's probably not on our side. Get it inside, and let's move!" With a sense of urgency, she yanked the van's sliding door open and scrambled in.

We trailed after Laurie into the van, squeezing ourselves awkwardly into the utilitarian but confined space. The sharp scent of antiseptic mingled with the lingering homey aroma of Laurie's coffee inside, an odd yet familiar combination.

"Ugh, this is ridiculous." Josephine planted her hands on her hips, annoyance etched into the lines of her face. "Laurie, enough with the cloak and dagger. Explain yourself this instant, or we're going back outside."

A deep, resonant woof echoed unexpectedly in response, causing us all to startle in alarm at the sudden sound in the close confines of the van.

Landon's head whipped around, his eyes scanning the dimly lit interior. "What the heck was that?"

Laurie's fingers grasped a light blanket that draped over an enormous crate. She yanked it off with one swift, fluid motion, unveiling the most enormous dog we had ever seen.

A colossal Great Dane stared back at us, its enormous tail thumping rhythmically against the crate floor as it wagged enthusiastically. The behemoth had to tip the scales at a solid 175 pounds, its gigantic paws resembling furry catcher's mitts. Sleek, gleaming black fur covered the powerful muscles that rippled as it rose to its feet, ducking its head to avoid the crate's low ceiling. Yet, despite its formidable size, the dog's eyes were gentle, round, and imploring, as though seeking our approval to come out and join the fun.

"That thing is as big as a horse," Josephine said.

I knew Great Danes were originally bred as boar hunters, but this one missed that memo entirely. The enthusiastic whacks from its tail echoed loudly through the confines of the van as it gazed at us with an open, guileless expression, appearing far more interested in befriending everyone it met than attacking any prey.

The Great Dane peered at Landon, tail still wagging, and gave a pleading little "woof." The big man's frown wavered, and his mouth twitched as he fought a smile while gazing into the dog's openly friendly face. "Well, he is handsome, I'll grant you that," he said.

The dog woofed again as if in thanks.

"So, I didn't bring him over just to show him off." Laurie grimaced, her gaze shifting between the enormous dog and us. "This is Tank. He belongs to Augusta Walton. The police brought him over to board until there's room at the county shelter."

Josephine gasped. "Do you have permission to remove him from the premises? That dog belongs to an arrested murderer. You can't just go for a joyride with him, Laurie!"

"Oh no?" Laurie scowled at her. "Now you care about the spirit of the rules, Ms. Go-Between to the police?" The two women stared at each other for a beat. "It's a dog. I'm taking him for a walk. We're allowed to do that. And while cats are manipulative little sociopaths that would lie if it meant an extra treat at bedtime, dogs just don't have that kind of conniving personality. If anyone would know the truth about what happened between Augusta and Ben, it would be Tank."

"I don't understand." Landon frowned, glancing from the dog to Laurie. "Why, exactly, did you bring him here?"

"I really need to spell it out?" Laurie asked. "I thought we could see if the talking plate works on dogs. I figured it was safer to bring him here than haul that thing into my office." She nodded at the duffel bag still clutched in my hands. "Frankly, if I got it there, I might never return it."

I gazed at the enormous Great Dane.

It seemed improbable that the cat plate would work

on a dog, yet hadn't everything we had experienced so far defied logical explanation? Who would have guessed a crystal drink tray would be an inter-species communication device for humans and cats?

I unzipped the duffel bag on the exam table, removing the silver talking plate. "I have no idea if this will work. We can try, but..."

"I know, I know." She shook her head, a frown creasing her brow. "Okay, I don't know. But Tank is very attached to Augusta, and by all accounts, I've heard, he was pretty attached to Ben, too. If any dog has information about that day..." Her voice trailed off.

"It would be him," Josephine finished.

Tank woofed softly as if in agreement.

"Are we really going to try and talk to a gigantic dog on that tiny little plate?" Landon asked. "How are you even going to get him on the thing?"

I shrugged as Laurie opened the crate. "Put his paw on the plate?"

Once free, Tank's tail wagged so vigorously that his whole body swayed from side to side as he jumped around, eager to greet each of us.

"This dog doesn't have a suspicious bone in his body," Landon observed.

"Danes are known for being friendly and affectionate," Laurie told him. "They're called the gentle giants of the dog world."

Tank padded up to Josephine first, nudging his huge head under her hand to request ear scratches and pets. Josephine obliged, a smile creeping across her face as she rubbed his silky ears. "Dogs are so much more interesting than cats."

"Oh, please. No one asked you," I told her.

Tank woofed in delight, then turned his attention to Landon. Before Landon could react, Tank had reared up on his hind legs, placing his front paws on Landon's shoulders in a semblance of a hug. Landon staggered under the dog's weight with an "oof!" and laughed as he ruffled Tank's fur.

When Tank finally approached me, he eyed me suspiciously as if sensing I was a cat person. But true to his friendly nature, Tank simply ducked his head and licked my hand, gazing up at me with those imploring eyes as his tail wagged. I grinned, scratching his neck and marveling at the feel of solid muscle rippling under my fingers.

"Okay, he's cute. But Josephine's right. He's not a pet. He's a small horse," I said.

"He's a big baby." Laurie smiled, shaking her head as she watched Tank dole affection to each of us. "Dogs are more popular than cats for a reason," she said. "All they want to do is love you."

"You might wanna tone down the doggie fan club before you and Ellie come to blows," Josephine said.

Tank turned his big, soulful eyes toward her, his tail still thumping, and let out a whiney woof that sounded like he hadn't eaten in days.

"You're such a big drama queen. I'll slip you some treats later if you behave, all right?"

At the prospect of food, Tank barked with excitement, instantly gravitating back to Josephine for more affectionate ear rubs and words of praise.

"I think you have an admirer for life now," Laurie told Josephine with a grin.

"Josephine, stop petting the dog and make sure the curtains on the back windows are closed tight, please." I placed the talking plate carefully on the van floor, motioning for Tank to come closer.

He did, sniffing at it.

The dog glared at me and whined when he realized there was no food.

"Oh, stop that," Josephine told the Great Dane. After swiftly securing the curtains to ensure no curious onlookers could peer in, she added, "It's not going to work. No one looking at you would think you've missed a meal a day in your life."

Landon looked toward the doors. "Is this van even soundproofed?"

"Does it really matter? If Tank manages to speak, no one's gonna know the voice belongs to a dog, anyway," Laurie pointed out. Her words carried a hint of wry amusement, highlighting the absurdity of our situation.

I squatted down, holding out a hand for Tank's enormous paw. "Tank, the talking plate allows cats to speak to us so we can understand them clearly. We hope it might help you do the same, big guy." I gazed into Tank's soft brown eyes, hoping he grasped at least part of what I was telling him. "Do you want to try?"

Tank barked as if signaling his understanding.

I gently took the Great Dane's enormous paw in my hands, placing it carefully on the surface of the talking plate. As soon as I did so, a bright silvery glow suffused the plate, shimmering and pulsing. It shined upward, casting an otherworldly light throughout the interior of the mobile clinic.

Tank gazed down at the talking plate in evident surprise, his expressive eyes widening. He lifted his head to peer at me quizzically as if awaiting an explanation for this strange new development.

Then a resonant baritone said, "That is very odd!"

We all gasped, staring at the dog in shock.

"I knew it," Laurie declared, her tone brimming with self-assured satisfaction. The smug grin spread across her face only added to the triumph surrounding her words. "Magic that only works on cats. Please."

Tank jumped, removing his paw from the plate, and barked — a perfectly normal dog bark. The glow of the talking platter faded, leaving behind a non-magical-looking polished crystalline silver tray once more.

"Tank, you have to leave your paw on there for us to hear you," I told him.

The dog stepped forward, and the light flared to life again.

"I have done so! I am talking like a human! With my head! And I am a good boy!" Tank panted, gazing up at us with his tail wagging, clearly pleased he had done as instructed, even though the result surprised him as much as us. "Am I a good boy?" His head tilted. "You should say I am a good boy."

Laurie's eyes were wide. "Okay, there must be more than one of these plates in the world because that Great Dane sounds just like that talking dog from that movie with the balloons."

"Well, I'll be," Landon said. He shook his head in disbelief. "A talking dog. Sure. Why not?"

I rubbed Tank's ears, grinning at him. "Good boy, Tank!"

I couldn't believe that worked.

"I am a good boy. Thank you."

"Tank, could you tell us about the day Ben died? Did your mistress actually hurt him?"

"He is not hurt. He is dead." Tank's brow furrowed as he whined sadly. "My mistress was home crying that day. She loved him and did not want to break up with him. And then she cried even more when the police came and said he was dead. I felt very sad for her. She would not even throw the ball."

We exchanged glances.

This was not the tale of a cold-blooded killer

grieving crocodile tears in case her dog learned how to talk so he could provide her an alibi.

"What do you think happened to Ben, Tank?" I asked.

Tank huffed. "I think the cat tripped him. He was always hissing and swiping for no reason. Cats are mean."

Laurie's expression shifted to a frown. "But the cat adored Ben. They were practically inseparable."

Tank snorted dismissively, his skepticism evident. "Cats don't love anyone. They are cats."

I chuckled.

Landon rubbed his chin thoughtfully. "Okay, so, if it's not the cat, who would be your next guess, Tank?"

Tank growled, the fur on the back of his neck rising. "That man Leo. Ben's old helper. I often smelled him around the farm, even though he should not be there anymore. I did not like how he watched the farm or looked at Ben or my mistress."

"Leo Barnett?" I asked.

"That is him. I do not know the reasons of men. I am just a dog. But that man Leo smelled of anger and bitterness and heat and dishonesty. And I heard him yelling at Ben in the back of the field, saying he deserved the farm. He told Ben this not long before Ben died."

"Thank you, Tank," I said, giving him another ear rub. "You've been very helpful."

"You are welcome!" Tank barked, panting happily. "I am always happy to help. And now, may I please have a treat? I think I deserve one. I am out of the little box, but this is still a big box. I do not like boxes. I am not a cat."

Josephine laughed. "All right, I did promise. Here you go." She handed Tank a dog bone treat, which he accepted with an enthusiastic chomp and woof.

The talking plate's glow faded once more as the Great Dane abandoned it to enjoy his treat and a thorough ear-scratching from Josephine.

Chapter Seventeen

Landon and I entered the isolation room, the cat platter tucked safely inside the duffel bag slung over my shoulder, to find Evie and Matt with Belladonna and Honey.

"Hey, you two," I said, but my greeting died on my lips as I took in the anxiety etched into the lines of my daughter's face. Her hair was askew, strands chaotically escaping in all directions from her usual wispy bun, and her eyes were wide. My gaze traveled down to find her hands clenching and unclenching at her sides, her fingers twitching restlessly.

"I can't find it," she said without looking at me.

Evie was frantically searching the room, peering under tables and behind equipment, a wild look in her eyes. Matt followed behind her, hands gently grasping her shoulders as he murmured in a soothing tone, "Breathe, Evie. It's okay. We'll find it."

My daughter's distress was almost palpable, radiating from her in waves.

When Evie glanced at me as if surprised to find me there, she hurried over. "Mom, the magic cat plate is gone. Did you take it?" Her words came out slightly slurred, and she swayed a little on her feet. "If you took it, I won't be mad, I swear. I won't. I won't be mad. But did you?" The panic and agitation poured off Evie, seeping into the air around us. "Oh my gosh, you didn't. It's gone!"

"Evie, everything is okay," I said, unzipping the duffel bag to retrieve the cat platter. It gleamed under the lights of the isolation room, its polished silver surface glinting as I lifted it free of the pack. "Yes, I borrowed it for a short while. I'm putting it back now. Everything is fine."

I went to the cubby and carefully placed the platter on its floor. Belladonna sniffed in its direction, her sun-kissed golden eyes suspicious as she watched me return the magic plate. Her plush ebony fur bristled, and she let out an irritated mrrow as if scolding me for daring to take the platter in the first place. Then her nose twitched.

"Someone needed to share some information with us, Bella. I'm sure you don't mind that." I offered her an apologetic smile. "There, you see?" I said, turning back to Evie. "It's back where it belongs, safe and sound. Everything's just fine."

Belladonna sniffed toward it again, her honey-golden eyes narrowing.

"Why did you take it?" Evie demanded, her words tumbling out in a rush. Her hands twisted anxiously at her sides, fluttering like fragile birds seeking escape. Her chest rose and fell with quick and shallow breaths as if she couldn't draw air deep enough into her lungs.

Landon watched her quietly from the doorway.

Matt's gaze locked with mine as Evie clung to him. His eyes bored into me, a sea of unspoken distress and desperation churning in his dark brown eyes. He had witnessed Evie's panic and distress before, but not as her boyfriend and not recently. When Evie had a good run, it was easy to get lulled into forgetting that she had issues at all.

"Evie, Laurie brought over a Great Dane named Tank. He belongs to Augusta Walton, and she's just been arrested for killing Ben Tyson," I said with a slow, careful cadence to my words. "Laurie thought the plate could also be used to talk to dogs, and she was right. He was able to talk to us. Just take a deep breath, Evie. Everything's fine now. The plate is back. Everything's fine."

Evie's gaze darted around the room as if seeking reassurance the platter was indeed returned. As her eyes bounced around, she said, "You went and talked to Tank without bothering to come to get me. You're trying to keep me from the case, aren't you? You don't trust me!" Her words held an edge of panic.

Evie was right.

At that very moment, I didn't trust her.

Telling her I didn't trust her at that very moment wouldn't help anything, however — in fact, it was very likely to make whatever emotional attack she was going through much worse.

So, I did what any good parent does in this situation. I lied.

"I assumed you were taking a nap after being in the emergency room, Evie, and we didn't want to wake you up after the day you've had. That's all."

"It's true, Evie," Landon added, supporting my half-truth. "We talked about whether to get you."

"And I just told you where and what we were doing. Surely I wouldn't have done that if I was trying to keep you out of the case. Your case, really." I studied my daughter with concern, noting the continued signs of distress and agitation in her features, movements, and speech. "I certainly wasn't all gung ho about investigating murders based on animal witness statements. That was your idea."

My words did little to reassure her.

Evie's gaze continued to roam the room, and her hands trembled like leaves clinging stubbornly to branches before a coming storm.

Matt shot me a worried look over Evie's head again, his arm tightening around her protectively. "She's had a rough day," he said.

No kidding, Matt.

I couldn't tell.

"She has," I agreed, suppressing my inner sarcasm.

Matt was still adjusting to the resurgence of Evie's ongoing health issues and the challenges accompanying managing a chronic illness, so I decided to cut him slack instead of chastising him for pointing out the obvious. I looked at my daughter and gently brushed a lock of hair away from her face. "Can I get you some water, sweetheart?"

"Yeah, okay," Evie grumbled, the tension seeming to drain from her limbs all at once. She sank down to sit on the floor, back sliding against the wall, posture deflating as if the anxiety had been the only thing keeping her upright.

Matt followed her down, settling beside Evie without releasing his steadying hold. Belladonna and Honey walked over to her and crawled into her lap, their warm bodies protecting the clasped hands.

Evie dropped her head. "I hate this," she said, the words muffled but audible. At that moment, she sounded so young, my little girl struggling in the face of obstacles no one of any age should have to try and overcome.

There were good days and bad, moments of vibrancy and joy, but others where the struggles of coping took their toll. Today was shaping up to be one of the latter, and all I could think was — what can I do? How do I make this right?

If I could have traded places and taken on her illness as my own to spare her suffering, I would have done so without hesitation. What parent wouldn't make that choice for their child?

But diseases didn't work that way. I couldn't make this right or better through sheer force of will alone. I could only offer comfort, share the burden as best I could, and remain by her side.

One breath, one heartbeat, at a time.

Seated at the kitchen table, I clutched a mug of chamomile tea with both hands, taking sips of the steaming liquid. The familiar floral scent wafted up, typically calming, but it did little to alleviate my frazzled nerves today.

The kitchen floorboards creaked, announcing Landon's approach before he appeared in the doorway. His brow was furrowed with concern, eyes shadowed as his gaze found me sitting at the table. The lines around his mouth seemed more profound, tugged down at the corners, and I wondered if the day's stresses had also left their mark on him.

"Are you okay?" he asked, stepping further into the kitchen. The words were gentle, as if he was afraid too loud a tone might shatter me.

I thought I should reassure him. Smile and say I was okay.

But the pretense felt like too much an effort, and what point was there in dishonesty with Landon, anyway? There was no hiding from those perceptive eyes or the caring they contained. He knew me better than that.

I set the mug down on the table. "I'm not the one having a difficult day."

"Oh, I think you are. You may not be the only one, though. I'll give you that." He pulled out the chair beside me and sat, reaching over to grasp one of my hands in his. "This affects you too. Any fool can see that. Is there anything I can do?"

I looked down at my hand in his and contemplated pulling away.

I didn't.

Instead, I shook my head, taking in a shaky breath. "No, I just..." My words trailed off, and I felt the sting of tears at the back of my eyes. There were no easy fixes for what plagued my daughter. No simple way for Landon or anyone else to make this right. I forced them away with another unsteady inhale. Shrugging helplessly, I said, "I'm coping." It was the most honest answer I could give.

Landon dropped my hand and rose from his chair to stand behind me. He placed his hands on my shoulders, fingers digging in to massage away the tension gathered there.

With a sigh, I dropped my head forward as his hands slid down to work at the knots beneath my shoulder blades, squeezing and kneading. The familiar scent of cedar that always clung to him wrapped around me, grounding me in its comforting familiarity.

I lost track of time, focused only on the feel of his strong yet gentle hands chasing away stress and soothing frayed nerves. By the time Landon stopped, circling around to crouch before me, some weight seemed to have lifted. I gazed at him through eyes that felt less likely to overflow, a hint of peace restored.

He brushed the hair back from my face like I had done to Evie earlier, tucking stray strands behind my ear. "Better?"

I offered him a smile. "Yes. Thank you."

Landon gazed at me expectantly, and for a moment, I worried he anticipated a kiss as a token of gratitude for his comfort and care. The thought prompted an odd fluttering in my stomach, one which I didn't have the time or energy to scrutinize.

To sidestep any awkwardness, I stood up from my chair and walked across the kitchen to place my used mug in the sink. Behind me, I heard Landon sigh, the sound faint yet undeniably audible.

Guilt tugged at me briefly, but then I mentally shook it off.

I had just let the man give me a neck massage. That was more physical contact than I'd allowed from any man since I had a husband.

Landon Rogers would have to respect and be satisfied with that as progress.

I turned to find Landon still crouched where I had left him, watching me with an unreadable expression. His eyes seemed to pierce through all my excuses and

second thoughts, glimpsing intentions I didn't have —
and, well, even if I did, I wasn't ready to think about
them yet. I cleared my throat, folding my arms over my
chest in an unconsciously defensive gesture.

"Thank you again for the neck massage. I should
check on Evie to see if she's feeling any better." I moved
to brush past him, anxious to escape that too-perceptive
gaze and the feelings it stirred in me.

"You know, you don't have to run from me, Ellie,"
Landon said, the words rough yet gentle all at once. "I
told you before. I'm a patient man. I can wait until
you're ready." He rose slowly to his feet, hand reaching
out to grasp mine, giving it a comforting squeeze. "You
go on and check Evie. I'll be here if you need anything
else."

With that, Landon released me.

I all but fled the kitchen, emotions in a tangle I didn't
care to unravel.

His parting words echoed in my mind, both reassuring and unsettling. What he said seemed like both a
promise and a warning of complications sure to come. I
had the sense of standing at a crossroads with paths
stretching out ahead — unsure of which one I would
take.

But that was a decision for another day.

I found Evie sitting in her second floor bedroom window seat, gazing over the backyard. Belladonna and Honey curled up on either side of her, and Matt sat in a chair a few feet away.

A hint of pink was returning to her cheeks, and she was no longer pale. The panic that had made her eyes glassy and unfocused earlier appeared eased, pupils no longer dilated by fear and distress. She looked pensive rather than frantic, fingers idly combing through Honey's sleek coat.

She noticed me and offered an apologetic smile. "So, I know you're not going to believe this, but I forgot to take my afternoon meds while we were at the hospital, and then I didn't catch up when we got home. Missed my stress stuff and the beta blockers. I guess anxiety was through the roof, and my blood pressure was up. So... yeah, I'm sorry for losing it earlier."

I clucked my tongue, a familiar sound of motherly admonishment and concern both. I stared at my daughter; I was still a little rattled by how quickly a missed dose of medication had plunged her into a temporary crisis.

"You must be more careful about missing those beta blockers, Evie," I said. "You know that can be dangerous." Her health and safety depended upon adherence to doctors' orders in a way most others never faced.

She heard me and then waved a hand, dismissing my concern.

Because, of course, she did.

"Look, I took them. Back off, Mom. I'm feeling better now, and we don't need to keep going over this. I apologized, and you've said it all before." Evie pointed the finger at me, expression sobering. "Change of subject. Did you notice how ungodly hot it was in that barn? I swear, I almost passed out just standing there."

I nodded. Landon and I had both commented on the stifling heat within the structure. It was hard to miss.

"I noticed, too," Matt said. "Evie mentioned it right away. Seemed weird for an abandoned old barn."

Evie leaned forward. "Exactly. Shouldn't it have been cooler in the shade?"

"Not necessarily," I said. "There was no airflow in there."

"Even if it was a little warm from being closed up, it wouldn't be that much hotter than outside, would it? I mean, there was no insulation, no ventilation. That big tree shades the roof." Her eyes narrowed in consideration. "Did either of you see any reason for the heat in there?"

I shook my head, realizing she had made a valid point. "No, there didn't appear to be any obvious heat source."

"I would swear it was at least twenty degrees warmer in that barn," Evie mused. "Maybe more. But why?" She tapped her chin, gaze distant as she turned over this new mystery. Some of the old enthusiasm returned to her eyes. A puzzle to solve, helping shift her mind from the earlier distress.

Okay, helping to shift my mind.

Because obviously, she was done with it.

Matt smiled, reaching over to squeeze Evie's hand where it rested on her leg. "You're right. That is weird."

"I wonder if the cops noticed how hot it was there yet. It might be worth mentioning to them. See if it means anything," I said.

"Oh, I did. They know. They didn't find anything, which shouldn't surprise any of us at all," Evie said, a hint of color rising in her cheeks. She was on a roll now with this new trail of speculation to explore. "We could go back there and take a look around ourselves. It has to mean something," she said. "The heat was outrageous."

"Are you out of your mind? You want to go back to the place that hospitalized you?" I asked incredulously. "Evie, you can't be serious."

"I just talked to Mario before you came up here. They didn't find that black garbage bag. I know it's there. We saw Tom bring it in there." She held up a cooling neck wrap. "Besides, I'll be prepared this time."

I looked at the object in Evie's hands and struggled to discern its purpose or function. It appeared to be a long, flexible wrap of some lightweight material. "What is that?"

"It's a cooling neck wrap," Matt volunteered, looking pleased with himself. "They have special cooling elements sealed inside the wraps that activate with water exposure. You wrap it around your neck. It stays chilled for hours and helps you stay cool and comfortable. A great alternative to constantly guzzling sports drinks or lugging around ice packs."

"Let's not knock drinking. A bottle of water would have solved—"

"Mom, stop. We stopped at Bowell's Sporting Goods on the way home from the hospital," Evie told me. "We got, like, ten of them. They're awesome. So, what do you say? Want to go take a hike?"

The spark was back in Evie's eyes — that glint of irrepressible mischief and glee that spelled looming chaos in some form. I didn't know whether to rejoice at seeing that familiar spark return or run for the hills in terror.

I stood near the doorway, watching Evie's resurgence. She was on the mend, coping mechanism found again. Ready to dig into the case we had no business investigating with her usual zeal.

Lord help us.

Chapter Eighteen

THE SUN DIPPED LOW IN THE TEXAS SKY AS WE made our way up the gently sloping hill toward the old Miller barn. Long shadows of mesquite and oak trees stretched across the overgrown grass, and a warm amber glow lit the ragged edges of scattered clouds drifting lazily overhead. The hot summer day had waned into a balmy early evening as a faint breeze carried the subtle fragrance of sun-warmed grass and honeysuckle.

Landon strolled beside me, hands shoved into the pockets of his faded jeans. His eyes scanned the area around the barn as we walked, taking in the details. "Looks like the police have already cleared out," he commented, voice tinged with surprise. "I would have thought they'd look a bit longer."

Ahead of us, Matt and Evie strolled side by side, heads bent together as they chatted. At Landon's words,

Matt glanced over his shoulder. "Why would they bother sticking around for long? I mean, they already arrested Augusta," he pointed out.

I took in our surroundings and realized this spot was perfectly secluded, nestled between two gently sloping hillsides covered in a thick blanket of overgrown grass and wildflowers. The rolling rises blocked views into this hidden hollow from the public park in the valley below and the dense woods of oak and cedar trees that bordered the long abandoned property. "What do you know about the Miller property?" I asked Landon. "Why did the Millers leave it?"

"There used to be a house down that way," Landon said, pointing to the right of the decrepit old barn. "Got blown away during that '97 tornado outbreak. You remember that?"

I nodded.

Anyone that lived in Central Texas in '97 remembered that.

"The Millers all made it thank goodness — they had a tornado shelter installed in the early nineties — but they lost everything when the tornado flattened their family home. Three generations of Millers grew up there. Anyway, that day scared Mrs. Miller so bad that she told Jeb she wasn't living here anymore. They picked up and went to California. That's where she was from."

"California." I raised my eyebrow. "Where they have earthquakes?"

Landon shrugged. "Guess that was less scary to her. Riding out a tornado in a fancy underground shelter while your home gets blown to Oklahoma can make an impression on anyone."

Matt and Evie wandered ahead along the overgrown dirt path, absorbed in lively discussion and debate as Landon studied my profile, brow furrowed in concern.

"What?" I asked.

"Are you okay with everything that happened today?" he asked. "With Evie, I mean."

His question made me sigh, another release of the fear and anxiety that had knotted my stomach since Evie's distress that afternoon. "You don't have to keep asking me. I'm as used to it as I'll ever be. As anyone can be. We've been dealing with this since she was a baby, and it just becomes part of life." My voice softened as I admitted, "But seeing her distressed like that never gets easier."

We walked silently for a few moments, each absorbed in our thoughts. The sunset blazed in vibrant shades of orange and pink, infusing the scattered clouds with color. Rays of golden light filtered through the canopy of oak branches above, dappling the ground at our feet. For a few heartbeats, the scene's beauty drove worries and cares away, allowing a sense of peace to settle over me.

Then Landon asked quietly, "What does a relationship mean to you?"

Well, so much for that peace I just found.

My steps slowed as I pondered how to answer this question, fraught with meaning and implication.

A relationship meant commitment, support, intimacy, weathering challenges and disappointments, and sharing joys. It meant a partnership on life's journey, facing uncertainties and unknowns together.

A partnership I never honestly had.

In many ways, I still felt like that young bride left so long ago, the one that struggled to build a new life — without child support — from the ashes of old dreams. The scars of love lost lingered, a reminder that as wondrous as a relationship could be, it also meant opening oneself to the possibility of deep pain.

I took a deep breath and gathered my words, hoping they might convey at least part of the tangled complexity behind such a simple question, but before I could answer, Landon continued.

"We spend nearly every day together and always go out for dinner. Honestly, Ellie, I feel like we're already in a relationship. I just...don't seem to have permission to be there for you when you need someone. I have to wait for you to open the door slightly." His eyes searched mine. "I don't want to pressure you, but I think I have the right to ask. What's stopping you from taking that last step? Why won't you just let me in a little bit more? Don't you know by now whether I'm someone you could care for?"

"Oh, Landon, that's not it at all. It has nothing to do

with how much I care for you." I stopped in my tracks, turning to face him. "I do care about you. You know that."

His eyes searched mine, filled with doubt and a flicker of hurt.

My heart twisted at being the cause.

I grasped his hands, hoping the gesture would convey my sincerity. "After everything I went through with my ex-husband, trusting someone new isn't easy. The scars run deep. But you... Landon, you're the kindest, most thoughtful man I've ever known. I love spending time with you and couldn't ask for someone better." As the words tumbled from my mouth, I blinked, realization dawning in a rush.

"Then what is it, Ellie?"

Yeah, Ellie.

What the heck was it?

My doubts and fears seemed foolish, considering the truth of my own statement.

"I do care about you, Landon. And I do want the chance to build something real together."

Before saying more, I leaned forward and stretched to kiss him.

And yes — Evie came by her ability to dramatically shift emotional gears in an instant quite honestly. She inherited that particular quirk from me, though in her, it manifested differently.

And more frequently.

Landon tensed in surprise, then gently folded me

into his arms. His woodsy scent surrounded me, familiar and comforting, as stubble grazed my cheek with a pleasant rasp.

Before his lips could touch mine, Evie let out a loud whoop of delight.

"Oh, my gosh, I thought you'd have grandchildren before you went on another date, Mom. It's about time!" she crowed, clapping her hands in exuberant glee.

A smile quirked the corner of Landon's mouth, and he pressed a quick, soft kiss to my lips before releasing his hold.

After weeks — okay, months — of hesitance and uncertainty, this first chaste kiss felt as inevitable as the sunset painting colors across the sky. It was a moment of beauty and connection I knew would linger in my memory long after this quiet summer evening had faded into night.

⁂

The Miller barn loomed before us, weathered wooden planks bleached pale gray from years under the relentless Texas sun. A blast of hot air rolled over us as we stepped through the yawning entrance. The heat was stifling, easily over a hundred degrees, and I frowned in concern at Evie.

"Are you feeling okay, honey? Not overheated?"

Evie waved off my worried questions, impatience flickering in her eyes. "Really, Mom, I'm fine. Stop hovering. Worry about yourself." Her gaze swept the cavernous interior of the barn, taking in details. Rusting farm equipment was still scattered about, relics of a working farm long abandoned.

"The glass jars that were over there are gone," she said, gesturing to a rough wooden table along the far wall. "But the heat is still here."

I studied the barn's cavernous interior, noticing the details Evie indicated were missing. My gaze caught on the tools hanging from the rough wooden walls, many dulled and worn with age and decay. An old pitchfork leaned in one shadowed corner, tines dulled to blunt points from years of use and rust patinaed a dusky orange-red.

The air held the scent of aged wood and dust, carrying a faintly metallic tang of rust. Generations of farmers might have toiled here, working this land, tending to their harvests and livestock with these well-worn tools. Now abandoned, the barn stood as a monument to simpler times and the tireless work of those who came before us. The marks of their labor echoed in the patina of rust and weathered wood surrounding us.

My gaze caught a gleam of silver on the rough wooden surface of the old table, oddly incongruous with the aged and rusting tools scattered about. It appeared to be some sort of clamp or bracket, with two curved bands joined in a circle at one end. A metal lever with a hinged joint pivoted over the open circle as if meant to lock something firmly in place when closed.

Beside me, Matt frowned at Evie in concern. "Are you sure you're all right?" he asked. "You're sweating a lot. Do you want to go outside for some air?"

Evie huffed out an exasperated sigh. "It's a hundred and ten degrees in here, Matt. Of course I'm sweating." She held up the thermometer she'd brought to prove her point. "And again — why is it so hot in here? I don't get it."

My gaze darted around the barn, looking for the source, but nothing seemed amiss. "There's no fire, no electricity," I said with a puzzled frown. "Where's all this heat coming from?"

Evie mopped at her brow with a handkerchief, her breath growing labored in the stifling air. Alarm spiked through me at this sign of distress, memories of past emergencies flashing unbidden through my mind.

"That's it. We need to get out of here now," I said. Striding over, I grasped Evie's arm, pulse racing at the heat radiating off her skin.

"Fine. I'll step out for a minute. Matt, Landon, keep looking while my mother interrupts everything I'm doing to make herself feel better." She shot me an exasperated look but didn't argue as I steered her toward the barn entrance. The blast of cooling air as we stepped outside was an instant relief.

I guided Evie to sit in the shade, waving off her protests that she was okay. Kneeling in front of her, I pressed my wrist to her forehead, pulse slowing in relief at finding her temperature normal. An errant lock of hair had escaped her braid, curling damply against her cheek, and I smoothed it back with a maternal caress.

"I know this is annoying, but you had me worried in there," I said, unable to keep the anxiety from my voice. "I wish you wouldn't push so hard."

"Mom, I'm okay, I promise." Evie smiled and patted my hand to reassure me. "Look, I even brought a water bottle this time." She held it up, uncapped it, and took a long drink. "I'm fine. Just give me a minute." Her physical health had given me countless scares over the years, yet it never seemed to weary her.

Landon emerged from the shadows of the barn, coming to stand beside me in the golden light of late afternoon. He ruffled his fingers through his hair, the dark wavy strands mussed and damp with sweat from the stifling heat within.

He huffed an exasperated breath, casting a bemused glance back at the weathered structure behind us. "Well, that place is just plain weird," he commented with a shake of his head. "It's sweltering in there, hot as the devil's armpit, but I can't figure out why it should be."

Matt joined us a few minutes later, swiping at the sweat beading on his brow. "I don't get it," he said.

Evie frowned, taking another sip of water. "There has to be a reason. Okay, come on. We're smart people. No idea is too off-the-wall. The roof is made of some heat-trapping material?"

Landon shook his head. "Just regular old tin. Wouldn't cause that kind of heat."

"Okay. Underground hot spring?" Evie suggested.

Landon shook his head again. "Not likely. No volcanic activity around here. Our 'hot' springs run around seventy degrees."

"Chianti Hot Springs can get to 113 degrees," I pointed out.

"Chianti Hot Springs is in the Chihuahua desert," Landon said. "Barton Springs is the closest to here and does not get anywhere near 100 degrees."

"Giant compost pile?" Matt offered.

"What, underneath the barn?" I asked. "No source for that. No smell, either."

Evie huffed in frustration. "Buried alien spacecraft?"

I couldn't help but laugh. "I think that only happens in the movies, honey."

"That's what they said in Roswell," Matt told me.

We continued tossing out guesses for several more minutes, each proving more implausible. Buried furnace, massive termite infestation, secret government testing site, fault line with lava. The ideas grew progressively more far-fetched and absurd.

Finally, Landon held up his hands in surrender. "I give up. We have no idea what's causing that heat, and we won't figure it out standing out here. Let's call it a day. I'm not sure we want to be here when it gets dark."

Evie frowned, clearly not ready to give up on solving this new mystery. But as the sun dipped lower, shadows deepened around us, and the logic of leaving before nightfall won out.

We returned to the cat shelter exhausted from the fruitless search of the Miller barn. Darla, bless her heart, looked a little resentful that she'd gotten stuck managing the cat rescue instead of joining our expedition. I couldn't blame her—solving mysteries was far more exciting than the daily tedium of cleaning litter boxes.

"How was the investigation?" she asked, a hint of bitterness in her tone.

"Frustrating," I admitted. "We have no idea what's causing that heat. We threw out every theory we could think of, and none of them make sense."

Darla shrugged, unimpressed by our failure to solve the mystery. "Well, while you guys were out playing Nancy Drew, I've been here managing the shelter. If you don't need anything else..." She let the question hang, brow arched in impatience.

Ouch.

"Darla, thanks for handling everything here today." I tried to infuse my tone with gratitude to smooth her ruffled feathers.

"Yep." With a curt nod, Darla headed off to finish her closing duties as Landon and I climbed the stairs to my second floor office.

We sank into the well-loved armchairs I'd salvaged from a thrift store's bargain bin, the rough, pilled fabric scratching lightly against my fingers. There was no sense in shelling out big bucks for furniture destined to double as a feline scratching post. My office chairs bore the battle scars of their secondhand status, their upholstery clawed and ripped, with tufts of stuffing daring to peek through here and there, each a tribute to an overzealous cat who'd left an indelible mark.

"Quite the puzzle, that barn," Landon commented, shaking his head.

"No kidding. I don't suppose you've stumbled on any brilliant insights since we're back in air-conditioning?" I sighed, leaning back in my chair and tossing the odd metal circle onto my desk.

He snorted. "Afraid not. I'm as stumped as you."

We chatted briefly about possible explanations until a knock at the door interrupted us. "Yes?" I asked.

Darla poked her head in. "Jessa Winthrop is here to see you."

Ugh.

Mayor Jessa Winthrop was the last person I wanted to deal with today. She and I had a... contentious history, and her unexpected visit filled me with anxiety. Still, refusing to see her would probably only make things worse. "Did she say what she wanted?"

"Only that she needed to speak with you urgently."

"Well, send her up, I guess."

Darla ducked out, closing the door behind her with a soft click.

I turned to Landon with a grimace, dread coiling in my stomach at the impending confrontation, just as he reached over to give my hand a reassuring squeeze, his callused fingers rough yet comforting against my skin.

"Whatever nonsense she wants to spout this time, I'm here if you need backup," he said, his eyes warm with understanding. "We're in this together, and that's how this works now. In case you didn't know."

His quiet words of support eased the tension in my shoulders.

Shoulders that tensed back up a few moments later as Mayor Jessa swept into my office in a waft of floral perfume, fixing me with a haughty stare. Ramrod straight and oozing authority, her gaze landed on Landon, and she frowned. "I wished to speak with you privately, Ms. Rockwell."

"Landon can stay," I said, unwilling to face Jessa alone.

She sniffed but didn't argue. "Eleanor, before I go any further, I just want to clarify that I know you came into possession of the Blackwell Plate."

The Blackwell Plate.

I'd never heard it called that, but I knew exactly what she meant.

"I'm sorry, Jessa. I have no idea what you mean." My pulse quickened at her vague reference to the cat platter, but I maintained an innocent expression, hoping she was fishing for information.

Her eyes narrowed. "Don't play games with me. I know Fiona left you that damn plate, and I know what it's capable of. Do you really think she never told her husband?"

"I honestly have no clue what plate you're referring to," I said, raising my hands in helpless confusion, palms upturned. Jessa and I had never gotten along, and there was no way I was going to admit to possessing a magical artifact like the talking cat platter, especially not to her. I did my best to feign utter ignorance, to appear as perplexed as if she'd spoken in a foreign tongue.

We went back and forth for several minutes, Jessa insisting she knew I had some magical artifact and me denying any knowledge of it.

Landon finally stepped in.

"There's clearly some misunderstanding here." His reasonable tone seemed to catch Jessa off guard, and she huffed out an impatient breath. "But it seems you ladies are just going around in circles. If that's all you came by to say, Mayor Winthrop, I think your business is concluded here."

Jessa fixed him with an imperious glare and then turned toward me, scrutinizing me for a long moment. Her eyes gleamed with suspicion, searching for any sign of deception — which I somehow managed to hide. I kept my expression carefully blank, willing my nerves to remain steady under her piercing gaze.

"Despite our significant differences and past, I did not come here to fight with you, Eleanor." Her gaze swung back and forth between me and Landon, eyes gleaming with resentment. "Augusta Walton did not kill

Ben Tyson. If you know anything that could help get her released, you are responsible for sharing that information."

"Mayor, I—"

"And if you fail to do so, you never deserved that damn platter in the first place." With that cryptic parting shot, Jessa swept out of the room in a flurry of floral scent and self-importance.

Chapter Nineteen

THE NEXT MORNING, I SAT IN THE COZY CAT CAFÉ sipping a cup of freshly brewed coffee and trying to make sense of Mayor Winthrop's bizarre visit from the previous night. Her strange insistence that I prove Augusta Walton's innocence in Ben Tyson's murder was perplexing, to say the least. I racked my brain for any shred of an idea why she believed I had any crucial information that could help exonerate Augusta, but I came up with nothing.

The fact that she correctly deduced my interest in the murder did set off a small alarm bell in my mind. Just a small one.

The sound of a jingle at the front door pulled me from my thoughts.

I glanced up just in time to see Dr. Laurie Gray stride in, a tiny Chihuahua nestled securely in her arms. Laurie's unexpected arrival with the little canine didn't

shock me in the least. Given her recent discovery I'd
expected the platter would serve as her secondary
recourse whenever medical mysteries left her scratching
her head.

"Morning, Ellie," Laurie said, making her way
behind the counter. "Do you have a minute?" She let her
voice drop into a soft, conspiratorial whisper. "I was
hoping to use the isolation room."

"Is everything okay?" I asked, nodding at the quiv-
ering bundle of fur in her arms.

"Poor little Nacho here hasn't been himself the past
couple of days. I was hoping that something here might
provide some insight into what's going on." She paused,
looking mildly embarrassed by her unspoken request.
"Something plate-shaped?"

"Come on." I nodded toward the stairs and moved
toward the second floor.

"You know, Ellie, you have so much space in this old
house. Have you ever thought about renting out some
rooms? To, say, a much beloved local vet?" Her eyes
sparkled with mischief. "My practice is bursting at the
seams and I was thinking about moving or building out,
anyway. Being closer to the...thing...would certainly
make accessing it easier when it was needed."

Her proposal, unexpected and somewhat astonish-
ing, caught me flat-footed, leaving me momentarily lost
for words. Letting space in the mansion had never
crossed my mind, yet I had to admit Laurie's suggestion
held merit. Having her nearby could serve as a valuable

asset, saving the new arrivals at the shelter from a more stressful journey to the vet's office.

However, the moment I swung open the door to the isolation room, any remnants of conversation about Laurie's idea splintered into oblivion. Belladonna voiced her displeasure with a harsh hiss, and the pungent, acrid stink of urine waged war on my nostrils.

"What on earth happened here?" I asked, my eyes watering.

Belladonna leaped onto the platter, which glowed at her touch.

"Upon detecting the unmistakable scent of canine upon this object, a surge of fury coursed through me. The smell is your fault for letting that vile beast use our platter," she spat. Her tail lashed in agitation, claws flexing. "The sheer magnitude of urine that Honey and I have had to deploy in order to mask the repugnant odor is so extensive that it is highly probable we have become severely dehydrated in the process!" She glared at the dog in Laurie's arms. "And lo and behold, here you are, introducing yet another canine into my hallowed domain! Such audacity is simply beyond the limits of my patience or tolerance!"

Her patience or tolerance?

What about my patience or tolerance?

My gaze was drawn to the splatter painting the walls — a vibrant declaration in yellow from the black feline. The nostril-scorching stench of urine scrunched up my features in a grimace. Trust Belladonna to broadcast her discontent in the most vividly expressive manner possible.

Even the most domesticated felines could, at times, revert to their primal, outdoor instincts and survival tactics in periods of heightened distress or irritation. Laurie's attempt at using the plate as a canine communication device had apparently set off one such incident, and Belladonna sought to reestablish control over her territory in the cat's instinctual language.

It made sense when you thought about it.

Belladonna tried to drive out the lingering intrusion of 'dog' with an overpowering announcement of 'cat.'

And man, was it overpowering.

I glanced at Honey. He looked nonchalant, but casually supportive.

Laurie's face crinkled in response to the bedlam in the isolation chamber, the picture of guilt painted across her features. "Ellie, I owe you an apology. I should've thought twice before bringing Nacho up here without any heads-up. I didn't—"

"It has nothing to do with that." I waved off her apology. "Don't worry about it. This didn't happen because of Nacho. Belladonna did this long before you brought that little dog in here." I looked at the cat. "And all the pee in the world won't change the fact that you, my dear, will have to learn to adjust. This place won't always revolve around your whims."

She glowered at me but said nothing, tail lashing in sullen silence. Turning her ire on Laurie instead she emitted an angry hiss. "Was this your idea, then? Dogs and plates? Bringing that vile beast into my space?" She swiped a paw at Laurie's arm, claws sheathed but still hard and fast enough to convey her annoyance.

Laurie instinctively recoiled from those outstretched paws, her expression a mixture of remorse and exasperation. "I only wanted to help my patients. I didn't mean to upset you, your highness."

Her wry tone mollified Belladonna not at all.

"Help that disgusting rat elsewhere," Belladonna spat. "The isolation room is for cats alone. I will not have my territory overrun by those foul creatures you call patients. If they are all ill, let them die. The world will be better for it."

I suppressed a grin, seeing Laurie's confused face clouded with embarrassment.

For all her skill as an animal doctor, placating an outraged talking feline was a skill Dr. Gray had yet to master. Belladonna appeared to relish every opportunity to knock overconfident humans down a peg, taking any deviation from her routine or whims as a personal insult.

Though there was a certain entertainment value in watching her high-handed tantrums, her dramatic displays could result in exhausting episodes that severely tested one's endurance.

Laurie turned to Belladonna, features schooled into a placating expression. "Belladonna, might I have permission to use the platter to speak with Nacho? I need to determine what's ailing the poor fellow before I can treat him."

Struggling to contain my laughter, I bit down on my lip as Laurie's vernacular took an amusing turn, veering more toward 'Bridgerton' than her typical speech.

Belladonna's eyes narrowed to contemptuous slits. "Absolutely not. Have you not caused enough trouble for one day? This room reeks of dog thanks to your idiocy, and now you wish to subject me to more indignity by bringing another canine in here?" She lashed her tail, glaring balefully. "Are you foolish humans incapable of listening? I said no dogs allowed!"

Laurie grimaced but persisted. "Might we strike a bargain then? There must be something I can offer you in exchange for use of the platter that won't inspire another...eye-watering outburst." Her gaze flitted to the spray-soaked walls.

"My urine smells of roses, not that your dull human senses could appreciate it." Belladonna's eyes narrowed, but a calculating gleam entered them. "And what will you offer me in exchange for this favor? I am not inclined to allow more infernal dogs into my space without proper compensation."

Laurie grimaced but seemed to breath a sigh of relief at the opening for negotiation. "What would appease you, Your Majesty? State your terms."

Belladonna sniffed haughtily, tail twitching as she pondered her options. "My demands are thus: a supply of sweetened heavy cream shall be left daily in the isolation room, along with catnip toys for amusement. Also, a scratching post topped with sisal rope, and a better plush cat bed for napping. And when I require attention or brushing, you shall come at my summons."

"Cats are lactose intolerant, Belladonna, and sugar is not good for you," Laurie pointed out.

"Sweetened. Heavy. Cream," Belladonna repeated as though it was a warning.

Laurie glanced at me, her eyes wide at the string of imperious requests. I shrugged. She nodded. "On days I need to use it, fine. I agree to your terms, O demanding one. But only when I need to use the platter."

Belladonna chirped in satisfaction, gazing up at Laurie through half-lidded eyes. "The platter is yours to use then, for the next few moments." She looked at Honey. "Come along."

Just like that, Belladonna's wrath had lifted, her temper soothed by the prospect of gifts and pampering. The cat hopped down from her perch and sauntered out the door, tail held high, leaving a bemused vet in her wake.

Laurie shook off her surprise and set Nacho on the platter, reviewing the list of Belladonna's demands with a wry chuckle. "That cat drives a hard bargain. But her price is one I'll gladly pay for continued access to the platter without this room smelling of ammonia."

Nacho gazed about in bewilderment as the platter beneath him began to glow an amber brown. His thoughts tumbled out in a rush, voice high and excitable. "Where am I? What is this place? It smells of cat, am I in hell? Why can I hear my thoughts?" He trembled, peering up at Laurie with confusion and fear in his eyes.

Laurie stroked his ears. "It's all right, Nacho. This is Eleanor's cat shelter — no, not hell. You can talk because of magic of the plate. It's allowing us to communicate. There's no need to fear anything here, I promise."

"Not even that demon cat? I think I should fear the demon cat." Nacho cocked his head, trying to make sense of her words. "Magic? A talking plate? My thoughts have never spoken aloud before...are you a witch?" His questions tumbled over each other in his anxiety and excitement. "Do all humans command such strange magic? Why did you bring me to this place filled with cats? Have I been bad? I don't wish to stay here, it's scary!"

The shrill, rapid-fire stream of his chatter was so characteristically Chihuahua. Nacho voiced each fleeting thought and emotion that darted through his nimble yet perplexed tiny brain. Laurie provided a patient, serene audience, letting his verbal cascade flow until he finally hit a pause.

"You have not been bad at all," she soothed. "I only brought you here to help figure out why you haven't been feeling well. Once you tell me, we'll go."

Nacho blinked up at her, still rattled by the unfamiliar experience of hearing his inner voice aloud but reassured by her explanation. "Not staying with scary cats? Truly?" At Laurie's nod, his trembling eased, tongue lolling in a grin. "You will fix me up, and then we go home? I like that plan!" His mood turned on a coin, anxiety shifting to optimism in a heartbeat. "I like home. I want to go home."

Laurie smiled, used to her little patient's mercurial shifts between emotion. "That's the plan. Now, tell me — what seems to have been bothering you these past few days? Your belly is a bit bloated, your mom said you've been lethargic and then very energetic and then lethargic again. Your blood work looks fine, though. Is there anything you can tell me?"

Convinced that his departure from the cat-ridden shelter was imminent, Nacho embarked on a fervent narration of his symptoms, his words tumbling out in another enthusiastic torrent. "I think I've figured out the cause of my strange feelings." Nacho squirmed, his eyes, a blend of guilt and excitement, fixated on Laurie. "I discovered Daddy's stash of giant marshmallows in the garage and I ate them!" His tail wagged in rhythm to his confession, a self-satisfied grin on his face despite the admission. "Well, not all at once. I've been making daily visits."

Laurie blinked, caught off guard by this revelation. "You ate an entire bag of marshmallows?"

"Giant marshmallows."

She struggled to keep a straight face, lips twitching.

"Nacho, those are not meant for dogs. No wonder your tummy has been upset."

Nacho's ears drooped, abashed by her scolding tone. "They were so squishy and tasty though. And Daddy left them out...I couldn't help myself. Am I going to get sick?" His bravado crumbled into anxiety at the thought. "Am I going to die? Can marshmallows kill me?"

"Maybe you should have worried about that before you ate them."

Nacho looked stricken.

Laurie smiled, unable to hold back laughter any longer. "No. You won't die. Limit treats to those meant for dogs next time!" Nacho's mood brightened at once. She scratched behind his ears, and he leaned into her touch, corners of his mouth lifting in response.

"No sick? I won't have to see the vet more?" At Laurie's chuckle and head shake, he yipped in delight. "Good! No more tummy troubles then. Marshmallows will be treats for good boys from now on."

"That's not what you said," I told Laurie.

"No, but it's a Chihuahua. Even with both of us speaking English you can expect things to get lost in translation." With an amused shake of her head, Laurie lifted our anxious little friend. "Ellie, you really should think about what I said. About my moving my practice here, I mean. This plate just saved this little guy a bunch of needles, and it saved his parents quite a bit of money on unnecessary tests."

"I'll think on it. The extra help could be useful, and

it might help the newer cats to have a vet on the premises just in case."

The pungent, biting aroma of urine caused my nose to crinkle. A formidable cleaning operation lay ahead, not just for me but likely a few volunteers as well. I grabbed the platter as Laurie thanked me again for its use.

"No problem," I told her as we walked out of the room. "I just want to drop it off in my office so I can get one of the volunteers to start cleaning. I'm glad we can afford hazard pay."

"I don't know how I managed without it before. The plate, I mean. That thing is going to be invaluable." She smiled, following me across the veranda to my office.

"You managed because you're a great vet."

"Yep. But I'm better with that thing."

Upon opening my office door, I was greeted by the sight of Belladonna and Honey perched on my desk like twin sentinels. My eyes instinctively scanned the floor and the walls, hunting for any hint of puddles or marks, but all seemed clean. I drew a deep breath, releasing it in a sigh of relief as no trace of ammonia tainted the air. I then fixed Belladonna with a firm gaze.

I expect no repeats of the mess you created back there. One meltdown a day is more than sufficient." The ebony feline returned my stare with an expression of pure innocence, as though she were the epitome of tranquility itself. As the reigning monarch of all feline drama queens, her expressions were a masterclass in inscrutability.

Laurie chuckled and moved past me into the office, reaching out to give Belladonna an appreciative ear rub. "You've caused quite enough chaos for one day, haven't you?"

Belladonna leaned into her touch, purring with delight at the attention. Her mood swings were as swift as they were unpredictable, her fury dissipating as quickly as it had flared at the slightest hint of affection or compliment.

I placed the platter on my desk.

The moment I withdrew my hand, Honey advanced, his claws making a soft clicking noise against the crystal-like surface. In response, the platter began to shimmer with an amber glow around his paws. His golden gaze met mine, a note of confusion in the cat's usually somber eyes. "Why do you have one of Leo Barnett's honey gates?"

A frown creased my forehead, his question throwing me into confusion. "A honey gate? I'm sorry, but I'm not following you."

Honey huffed, and the magical glow surrounding his paws flickered momentarily. Taking a confident step forward, he inclined his head toward the silver trinket I had discovered in the old Miller barn. "That's a honey gate. It carries the scent of Leo Barnett. I'm not sure how it ended up here."

I followed Honey's gaze to the small silver object I

had found. A honey gate? I picked up the metal piece, turning it over in my hands. "What's a honey gate?" I asked.

Honey sat down, wrapping his tail around his paws with a sigh. "A honey gate is a simple valve used by beekeepers to control the flow of honey from an extractor or from storage," he explained in his usual solemn tones. "When opened, it allows honey to pour out so it can be bottled. This one smells of Leo Barnett."

Laurie came to stand beside me, peering over my shoulder at the object in my hands. "You're sure it's Leo's?" she asked, echoing my own silent question.

Honey sniffed, whiskers twitching. "I know Leo's scent well. I was Ben Tyson's cat. Before he died and sent me to the shelter." A hint of wistfulness entered the ginger tom's voice at the memory of his former owner. "Leo worked for Ben. I remember the way he smelled."

"Where did you find this?" Laurie asked.

I set the honey gate down on my desk. "The old Miller barn by the park. We were poking around yesterday looking for anything the police might have missed." I turned to my computer, typed in *honey extractor*, and landed on a beekeeping store. "Mario said that Ben was killed with a honey extractor, but that...I don't see how." The web site showed us a large stainless steel pot with three legs and a crank on top. "According to this, you put frames in it to get the honey out. How could someone have killed him with this?"

We scrolled up and down the page scanning the extracting tools.

"There," Laurie said, and pointed. "That's the only thing on this page you could hold in your hand and beat someone with."

Laurie was right.

It was an uncapping roller, a strange instrument that resembled an old-fashioned washing wringer.

On the large extractors, it appeared the beekeeper would drop a honeycomb frame into it and slide it between the rollers inside the metal tub by cranking the handle to spin them. The sharp teeth on the rollers would pierce the delicate wax caps on the honeycomb, leaving the honey exposed. The stray wax pieces fell through into a tray below the rollers, leaving the honey-comb intact but ready for extraction.

The uncapping roller did the same thing, only manually.

As I flipped through the beekeeping tools, my eyes fell on the tools for storage.

I stared in shock.

"I know what's happening at the Miller barn," I whispered. I snatched up the honey gate from my desk. "Come on. Let's drop that dog off and get out there. I want to make sure I know what I'm talking about. Because if I do, I might have solved this case."

Chapter Twenty

I was back on the hiking trail that wound through the thickets of oak and cedar trees, their gnarled branches intertwining to form a canopy overhead that protected us from the midday sun. Dappled sunlight filtered through, painting the path ahead in patches of gold. We hiked in comfortable silence.

After a few minutes, Laurie glanced at me, her finely plucked eyebrows raised in a questioning arch. "So, will you explain why I'm exercising on my lunch hour?"

"This isn't exercising."

"It's hiking. That's exercising."

I hesitated, uncertain if I should share my thoughts just yet. It wasn't anything concrete or momentous, not yet. Little offhand remarks and subtle hints that various people had said over the past weeks were coming together in my mind, pieces of a puzzle slowly joining to form a hazy image that I couldn't quite make out.

For example, Landon's story about the Millers and how they survived the 1997 tornado in a "fancy" underground shelter. At the time, his story seemed an innocuous bit of small talk.

But now I wondered if there wasn't more to it.

After all, installing a tornado shelter under a rambling three-story farmhouse that had stood for generations would be nearly impossible. But installing one under the old barn out back, with its cavernous interior and dirt floor, would be easy as pie.

And if there really was a secret tornado shelter hidden beneath the dusty floorboards of that barn, it would be the perfect place to discreetly hide anything from prying eyes. A 'fancy' shelter might even have amenities like electricity, ventilation, and temperature control — which could account for the stifling, unseasonable indoor heat.

My suspicions grew like weeds, threatening to choke out any last shred of ordinary logic or good sense, and I could be wrong. I didn't want to say anything definitive until I had a chance to at least confirm one of my suspicions.

"I'm still piecing some things together," I said finally. "I saw something yesterday that might explain some things, but I want to check it out again before making wild guesses. Suffice it to say we're going to the barn to see if we can spot a tornado shelter entrance."

Laurie nodded, used to my propensity for keeping things close to the chest until I felt confident enough to share them. "Fair enough." She glanced over at me again. "So, have you given any more thought to my proposal?"

A frown creased my brow. "Are you asking if I've given it more thought since we traveled here from the house a mere thirty minutes back? Nope, nothing."

"Honestly, Ellie, how long do you need to think about it?" Laurie pressed on as we walked, pointing out the benefits. "You'd have a vet on call all day. The shelter could offer free spay and neuter services with me right there. The non-profit would get the income from my rent instead of some wealthy developer I never see who's likely just using it to buy his tenth sports car."

I did see the merits in her arguments.

I mean, who wouldn't?

The free services Laurie wanted to offer would help curb unwanted litters and support the local community. Having a vet on-site would provide peace of mind, enabling us to accept more medically fragile residents. And the steady income stream in the form of rent would provide financial stability for the shelter beyond Fiona Blackwell's gift (considerable though it was.)

"It's not a bad idea, but we'd have to make sure there's adequate space and facilities for a vet clinic. And we'd need to ensure the zoning allows for it. I don't want the shelter slapped with code violations or fines." I turned to Laurie with a wry smile. "You'll also have to promise not to wake us up at 3 a.m. for an emergency platter call."

"Can't promise that. If it's an emergency, the

animals come first. But early morning anything won't be my first choice," Laurie said with a chuckle. "Don't worry. I plan to keep regular business hours." Her expression turned earnest. "Look, I don't mean to be a pain about this, Ellie, but I have to decide whether to renew my lease in the next few days, so time's really of the essence here."

"You know what? Let's just do it," I said. With careful planning, it just might work out for everyone involved, two-legged and four-legged alike.

"Really? That's awesome," Laurie replied, her smile returning. She gave my arm an affectionate squeeze. "Thank you, Ellie. This means a lot to me."

I nodded, hoping we could make it work.

Not too long after, the ancient Miller barn loomed into sight. I swiveled toward Laurie, caution lining my words. "Every time we visited here, that barn has felt like a veritable oven, so don't linger too much, or you could overheat. Get air if you need it. Drink water." I held up the water bottles I had brought.

Laurie frowned. "How hot is 'incredibly hot'?"

I grimaced. "You'll see."

We made our way inside the barn. Almost immediately, a wave of stifling heat enveloped us. Laurie pulled a face. "Jeez, you weren't kidding. It's like we stepped into a preheated oven."

"Told you. Remember, we're looking for something that would lead to a tornado or storm shelter," I said, not knowing the difference.

We started our search, examining the floor and walls for any indication of a hidden door or access to a subterranean refuge. The floor, littered with hay, was challenging to navigate — secrets aren't easily spotted in such a mess.

We spent a few minutes looking until Laurie's voice pierced the silence.

"Ellie, I think I found something," she announced, stooping beside a pile of old blankets in the far-off corner. As I bridged the distance, she whisked the blankets away to reveal a concealed trapdoor. Its wooden face was tucked neatly into the barn floor.

"Nice work," I said.

"It actually feels hotter over here," she said.

"There might be a reason for that," I told her as she grasped the iron ring handle and pulled. The trapdoor opened with a groan of protest, revealing a set of concrete steps descending into darkness. A wave of even hotter air rose up to greet us. "I think this might be storing honey."

"Honey?" Laurie peered down into the inky black hole. "Do we have a flashlight?"

I shook my head. "I have the flashlight on my phone."

"Next time, we need to bring a flashlight." Laurie glanced at me, eyebrows raised. "Shall we?"

"Let's go," I said.

With caution guiding our every step, we navigated our way down the steep concrete staircase. The faint illumination from our phones struggled to penetrate the thick blanket of darkness.

When we reached the stairs' foot, my shirt clung to my back, dampened by sweat.

At the base of the stairs, we were greeted by a second door which, upon opening, revealed what appeared to be the tornado shelter that had once served as a safe haven for the Miller family over two decades ago. It was a single room, roughly fifteen by fifteen feet in size. As I swept the harsh, sterile light from my phone across the room, I whispered, "I was right. I knew it."

"Right about what? What is all this?" Laurie asked.

The shelter was filled with an odd assortment of items — stacks of beehive frames, bags of sugar, uncapped bottles of honey. In the center of the room were several honey storage tanks, hulking cylindrical vessels that stood nearly four feet tall, constructed of gleaming stainless steel.

"It's an underground honey...um, thing," I said, shifting my attention to the wall. I located a light switch and flipped it on. "The heat in here is from those tanks. See the cords? They have heaters to heat the honey," I explained, gesturing in their direction and pointing to the black cords trailing from their side. "The space is too small for the tanks and the heat. Add the lack of air circulation down here, and you get this stifling inferno."

Laurie grimaced, wiping beads of sweat from her brow. "This place is unbearable. I'm turning off those heaters before we bake to death." She strode over to the cords trailing from the honey tanks and unplugged them all. "Hopefully, that will cool things down a bit in here."

As Laurie busied herself with the heaters, I took it upon myself to survey the perimeter of the modest room. Tucked away in a corner, a mound of discarded clothes drew my attention. I reached down and picked up a shirt from the top of the pile. Unfolding it, I was met with the bold logo "Ben's Honey Pot" emblazoned across the back — a staff shirt.

For Ben Tyson's store.

"I think this place was set up by Leo Barnett to process the honey he's been selling at the farmers' market. Look—" I pointed to the beehive frames stacked in the corner, each stamped with the Tyson name. "Leo was stealing frames from Ben's farm. All this honey — it's stolen."

Laurie's eyes widened. "Wow. I need to call Mario — the police clearly never found this place." She pulled out her phone but frowned at the screen. "No signal." She strode toward the trapdoor, pausing on the bottom step. "I'll run up and call from outside."

I nodded as Laurie ascended the steps two at a time and disappeared above.

Had Ben discovered Leo's theft and threatened to expose him? Have him arrested? Is that what led to Ben's murder — Leo's desperate act to silence him and keep this illegal operation hidden?

Just then, my gaze landed on a black garbage bag tucked haphazardly behind an empty honey tank against the wall. It was a bag identical to the one Evie had spotted in Tom Coleman's possession, possibly the same bag she'd seen him carry into the park—and subsequently into this barn.

I frowned.

How would Tom Coleman know about this place?

And why would he bring something here?

He must have been here in this room while Matt and Evie were upstairs. That's why they never saw him in the barn, and they never saw him leave.

I moved toward the bag, curiosity pulling me in like a magnet. With a swift tug, the bag fell over, releasing its contents onto the concrete floor. A clatter echoed around the room as an uncapping knife and an uncapping roller tumbled out. The blade's sharp edge and the roller's jagged surface gleamed ominously.

But it was the stains on the tools that truly sent a jolt of shock through me.

They were dark and dried, bearing an uncanny resemblance to blood.

Why would Tom Coleman stash bloody bee tools in Leo Barnett's concealed honey processing hideout? Was he covering for his wife, Nina?

Did she kill Ben?

Was he framing Leo?

Lost in my thoughts, I was still eyeing the objects when the shelter's door swung open with startling abruptness. Whirling around, I found Laurie descending the stairs, her hands raised in surrender and a grave expression etched on her face.

"Stay calm. No sudden movements," she warned in a hushed, urgent tone. Her eyes darted over the bag and its contents, the dried crimson stains on the tools not escaping her attention. She sucked in a sharp breath, her eyes widening slightly. "He's armed."

A crease formed between my brows, confusion, and alarm intermingling in my features. "Who's armed?" The words tumbled out of my mouth, my voice barely above a whisper.

❧❦❧

From behind Laurie, Tom Coleman materialized through the doorway, his lips twisted into an unsettling smile. He gripped a pistol tightly in his right hand, its muzzle ominously aimed at Laurie's back.

"Good afternoon, ladies," Tom greeted us, his voice carrying a deceptive cordiality that did little to conceal the threat he posed. "Perfect weather for a leisurely walk, wouldn't you agree?"

Laurie's eyes were wide with terror, her hands suspended in the air. The sight of the firearm caused me to inhale sharply, my heart pounding in an insistent rhythm against my ribcage. A grim thought crossed my mind — if I managed to get out of this alive, Landon would undoubtedly never let me hear the end of it.

"I do apologize for the intrusion. But when I saw the good doctor here, and you were nowhere to be found, it was clear to me the two of you discovered Leo's little hideaway, and, well—I couldn't have that."

His seemingly polite demeanor failed to mask the madness glinting in his eyes.

Tom gestured at Laurie with the pistol. "I wish the cat women hadn't dragged you into this, Dr. Gray. You've always been a valuable member of the Tablerock community, and it seems like such a waste to have to kill you." He pivoted to face me, his smile unwavering. "But you and your daughter just couldn't stop poking around, could you?"

A wave of panic crashed over me. I glanced briefly at Laurie, my eyes silently conveying an apology.

Laurie nodded slowly, her face pale. "All right, how about we just calm down? I don't know what you think you caught us doing, and I really don't have any idea what any of it has to do with you—"

"You didn't tell her your daughter and her boyfriend followed me out here the other day?" Tom asked me. He motioned toward the black plastic bag on the floor at my feet. "Even if you haven't put it together yet, Miss Ellie, once you found that bag and saw the bloody tools, I can't believe it would take long for you to realize who killed Ben Tyson."

An image flickered through my mind, Tom

assertively grasping his wife, Nina, in the middle of the restaurant. "You did."

"No, Ellie, I don't believe he did," Laurie countered with conviction. "He wouldn't do something like that. He and Ben were friends. Sort of."

"Were we?" Tom's eyes widened, and his expression was the picture of innocence. "Did I kill Ben Tyson?"

"Yes, you did," I said, my voice wavering slightly. "You killed Ben Tyson because Nina used to be involved with him. Or was involved with him. And you knew you could frame Leo Barnett, considering his history with Ben. You'd eliminate the competition and become Tablerock's only honey producer."

Tom's smile faded, his congenial mask slipping away to reveal the menace beneath. "Clever girl—"

"I'm half a century old, Tom," I told him hotly. "I'm no girl."

"I didn't truly suspect dear Nina of having an affair — or that the police would be so stupid that they'd arrest Augusta. Ben simply posed a threat to my business that needed to be eliminated. Ben could have won that stupid lawsuit he filed against my wife, and lord knows she would never shut her mouth. Leo Barnett's history made him the perfect scapegoat. Framing him allowed me to kill two birds with one stone, so to speak."

A chill ran down my spine at his callous admission. Tom Coleman was utterly ruthless and without remorse.

"As for you, Doctor, I do apologize for what I'm about to have to do. But dead bodies can attract atten-

tion, even when the police have a suspect in custody."
Tom motioned at Laurie with the pistol again. "Since
you discovered Leo's little operation here, well—loose
ends must be tied up."

Panic surged through me. He was going to kill us. I
had to do something, and fast—but what? I was
unarmed, and Tom had a gun.

Laurie's eyes were still wide, her face still pale. But
her voice remained steady as she said, "There's no need
for violence, Tom. Ellie and I will keep your secret. You
have my word."

Tom let out a humorless laugh. "My dear doctor, do
you take me for a fool? I can't have the two of you
running around knowing what really happened to Ben
Tyson. Why, you might let it slip to the police, and then
where would I be?" He shook his head. "No, it's best if
this little mystery disappears with the two of you. A
tragic accident, suffocation in an old tornado shelter.
Perhaps a fire in the old Miller barn. Leo killed you both
when you discovered his secret. No one will question it
— Mario knew you were poking around like Cagney and
Lacey."

My mind raced as Tom rambled on about ways to
stage our deaths.

We had to distract him and get that gun away
before he could carry out his sinister plans. But how?
Tom's hand remained steady, the pistol barrel unwaver-
ingly pointed at Laurie. He might just squeeze the
trigger with one false step, one hasty action. I had to

think of something fast, or we would never leave this place alive.

As Tom rambled on, an idea struck me.

The honey tanks.

Their heaters were unplugged, but the heat in this place was still incredible. If I could reach them without Tom noticing and push them over, the honey likely had enough residual heat to burn him. It would distract him, at least. Give us time to make a run for it.

I hoped.

While Tom pontificated, I caught Laurie's eye and gestured at the tanks, hoping she understood my plan. Her eyes widened, but she gave a quick nod.

Laurie and I hurled our weight against the nearest honey tank without missing a beat. It wobbled precariously before crashing to the floor, its contents — thick, golden honey — splashing out in a tidal wave across the warm concrete floor toward Tom Coleman.

Caught off guard, Tom stared at us in shock, a bellow of rage erupting from his lips. I was afraid he would reflexively squeeze the trigger of the gun he held, but it appeared the pain of the burns on his ankles already commanded his full attention. As the second tank toppled over, his screams of agony pierced the air as the scorching liquid splashed against his skin

Laurie and I ran around him and bolted for the exit, stopping long enough to close and lock the door. We scrambled up the steps and out of the shelter, slamming the trapdoor down behind us

As we stumbled out of the barn, our lungs gasping for fresh air, the muffled echoes of Tom's tormenting screams echoed faintly behind us.

We darted into the open, only to run headlong into Mario, Landon, and the Tablerock Police. The sudden appearance of familiar faces, the scent of fresh air, and the sound of our ragged breaths starkly contrasted with the sticky-sweet horror we'd just left behind.

Chapter Twenty-One

Mayor Jessa strode into the cat café, her unsensible high heels clicking briskly against the wooden floor. Her gaze swept the cozy interior, lingering briefly on the cats lounging in various perches and nests.

With purposeful steps, Jessa made her way to the counter where I stood cleaning up after the lunch rush. "Ellie, do you have a moment? I wanted to talk to you about something important."

Her tone was uncharacteristically polite.

I glanced up from wiping down the counter, surprised by the seriousness etched into the mayor's usually fake-friendly features. Apprehension stirred within me. After the past few days, the appearance of the vindictive mayor that claimed to know the secret of the magic plate did little to settle my nerves.

"How can I help you?" I asked, keeping my tone light. I tossed the rag into a bin beneath the counter.

Jessa leaned in, folding her arms in front of her. "I wanted to speak with you in person about the horrible events of the past few days. As you know, the entire town has been shocked by Ben Tyson's murder, Tom's arrest, and the drama surrounding it." She paused, hesitating. "The truth is, Ellie, I wasn't sure that Augusta would get herself out of the fix she was in without your help, and friend or not, she's important to wedding event bookings for her cakes."

I stared at the mayor.

"Which boosts tourism dollars," she added (as if that clarified things.)

I frowned, uncertain where Jessa was going with this line of conversation. After Tom Coleman's attempt to kill Laurie and me, her tourism concern seemed... oddly misplaced.

"With that in mind," Jessa continued, "the city council and I were hoping you might consider...well, downplaying certain details about the case when speaking with any media." She gave me a cold smile. "You know, focus on the fact that the killer was brought to justice, but avoid mentioning the...messier parts of how it all unfolded. Like the fact that the police seemed completely unable to solve the case. Or that Augusta was arrested at all."

After everything we had been through (and Augusta had been through,) the notion that Jessa cared more about tourism dollars than the state of her citizens sparked annoyance within me. I folded my arms across my chest, leveling Jessa with an even gaze.

"With all due respect, Mayor, I'm not planning on doing any interviews." I shook my head. "While I believe the public deserves the truth about what happened, not a sanitized version meant to make our town appear safer or quainter than it is, I won't be volunteering that information to the press."

Jessa's smile faded, a flicker of irritation passing over her features before she reined it in. She inhaled slowly, considering my words. "You and I both know there's a lot of things about this case that we need the public to remain unaware of, Eleanor. So don't act like you're looking down at me from your high horse." Her tone took on a sharp quality. "If you're taking over for Fiona Blackwell, however, you'll need to learn to keep your trap shut."

If I'm taking over for Fiona Blackwell?

What on earth did that mean?

I gave her a wan smile. "I'm sorry, Mayor Jessa, but I have no idea what you're talking about." I spread my hands out on the counter, meeting her gaze directly. "Whatever Fiona Blackwell did or didn't do when she was alive, I couldn't say. I barely knew the woman."

"And yet you have all her money," Jessa shot back.

No, the cats had her money.

And to be more specific, one particular cat — who chose that moment to leap up onto the counter like a feline ninja, puff herself up to twice her size, and let out an angry hiss in the mayor's direction.

I scooped her up under her belly and dropped her onto the floor with a thump.

"Horrible animal," Jessa muttered.

Belladonna stalked off, tail high in the air, no doubt planning how to get revenge for her wounded pride.

With a resigned nod, Jessa Winthrop stood up straight, adjusting her blazer. "Very well. If that's how you want to play it, then that's how we'll play it, Ms. Rockwell." She sighed. "I hope you know what you're doing."

I didn't.

But only because I didn't know what the woman was talking about.

The mayor turned on her heel and strode out of the café, the door swinging shut behind her with a jingle of the bell. I watched her go, wondering what she meant... and what her intentions were.

Later that afternoon, familiar faces gathered in my office — Josephine, Laurie, Evie, and Mario. It brought a sense of comfort after the rather traumatic events of the previous day (and a sense of stability and normality after the weird visit from the mayor.).

We sank into the well-worn, plush armchairs and sofa.

Evie squeezed my hand, her bright eyes shining with relief and pride. "I still can't believe what you and Laurie dealt with yesterday. I swear, you're the bravest women I know. I am a little jealous, though — that's twice you wound up in the center of this big drama at just the right time."

"She solved a murder at the point of a gun," Laurie pointed out. "Don't envy that, Evie. That's not the ideal way to do things."

"Laurie's right," I said, uncomfortable with the praise. "It's more like we were fortunate. I'm not sure what would have happened if Laurie hadn't managed to call Mario when she went outside."

"Nothing would have happened," Evie said.

"She's right," Laurie agreed. "We already had him honey-roasted."

Josephine sighed, folding her glasses briskly and tucking them into her jacket pocket. "Well, I'm not patting either of you on the back. That was incredibly reckless. The next time you get a hankering to poke around in abandoned barns or confront murder suspects, call the police first or, better yet, call the lawyer you elected as a go-between to give information to the police. Which you didn't do." Her acerbic words carried the potent bite of concerned relief. "I can't believe you just went off without calling anyone. Reckless."

"We didn't go there expecting to confront anyone," I protested, exchanging an incredulous look with Laurie. "We just wanted to look around the old Miller place again. Well, I did. I knew there had to be a reason for that weird heat, and I wanted to find out before I went to the police. They'd already been there, and they hadn't found anything." My eyes went skyward of their own accord. "You would have done the same thing, Josephine, and you know it."

Josephine snorted at that. "Yes, because strolling into overheated abandoned barns in the middle of nowhere that are connected to a murder is what people do for fun."

I couldn't argue with that.

Trouble did seem to have an uncanny way of finding us lately.

"Look, whether we should or shouldn't have, we did, and it worked out. I'm just glad Mario showed up when he did," Laurie said. "If he hadn't gotten my call and Landon hadn't been coming to check on Ellie —"

"We would have been fine," I insisted. "As you pointed out, we'd already dealt with the situation. I'll admit honey-roasting a murderer isn't a typical way of dealing with a life or death situation, but it worked out well."

"Speaking of Landon, where is he?" Josephine peered around the room, scanning for any sign of the burly contractor's familiar figure. "I would have thought he'd be hovering like a mother hen over his new girl-friend after yesterday's excitement."

"Girlfriend?" Laurie asked, shocked. "Who's Landon's girlfriend?"

"She is." Josephine pointed at me. "Evie told me."

"Since when?"

A faint blush rose in my cheeks at Josephine's statement. After everything Landon and I had shared, his absence felt conspicuous and stung more than I cared to admit. "Landon and I just agreed to start dating. I'm too old to be anyone's girlfriend," I insisted. "And he had some work obligations today that couldn't be rescheduled."

"Uh huh." Josephine's eyes gleamed with amusement, seeing through my pathetic denial attempt. "Well, at least you ladies handled that madman and got out of that death trap shelter in one piece, thanks to your quick thinking. Tom Coleman is behind bars where he belongs."

"And we have Ellie and Laurie to thank for that," Mario said. "If only we had looked into Tom Coleman more closely. We looked at Nina, yes, but not Tom. The signs were there — we just didn't put them together in time."

"Don't blame yourself, Mario," Laurie said. "No one suspected Tom. He hid in plain sight."

"Plain site my rear end," Josephine said. "I think your boss really needs to check his misogyny. You laser-focused on the women in this little drama and ignored all the murderous, criminal men. Why was that, do you think?"

Mario's eyes slid over to Josephine, but he shut his mouth.

"Well, the important part is that the two-woman

crime-solving team of Mom and Laurie figured it out in the end," Evie said. "And both Leo and Tom are in jail."

"I think we all had a lot to do with that. It wasn't just me and Laurie."

As unorthodox — and slightly bumblingly dangerous — as our methods might have been, we had somehow helped crack the case wide open. With the threat of Tom Coleman eliminated, I hoped Tablerock might finally return to the sleepy peace we had known before Fiona passed away — at least for a little while.

The familiar jingle of bells chimed from below, announcing a new arrival to the cat café. I glanced at Evie in surprise. "Aren't you supposed to be working the closing shift at the café today?"

Evie shrugged. "Technically, yes. But Matt's handling it." She grinned, eyes glinting with mischief. "Come on. After everything that's happened, we deserve to get out of here for a while. Let's go get a celebratory lunch at the Grackle Tavern."

The others chimed in, voicing their enthusiastic agreement with Evie's suggestion. We had certainly earned a respite from the chaos and drama of the past few days.

As the group exited my office and descended the stairs, Evie slowed her steps to match mine. She slid her arm around my shoulders, giving me a quick side hug.

"What was that for?" I asked, touched by this spontaneous show of affection.

Evie smiled. "Just glad you're you. My crazy, unstoppable, mystery-solving mom." She laughed. "Who else would I get into so much trouble with?"

I had to laugh at that, draping an arm around her waist in return. "You're stuck with me, kid," I said, and together we made our way down the stairs to join the others. However unorthodox, our mother-daughter sleuthing team made quite the pair.

A knock at my office door startled me out of my work-induced stupor. I glanced at the clock, surprised to find it was already after 7 p.m.

"Come in."

Landon pushed open the door to my office, his hands nonchalantly tucked in his pockets. The usual contours of his face relaxed into a smile upon spotting me. "Evening, Ellie. Am I interrupting something important?"

"Not at all. Please, make yourself at home." As he stepped into my office, a cloud of cedar and sandalwood fragrance wafted in, filling the room with its soothing and familiar scent. The aroma clung to the air like a warm embrace, bringing a momentary calm. He reached down, held out his hand, and guided me out from behind my desk to the sofa in my office...

Where an unexpectedly tense silence descended.

When Landon materialized at the ill-fated honey-roasting yesterday, he'd remained uncharacteristically quiet as chaos swirled around us. The carpenter stood beside me in silence as the police and paramedics escorted a handcuffed Tom Coleman from the premises, and Mario recorded everything Laurie and I had seen.

And, as if ironically summoned by some unspoken signal, Leo had conveniently appeared, ready to be apprehended for the felonious theft of Ben Tyson's honey.

When finished, I had braced myself for Landon's inevitable lecture on recklessly hurling myself into yet another dangerous situation, but no reproach passed his lips.

Not a single word, not a hint of chastisement.

His silence was confusing, leaving me wondering what thoughts were swirling behind those expressive eyes. An unsettling void lingered, a nagging question mark hanging suspended in the air between us.

A void I suspected was about to be filled.

Landon cleared his throat. "I wanted to check on you. After everything that happened yesterday..." His voice trailed off, gaze searching mine. "Are you okay?"

"I'm doing better. Really, I'm fine. I'll be all right. You don't need to worry about me."

"Of course, I'm worried about you." Landon reached over to take my hands, callused fingers intertwining with mine. "Do you know how much you mean to me, Ellie?" He paused, hesitating. "Sometimes I wonder whether you think I'm just some casual guy that doesn't think much of relationships. I'm not some casual guy, Ellie."

"Of course not. Of course, I don't." The words came out barely above a whisper. "I'd never be with you if I thought that was the type of man you are."

Landon's eyes brightened, a smile tugging at the corner of his mouth. "Yeah?"

I nodded, giving his hands a gentle squeeze. "I know what you're going to say, too. I should have called you before Laurie and I went to the Miller barn, and I should have at least called the moment we found that trap door." I sighed. "You're right. I should have. I should have called everyone. I just didn't want to be wrong and waste everyone's time."

"I would never feel any time spent with you is wasted." Landon gazed at me earnestly. "I told you. Whatever comes, we'll face it together. But for us to do that, Eleanor Rockwell, you have to let me know what you're running headlong into."

"I'm sorry. You're right. I'm just used to doing things on my own."

Landon's smile lit up the room as he leaned in close, his breath warm against my cheek. "Well, get unused to it, ma'am," he murmured, lips grazing my ear.

Oh my.

When his mouth found mine, all lingering doubts and worries faded, leaving behind the blissful realization of how perfectly his arms seemed to encircle me — as if I had found a place I was always meant to be.

Landon's kiss was a slow, lingering whisper against my lips, each movement carrying a depth of consideration as the stubble on his face grazed my skin. It was rough yet oddly captivating, adding an alluring contrast to his tender sweetness. The man was a thrilling dance of contradictions—soft and hard, gentle and intense—all at once. His touch stirred a whirlpool of feelings within me.

Landon leaned in to rest his forehead against mine when we finally broke apart. His eyes were mere inches away, bright with affection as a smile played about his lips. "How's that for a start at getting unused to going it alone?"

"Not bad, for a start," I teased, rewarded by a rumble of laughter escaping his chest.

Landon raised a brow, his smile turning sly. "Well, if that's your way of asking for more practice—"

I swatted playfully at his chest. "Behave yourself!" The worries plaguing me seemed to have faded, leaving a giddy warmth behind.

This lighthearted respite was a balm, easing the turmoil of the past days and reminding me what still remained despite the chaos — what we had built here together, side by side. This cat shelter, the friendship foundations of this new relationship... "Thank you," I said, "for being here. For understanding."

"Where else would I be?" He ran a thumb along my cheek. "No thanks needed. Not to sound like a broken record, but we're in this together from here on out. Promise?"

I nodded, leaning into his touch. "Promise."

Landon smiled, stealing one last quick kiss before rising from the sofa and holding out a hand. "You've probably put in enough hours here today."

I accepted his proffered hand, letting him pull me to my feet. "Are you suggesting I play hooky from responsibility?"

"That's exactly what I'm suggesting, though I don't think you're playing hooky. It's past dinner time." His eyes gleamed with a hint of mischief. "End your work day. Come on — let me take you out for dinner at that Hibachi Sushi place you like."

Hand in hand, Landon and I made our way out of the office and down the stairs. The familiar jingle of bells announced our departure.

Whatever adventures lay ahead, come what may, it felt like we just might face them together.

⚜

Thank you for reading! I hope you enjoyed the second book in the Silver Circle Cat Rescue Mysteries!

"Nugget, Coins, and Murder" is the next book in the series. Follow Ellie, Evie and the gang as they become convinced the Tablerock Police are sweeping a murder under the sisal rug!

KEEP UP WITH LEANNE LEEDS

Thanks so much for reading! I hope you liked it! Want to keep up with me?

Visit leanneleeds.com to:

Find all my books...

Sign up for my newsletter...

Like me on Facebook...

Follow me on Twitter...

Follow me on Instagram...

Thanks again for reading!

Leanne Leeds

Find a typo? Let us know!

Typos happen. It's sad, but true.

Though we go over the manuscript multiple times, have editors, have beta readers, and advance readers it's inevitable that determined typos and mistakes sometimes find their way into a published book.

Did you find one? If you did, think about reporting it on leanneleeds.com so we can get it corrected.

Artificial Intelligence Statement

Portions of this book were created with the assistance of AI tools used for editing, proofreading, and refining the text. However, the ideas, storyline, characters, and overall creative vision remain my own original work.

While some aspects of the cover image were generated using AI tools, it was done so under my creative direction and curation.

I want to acknowledge the use of these technologies as part of my creative process, while affirming that the essence of this work comes from my own imagination and effort.

Leanne Leeds

www.ingramcontent.com/pod-product-compliance
Lightning Source LLC
Chambersburg PA
CBHW011716240626
47153CB00009B/2884